ROGUE SOUL

Linsey Hall

Linsey@LinseyHall.com
www.LinseyHall.com
https://twitter.com/HiLinseyHall
https://www.facebook.com/LinseyHallAuthor

**BONNIE
DOON
PRESS**

ISBN 978-1-942085-20-1 (eBook)
ISBN 978-1-942085-21-8 (Paperback)

Books by Linsey Hall

Braving Fate
Soulceress
Rogue Soul
Stolen Fate

DEDICATION

To Cathy and Bob Hall, for being inspirational examples of
hard work and perseverance.

ACKNOWLEDGEMENTS

Thank you so much to all the people who put their time and effort toward helping me develop this story. As always, thank you Ben, for helping me create this book. Emily Keane, for reading every story I've written, no matter how busy you are. I think this is the book you had to squeeze in while studying for the bar, and I appreciate it so much.

Thank you, Doug Inglis. This was the first story we worked on together, and at least half the cool stuff that happens at the end is due to your astounding imagination. Thank you to Carol Thomas for reading this story and always being there for me.

Thank you to Megan McKeever, Simone Seguin, and Jena O'Connor for various forms of editing. The story is much better because of your expertise.

Dear Reader,
I love this story. It's my most adventurous yet, full of history that I adore and a hero and heroine who stole my heart. I hope you enjoy it.
Happy reading,
Linsey Hall

GLOSSARY

Aether - The invisible substance that connects the afterworlds and earth. It is both nothing and everything.

Aetherwalking - A method of traveling through the aether to access the afterworlds or different places on earth. Some Mytheans have this power and can bring another person with them.

Afterworld - A heaven or hell created by mortal belief. Mortals can access them only through death. Some Mytheans can aetherwalk to them.

Immortal University - An organization created thousands of years ago to protect Mytheans and keep them secret from mortals. It was initially founded as a true university, hence the name, but over time it morphed into an institution with greater power and responsibility. The university's primary goal is to maintain the secrecy of Mytheans and to keep the gods from warring to obtain more followers. They do this primarily through diplomacy. The university also provides services to Mytheans that they can't get elsewhere, lest mortals figure out that their clients never die. Things like education, health services, and banking.

Mortals - Humans. They are unaware of the existence of Mytheans or that all heavens and hells truly exist. They are immortal in the sense that their soul will pass on to whatever afterworld they believe in.

Mythean - Supernatural individuals created by mortal belief. They are gods and goddesses, demons and monsters, witches and other supernatural creatures. They are immortal in the sense that if they live on earth, only beheading or grievous injury from magic can kill them. If they are killed their soul will pass on to an afterworld. Secrecy from mortals is one of their highest priorities. Some Mytheans, particularly species of demons and some gods, are trapped in their afterworlds. Others have access to both earth and the afterworlds.

Mythean Guardians - Powerful mortals made immortal, or other supernatural beings who serve at the Praesidium. They protect those mortals and Mytheans who are important to the fate of humanity.

Otherworld - The Celtic afterworld. The Celtic gods are forbidden from traveling to earth because they believe that they are required to be in Otherworld to keep it functioning.

Praesidium - The protection division of the Immortal University. Mythean Guardians work here. Their job is to protect those important to humanity and maintain law and order by keeping Mytheans secret from humans and keeping the gods from warring.

Sila Jinn - Derived from Arabian mythology, a Jinn is a supernatural spirit in a class below that of angels and devils. A Sila is a female Jinn who can shapeshift, aetherwalk between all afterworlds, and manifest some types of magic.

Soulceresses - Mytheans who fuel their power by draining the immortal power of other Mytheans' souls. When fueled by the power of others, they can manifest their magic with a thought. They are hated by other Mytheans because of this. They also have the ability to see the evil in a person's soul.

CHAPTER ONE

The Caipora's Den
Edge of the Amazon River, Brazil
Present Day

Andrasta, Celtic goddess of victory, swallowed hard, her gaze transfixed by the man in the makeshift boxing ring. *Was he that handsome when I tried to kill him? Or that brutal?*

She honestly couldn't remember. It had been more than two thousand years since she'd seen him last, and she barely recognized him. Dim spotlights gleamed off sweat-slicked muscles and highlighted the feral brutality with which he pounded his opponent. No gloves protected his big hands, just white fabric wrapped around knuckles. They were spotted with blood.

She swallowed hard again, unable to look away.

She'd known she would find him here when she'd strolled up to the Caipora's Den, a little dive bar perched on the edge of the Amazon River. But she hadn't expected the outdoor boxing ring surrounded by a horde of cheering

Mytheans or that her prey would be inside it, pounding his opponent into a sack of broken bones.

She'd never before been to the bar, which catered only to the supernatural beings who lived secretly alongside mortals. The building itself was ramshackle, and she had a feeling that it was just as run-down on the inside. The outdoor lot in which she stood was pressed between the building and the river. It housed the boxing ring and nearly a hundred Mytheans, most of whom looked human even though they weren't. They screamed and cheered as punches landed with fierce smacks.

"All right, that's enough," hollered the ref, a big ugly brute who stepped forward to end the fight. The man she'd come for stood over his collapsed opponent, his heavily muscled chest heaving. He was declared the winner—no surprise, considering his opponent didn't look like he'd be getting off the floor anytime soon.

She sank back into the crowd when he turned to exit the ring. Though she wanted to watch him, to devour every hard inch with her eyes, she didn't want him to see her before she could approach him on her terms.

Their past was a pit of snakes, so confusing that even she couldn't figure head from tail though she'd lived through it. She wouldn't be surprised if he was pissed as hell, considering the arrows she'd sent through his heart the last time she'd seen him. Not that he hadn't wronged her. He had. He'd started the nightmare that had ended in her stealing his godhood for herself. Worse, they'd cared for each other. Until it had all gone to shit, at least.

And now she needed his help.

She turned and pushed her way through the crowd, toward the small bar pressed against the outside of the building. She needed to buy herself some time to recover from the sight of him but didn't want to do it inside the bar where she might lose track of him. Seeing him again made her shaky, even though it had been so many years. She just needed a minute to catch her breath, that was all.

She squeezed between two Mytheans of indeterminate species and reached the bar—which was more of a table with some liquor bottles and a cooler, but it would do.

"A beer," she said to the bartender, a beautiful brunette who had the slightly feral face of some kind of shifter. Ana had never been any good at identifying Mytheans since she rarely got away from her own kind.

The bartender handed over a sweating glass bottle and hissed, "On the house."

Anaconda Incantada. The sound of her voice gave away what her features did not. She was a snake shifter.

And it had better be on the house. There had to be some perks to being a god, since everything else had been a disappointment. Although Ana never tired of Mytheans fearing or bowing to her. Some watched her warily even now, and she appreciated it all the more for not having had it when she'd been mortal.

"How often does this happen?" Ana asked the bartender, hiking a thumb at the ring.

The shifter shrugged. "Every night."

"Know anything about the fighters?"

"Not the loser. But the winner, he's never lost. Fights pretty often. Seems to like it. Keeps to himself otherwise."

3

Ana nodded and turned to look for her prey. The beer slid refreshingly down her throat, and she sighed in pleasure at the smooth taste of the infrequently allowed delicacy. Focusing on the taste helped calm her nerves just a bit. She was raising the bottle to her lips a second time when she spotted him standing off to the side of the crowd near the jungle that crept up to the dirt lot.

It had been two thousand years since she'd seen him last, when she'd thought she'd killed him and taken his place as a Celtic god. Those years had been kind to him, considering that he was still alive. Almost as kind as the way-too-hot woman draped around him, sucking on his neck while he unwrapped the bloody cloth from his hands.

Ana stifled the strange little twinge in her chest. She'd cared for him once, and he for her, but that was so long ago the memories had gone to dust. Or so she told herself. She took one last swig of the beer to chase them away.

Now or never. If she wanted a permanent escape from Otherworld, the land of the Celtic gods and what felt like her eternal prison, there'd be no more dawdling, no matter how nervous she was about his reception or willingness to help her.

She needed him. Admitting to it scraped something raw inside her. But after two thousand years, she wanted out more than she wanted her pride.

Ana sucked in a deep breath and wound her way through the crowd. When a *lobisomem* got handsy as she passed, an elbow to the gut halted his straying paws, and a glare stopped another. Fancy Brazilian name or not, they were dogs like the rest of their werewolf brothers. Within moments, she'd reached the edge of the crowd and stood before the now-kissing pair.

She squashed her nerves as she gazed at the strong profile of the man she'd never been able to forget—whose mouth was glued to the woman's. He was a bruiser, even from the side, a contrast of hard features and short ginger hair. He looked rougher than she remembered. Bigger, too.

"Camulos," Ana said. She glanced dismissively at the sultry woman now trying to swallow his tongue.

"Cam," he said absentmindedly as he drew his face away from the woman's to look at Ana. His brows shot up, his gray eyes widening the barest fraction. A scar sliced through one of the brows.

"Recognize me?" she asked, absorbing the fact that he no longer went by Camulos.

"Andrasta," he rasped, shock plain on his face.

Did she hear his breath catch?

Hers certainly did. He looked every inch the god he'd once been—strong and powerful, with broad shoulders and big arms that looked like they'd been cut from steel. A man comfortable with the mantle of worship, even if he no longer carried it.

Ana shot a pointed glance at the other woman.

"Luciana," he said, drawing the woman's mouth away from where it had suctioned onto his neck.

Ana's eyes zeroed in on the huge hand that cupped the back of Luciana's neck, then looked back to realize that he'd kept his gaze trained on her own face.

"You need to go," Camulos said to Luciana.

Luciana pouted at him, then turned to look at Ana.

"A goddess?" Her brows shot high. She no doubt noticed the small glow emitting from Ana's skin and marked her as one from Otherworld. Her lips twisted in a sneer. "I thought you Celtic gods never left your cold realm."

She'd be right, Ana thought bitterly. Cold and emotionless, that was Otherworld, and she was trapped there except for a few times a year when she could sneak out without the other gods noticing. But that's what she wanted to change.

"Beat it, sister," she said, trying out some earth slang she'd seen on a TV show. Sneaking a laptop into Otherworld and firing up movies with her magic was one of the few ways she stayed sane.

The woman pouted, gave one last longing glance at Camulos, and then moved off into the crowd.

Camulos gave her a hard, searching look, his shock now masked. He didn't make a move to kill her—which was good. Not that she'd let him. But still, it was promising. He might have cared for her once, but after what had happened at the end, she wouldn't be surprised if that had been pushed out by anger.

"Come on. Let's get a seat inside." He jerked his chin toward the ramshackle bar.

Ana nodded and turned to lead the way. This time, with the huge male of indeterminate species following closely behind her, the crowd parted in waves to let her pass. Camulos was so close on her heels she swore she could feel the heat of him. It made the fine hairs on her arms stand on end. She tried to ignore it.

The smell of sweat and stale beer assaulted her nose when she walked into the bar. It was even more crowded than the outside, with dozens of volatile Mytheans partying and fighting in the dark, smoky space lit only by bare, dangling light bulbs.

She blinked. Wow. This was so different from Otherworld. Gross, definitely, from the smell to the cleanliness of the occupants.

But it was great. It was nothing like Otherworld, and she *loved* it. There was one small unoccupied table in the corner, but it was far enough from the main crowd to suit her.

They hadn't so much as settled at the table when a beer appeared in front of Camulos, carried by a smiling waitress whose eyes didn't stray from him. He ignored it and spared her only a curt nod.

"How the hell did you find me?" he asked when the waitress slunk away.

His rough voice sent a shiver down her spine. That first tingle of attraction hadn't been a fluke, after all. Damn it. This was what had gotten her in trouble so many years ago. Insane attraction that had blinded her to the danger she'd stepped into.

She dragged her mind back to the present. "More importantly, how the hell are you still alive? I thought I killed you."

His big hand clenched on the table. Scars sliced across his knuckles.

She tried not to squirm in her seat as his eyes roamed from her face down to the hint of cleavage she knew peeped above the top of her leather breastplate. She always wore it, but then she spent most of her time in temperate Otherworld or Scotland. It was damn hot in the jungle.

Finally, his gaze dragged back to hers. The sight hit her straight in the solar plexus. Damn, he looked good, no matter how wary or how harsh his gaze. His short reddish-blond hair glinted in the dim light that struggled to illuminate the seedy bar with its sticky seats. He still looked like a damn god, no matter what he'd turned into.

"You didn't kill me," he said, one corner of his mouth hiked up.

"Then what the hell *are* you? How are you immortal?"

"Why would I tell you that?"

So it was going to be this way? A game of chance where neither showed their cards? But it suited her too, since she had no idea how she felt about him. She glared at him as a Jurassic-sized fly buzzed around her head, as annoying as the questions hanging in the air between them. She still didn't fully understand everything that had happened those many years ago when she'd taken his place as a god by sending an arrow through his heart. Twice. She flinched at the mental image that came with the thought—him dying in the snow, his blood soaking through the knees of her dress.

"Aren't you afraid of me?" he asked.

"Nope." If she was going to be afraid of anyone, it would be him—with his huge body, scowling face, and potentially deadly grudge against her. But she wasn't. She could take care of herself, damn it. Being afraid was a thing of the past.

"Cocky."

"Yep." She wasn't the same girl he'd once cared for, however briefly. After they'd gotten caught in the crosshairs of the gods and her whole life had gone to hell, she'd changed.

"Anyway, it worked out for the best." He raised his smudged glass in toast to her.

"Really?" Her brows shot up. He truly thought their past—trading places so that she became a god and he went to earth—had worked out for the best?

He nodded, but she had a hard time believing him.

"Why? You should have loved Otherworld. You're a god," she said.

"Not anymore."

"Yeah, but you get what I mean," she said. "Otherworld, the coldness there, shouldn't have bothered you since you were born a god. The power, the perfection. It was all yours. Without all the downsides."

Like the soul-sucking loneliness of a place with no emotion. No one could care about anyone else. She was a fluke, a god with the ability to feel because she'd once been mortal. But there was nothing to feel there. No joy, no love, no fun. No way to distract herself from the misery of being trapped. All the other gods, they were perfect for it. Automatons in their impeccable world. But not her.

"So why would it be better for you on earth?" she asked when he didn't respond. He had less power here and had to hide from the other gods. And earth was messy and miserable compared to Otherworld. But it was that ability to be miserable, and alternately joyful, which made her want to return. "There's nothing for you here."

His gray eyes darkened, his expression effectively closing the subject. "That's my business, not yours. Why the hell are you here?"

"I want out."

"Are you kidding? Do you know what will happen to you when the other gods figure out you've tried to run?"

What was it about his voice that made her want to squirm in her seat? The mixed accent from his long life sounded exotic somehow and a hint of roughness dragged across her skin.

She shivered. "I've snuck out before."

"For a few hours maybe, and not with the intent to flee." He nodded smugly and she knew he must see acknowledgment in her eyes. "When they figure out that you're gone and don't intend to come back, you'll end up chained to the most desolate tor in Blackmoor for a thousand years while ravens circle for dinner."

Ana swallowed hard. The knowledge of the great rock formations where lawbreakers were punished was something she'd tried not to focus on when she'd decided to run. Blackmoor was the most desolate place in Otherworld, all scrubby ground punched through with granite tors and howling wind and rain. She had about a day before the other gods figured out she was gone. At that point, she'd be considered a deserter and they'd hunt her down.

"I'm aware of the risks." She tried to make her voice hard. "I want out."

"What the hell do you expect me to do about it?"

"You cared for me once." She didn't want to play that card—not after how it had ended between them—but she was desperate.

Truth flashed in his eyes, then his jaw hardened. "It was a long time ago."

It had been. But seeing him was dredging up emotions she'd forgotten she'd ever had. She tried to force them to the back of her mind and focus on her goal. "I want to know how you became mortal."

"Not mortal."

"Damn it, you know what I mean. I just don't want to be a god anymore. You stole my life when your obsession with me attracted the attention of the other gods. I want my life back."

"I don't owe you a thing." He raised his glass and his strong throat worked as he swallowed, drawing her eyes to it. She couldn't help but notice the way his worn shirt stretched over his broad chest. She scowled at her own interest. Long ago, that same interest had gotten her into trouble.

"Fine. I'll just have to convince you," she said.

He didn't respond, just smiled and folded his muscled arms over his chest. She sighed, then tensed when he swung his feet up onto the chair next to her.

Her breath caught in her throat. She could almost feel the heat of his thighs close to hers. Her leg tingled, her skin prickling. Something low in her stomach tightened, and it reminded her that this was one of the reasons she wanted to be back on earth.

Fates, her nerves were on edge, and he wasn't helping matters. She'd spent nearly every day of the last two millennia in Otherworld—the dullest, loneliest place in all of creation. As much as she loved the hustle and bustle of the Mytheans and mortals on earth, there was way too much of it in this bar. Her senses were on overdrive, and the air fairly buzzed with emotion from the dozens of volatile Mytheans carousing around her.

She swallowed hard and met his eyes. His smile reappeared, as if he knew what was going on inside her head. Inside her body.

"I need some air." She jumped to her feet. "Come on."

As soon as he stood, she spun and headed for the front door of the bar, hoping it would be quieter than the fighting ring out back. She had to cool down or things were going to get out of control.

CHAPTER TWO

Cam kept close behind Andrasta as they walked through the crowded bar, glaring at a couple of *lobisomems* who leered at her. Satisfaction kicked up the corner of his mouth when they turned and slunk away. Damn dogs.

But as soon as he looked at Andrasta's back, he felt the grin slide from his face. His heart thudded too hard, an unfamiliar pounding against his ribs. *Damn it.* It was a sensation he hadn't recognized when he'd first met her two thousand years ago. He'd been cold and emotionless, as a Celtic god should be. Until he'd seen her.

He tried to keep his eyes on the back of her head and off the curve of her waist and hips, which rolled with an unusual kind of grace despite the bow and quiver of arrows strapped to her back.

She wasn't dressed well for the sweltering heat of the jungle. Though her leather breastplate left her strong shoulders and arms bare, the raw leather pants that molded to her enticingly curved ass would be stifling. He tried to keep his eyes off that as well. He hadn't seen her in millennia, and he sure as hell had never seen her in clothes like this.

They reached the rickety door and he followed her out into the sticky heat, sucking in air so humid he nearly drowned. The lonely bar sat in the middle of nowhere, the jungle pressed against its back. A small village inhabited by Mytheans was located a bit deeper in the jungle. Magic hid both from mortal eyes.

Once the door swung closed, the light dropped to almost nothing, the only illumination provided by a sliver of moon hanging over the edge of the jungle canopy. Monkeys and insects screeched in the night, vying to be the loudest in the forest.

Cam was on Andrasta in seconds, gripping her firm biceps and swinging her around to press her against the wall of the bar. She gasped, and he had to stifle his own. Electricity shot up his arms where he touched her, a stronger version of what he'd felt when he'd first looked up and seen her standing across from him.

Damn it. It pissed him the fuck off.

"You have one more chance." He bit out the words through clenched teeth. "How did you find me?"

He'd been wearing a cloaking charm for the last two thousand years, ever since he'd left Otherworld; it should have kept him hidden from her eyes and those of the other gods. It was a huge problem if the gods could find him. The kind of problem that would end up with him dead.

"I don't know." She wriggled against him. She was strong, but her struggles only pushed them together, her curves and muscles straining against him. Something dark within him surged, and he nearly groaned at the contact.

14

Fuck. He hadn't felt anything this powerful since he'd spent that time with her two thousand years ago. Hell, he'd forgotten it was possible to feel something so strongly.

"Settle down," he muttered, trying to ignore the erection hardening against the front of his pants. If she could find him, then the other gods could. And if she didn't stop her damn struggling, he'd get distracted and he'd run out of time—time he desperately needed to figure out what the hell was going on and then to get out of here.

"Do the other gods know I survived?" he asked.

Though she was cloaked in shadows, he caught glimpses of her full lips and the shine of her honey-colored hair. *Focus.*

"Yes." Her green eyes widened and she stilled, seeming to realize he'd grown fully hard against her, his cock pressing achingly into the softness of her stomach.

What was it about her that did this to him? He was thousands of fucking years old, he should be able to control himself. She made the idea laughable. But damn, she smelled good. Like the forest: cedar and pine and green leaves. Strange, and not particularly feminine. But so like her that he couldn't get enough of it. It threatened to drag his mind back into the past, to when they'd first met. He resisted inhaling too deeply, deciding it was better to breathe through his mouth instead. Better yet, he released her and stepped back, inhaling deeply of the jungle air to try to clear his head.

"Do they know where I am?" Though he could take on a few of the gods at a time, if they all rose up against him, he was fucked. While the rules that kept Otherworld functioning had prohibited them from killing him when he was a fellow god, as a demi-god he was fair game.

"Not yet, but if you don't help me, I'll see to it that they do."

"Threatening me, are you? We'll see about that. How did you find me?"

"I had a vision of you. Here, with a bow." She nodded to the bar. "Smaller than the one you once used."

"Fuck." He never should have picked up the bow yesterday, but it had been so long since he'd held one that he couldn't resist. He hadn't even shot the fucking thing, but his lapse in judgment had been enough. One of the conditions of his cloaking charm was that he stay away from the things that were most closely associated with his time as a god. He'd learned the tip from a witch—not the one who'd given him the charm, gods damn her—and thank fuck he had. Apparently it had been excellent advice, as just picking up a bow had put him on their radar again.

Sloppy. He was getting sloppy after so many years on earth.

"I think I sensed you first because I sent you here," Ana said

It made sense. Taking someone's life, sending their soul elsewhere, was a powerful thing. It linked them. But it'd only be a matter of time before the other gods found him. He had to get his cloaking charm renewed before they did.

"Help me find a way out of Otherworld." Desperation was thick in her voice. "Permanently. I renounce my godship. I need your help."

She needed him. How the hell was he supposed to ignore that? Their past was fucking complicated, but part of him felt like he owed her. "You can't renounce your godship."

"But there has to be a way out. You found one, and I want it too."

"I can't do that. I don't have that power."

Ana groaned and nearly stomped her foot. She couldn't take no for an answer, not after so much time spent searching and dreaming of a way to have a real life. If the other gods found them before she could convince Cam to help her regain her humanity, she'd be forced back to Otherworld. Failure meant a fate she'd happily trade for death if she could.

"Someone has that power, and you know who it is. Take me to them," she demanded.

"Or what?" His voice froze with a deadly cold.

"Or I'll tell the other gods where you are. I meant it when I said it. I've got nothing to lose. If the other gods catch me deserting, I'm worse than dead. If you don't help me, I'll tell them where you are. You know I can be back in Otherworld in an instant." She snapped her fingers. It was the only card she had in her hand, and she had to make him believe her.

He cursed, spurring the monkeys on to greater howls. The jungle had as much energy as the bar, but it didn't bother her like that of the Mythean energy inside. What did bother her was the man who towered over her, even though he'd stepped back. She wasn't used to feeling small or helpless. She'd left that behind along with her humanity. But he made her feel that way, and she hated the fact that it caused her blood to sing through her veins and her skin to heat.

"Well?" she prodded.

"Fine." His voice carried the harshness of boulders scraping against each other as the earth moved. "Druantia created the potion that allowed me to Fall. I sought her out after meeting you, when I realized the gods were plotting against us."

The name was familiar. She was the most powerful Druid priestess and the one who'd facilitated communication between gods and mortals back when mortals still worshiped Celtic gods.

"She's your friend, so you think she'll give me the potion?"

"She's not my friend. She does a job for me when I need her to, and if you pay her, she'll do it for you too. She's difficult and a pain in the ass, but her services can be bought."

"Excellent. Take me to her and I promise I'll leave you alone. You can have your life"— she gestured to the bar and he scowled—"back to normal."

He thought about her offer for a moment and nodded. "I'm not actually helping you. I need a new cloaking charm, and you can tag along, but you're on your own. I'm not taking care of you along the way."

She scowled at him. "Please, like I need you to protect me. I killed you, remember?"

"Don't remind me."

CHAPTER THREE

Cam watched Andrasta step onto the deck of his boat, a strange feeling in the pit of his stomach at the sight of her entering the place he'd called home these past few decades. He hadn't had another person on his boat in years. He preferred it that way. The jungle allowed him to keep to himself, no questions asked. The towns allowed him to find the occasional woman when he wanted one, but otherwise he was left alone there as well.

So what the hell was he doing, letting her tag along? He hated traveling with others. Not to mention that he'd expected never to see her again. Yet here they were, about to spend the next two days traveling downriver to the nearest airport. After they flew to Scotland, it'd take at least another few days to find Druantia.

He'd fallen hard for Andrasta when he'd met her two thousand years ago. He'd been a stone-cold god, incapable of emotion—until he'd laid eyes on her. She roused things in him that were hard to control. And if he were honest with himself, he hadn't felt like that about anyone since her.

But he couldn't afford to be distracted by her now, not when all his attention needed to be on getting them safely to Druantia before the gods found them.

"You coming?" She looked back over her shoulder at him.

He shook away the thoughts and stepped off the ramshackle dock he tied off to every time he visited the Caipora's Den. He'd take her to Druantia, get his cloaking spell renewed, and then he could get back to the work he was meant to be doing. He had responsibilities he couldn't screw up.

"We'll find Druantia in Scotland, right?" Andrasta asked.

"Yes. It's been two thousand years since I've seen her last, but she'll be somewhere in the north." He'd called a couple contacts on the walk to the boat, hoping they'd know where she lived now. "I'm waiting on some information about her whereabouts."

"I can call my friend Esha and ask. She knows a lot of high-ranking Mytheans in Scotland. She might be able to find her."

He nodded. "Good."

"It's too bad we can't aetherwalk," Andrasta said as he moved to the stern of the boat.

He grunted his agreement. The aether, that ephemeral substance connecting earth and the afterworlds, allowed certain Mytheans to travel through it by aetherwalking. Andrasta had the ability, and she could take him along as well. The only downside to that plan—and it was a major downside—was that the aether linked everything. If she entered it to travel, the gods could find her. And him.

So it looked like they'd be taking the slow route.

"How long have you had this"—Andrasta peered around with a dubious expression—"vessel?"

"A while." He liked the old girl, and though he wanted to defend the *Clara G.'s* honor, he didn't want to give Andrasta any encouragement to keep talking. He'd always liked her voice, full of the joyous way she viewed the world. If he wanted to keep his wits about him, he couldn't be distracted by mooning over her as he'd done so many years ago.

Cam set about untying the lines to free the boat from the dock, the action as much muscle memory as it was conscious act. He didn't let the dark slow his progress. Andrasta had taken the aether to get here. If the gods were looking for her, this was where they'd show up, since it was the last place her energy led. Getting out of here soon was at the top of his list.

"You can have the bunk." He nodded to the little cabin built onto the aft end of the boat, which housed a bed and his clothes. The rest of the boat was open air.

With a flick of his wrist, he untied the last line at the bow, then bounded up the small ladder to the raised pilothouse situated in the forward end of the boat. The *Clara G.* was primarily flat deck space, with just the little cabin at the stern and pilothouse at the bow.

He flipped on the big lights that would help illuminate the river. It was wide here, the water moving sluggishly downstream. He threw on the engine and pulled smoothly away from the dock. He'd let Andrasta explore while he got them far enough away from the Caipora's Den that he could breathe freely again.

"What kind of boat is this?" Her head popped up on the ladder leading to the pilothouse.

He sighed. So much for exploring the main deck. Not that there was much to see down there. But he didn't want her squeezing into the tiny pilothouse; she'd be too close.

"Get on the roof." He jerked his head backward to indicate that she should climb on top of the flat roof, which was supported by piping. It didn't enclose any space on the main deck, but it did provide shelter from the rain.

He could hear her climb onto the steel roof and walk around the flat space he used as a deck whenever he wanted to relax or needed a bit of extra cargo space.

"What kind of boat is this?" she asked again. Her voice came from too close behind him.

He glanced back to see her standing with her arms folded over the half wall of the pilothouse, staring at him. He turned to face the river, but the back of his neck prickled under her gaze. Normally he liked that the breeze flowed through the pilothouse, which was essentially just a chest-high box with a roof several feet overhead. Now, he wished for windows. Thick ones.

"Steamboat originally. But now it's powered by diesel," he said.

"An old one?"

Always so curious. He felt a grin tug at the corners of his mouth, but he stifled it. "You could say that. It's one of the mini riverboats from the Klondike gold rush back at the end of the nineteenth century. Found it rotting away in a barn up in the Yukon Territories about fifty years ago. Couldn't save the wooden paddle wheel, and the engines and boiler had been stripped, but the rest of the steel hull was sound. Brought it down here, gave it a couple outboard engines and some modernizing, and it's been faithful ever since."

"Really?" Excitement laced her voice. "How do you think the diesel engines compare with the original steam propulsion?"

"You like engines?"

"I like technology, and steam was the biggest thing to hit humanity since the wheel."

She was clever. "Diesel is less exciting and less dangerous, but more reliable and easier to maintain. But I do miss steam sometimes."

"That's what I figured. There's just something so romantic about steam. How'd you get it all the way down here?"

Steam was more romantic? She was clever *and* weird. He'd almost forgotten how much so. He grinned as he said, "I shipped it overland, like that movie. The one where they carried the steamboat over the mountains into South America."

She made an impressed noise in the back of her throat. Or did he just choose to interpret it that way? He scowled.

"*Fitzcarraldo?* Wouldn't it have been easier to put it on a cargo ship?"

"Sure, but I've got nothing but time and wanted the challenge. You like movies?" *Fitzcarraldo* was an unusual one. He had no idea they had movies in Otherworld—but then again, he hadn't been there in two thousand years.

"Yes. I need something to pass the time up there, don't I? My friend Esha gave me a laptop that's loaded with movies and television shows. It's how I keep in touch. With earth."

The tinge of sadness to her voice tugged something within him that he quickly ignored.

"How big is this steamship?"

"Boat. It's a steamboat. Steamships go on oceans, steamboats go on rivers."

"Oookay then. I guess you like boats."

He shrugged. But yeah, he did. About as much as she liked technology. There hadn't been any significant bodies of water in Otherworld. Nothing other than small rivers and a few ponds. When he'd ended up on earth permanently, oceans had fascinated him, along with the lakes that were as big as seas and rivers so wide you'd have sworn you were at the beach. A passion for boats had followed shortly behind.

"So, how big?"

He sighed. "Don't you have something else you want to be doing? Instead of bothering me?"

"Nope. Too dark to see much. I'd rather hear about the boat. How big is it?"

He sighed. "Fifty feet. Small open-air galley below the roof you're standing on, bunkhouse with a bed behind that if you're feeling tired." Which he wished she was. She could have his bed, as long as it kept her away from him. He'd take the hammock tied in the open air of the bow, but odds on him sleeping, with the gods possibly on their tail, were slim.

"I'm not tired. Too keyed up being on earth," she said.

"Speaking of, how long 'til the gods start looking for you?" *And me.*

"A day. I've never come to earth for longer than twenty-four hours. That always seemed to be a safe amount of time. I figure they'll start to notice I'm gone once I miss a meeting. There's one tomorrow."

"They still have those?" He'd hated the damn things when he'd been there.

"Yeah. They're no longer for accounting for worshipers, since we don't have any alive anymore. Though the recent interest in Druids has given us a bit of power. Now the meetings are mostly for managing the mortals who came to Otherworld when they died and to keep track of the gods. So we don't leave." The last sentence was delivered with a scowl he could hear.

"The council is still obsessed with keeping the gods in Otherworld, then?" It had been the most important law when he'd still been a god.

"Yeah, I don't get it. Greek and Roman and Norse gods get to go to earth whenever they want. But not us Celtic gods. No, *Otherworld is weakened without our presence.*" Her voice had lowered, and he huffed out a small laugh at her impression of Hafgan, one of Otherworld's eldest gods.

Even at more than two thousand years old, Andrasta was the youngest Celtic god. He wasn't surprised that she hated Otherworld. He'd been born there. Never known anything different, and therefore never felt a need to leave. Not until a young mortal's skill with a bow had caught his attention. Then he'd gone to earth, met Andrasta, and fucked everything up.

"Anyway, on to happier topics. I'm going to have fun while I'm here on earth, damn it. You said that we're two days out from the airport? Where's our next stop?"

Fun? No. They'd be heading hard and fast toward Scotland and the potion that would get her out of his life. There'd be no time for fun. "Little town called Havre. Got some business I have to tie up if I'm going to be away a while. Not much going on there. We'll be in and out."

"What kind of business?"

Fates, she had a lot of questions. He'd never met anyone so chatty. But on her, he kind of liked it. He scowled. "Wouldn't you rather take a nap?"

"Jeez, you're grumpy. I don't remember you being this grumpy."

"My business is in pharmaceuticals." Talking about the present was better than thinking about the past.

She laughed, a disbelieving sound swallowed by the shrieks of the howler monkeys. "Really?"

"Yeah. Good money."

"Don't those companies charge a fortune for sick people to get well?"

He shrugged. "Like I said. Good money."

"But you just work for them, right? You're not the boss or anything."

He could tell from her voice that she didn't want him to be the evil mastermind behind the operation. He couldn't give her the answer she wanted, so he just shrugged.

She didn't say anything for a minute, but the waves of censure coming off of her were unmistakable. It didn't bother him. Not at all.

"Go down below, Andrasta. There's a rough patch of river coming up and I need to concentrate."

She sighed. "Fine. You're no fun anyway."

He watched out of the corner of his eye as her pale form disappeared down the ladder, taking with her the forest scent that complemented the earthiness of the jungle. She'd probably notice that there was no rough patch of river, but by then she'd be pissed enough to stay away. It'd be for the best. He couldn't allow himself to get used to her presence. Or worse, start to like it.

"Do you have anything to drink?" Ana hollered at Cam once she reached the main deck.

She walked the few feet to the bow so that she could look up at him in the pilothouse. It stood on sturdy wooden legs about six feet above the deck and gave him an exceptional view of the river. A view that he kept his steely gaze nailed to instead of looking down at her. She propped her butt on a huge metal piece of machinery sticking up off the bow.

"Ass off the windlass," he yelled down at her.

"Fine." She took her weight off the machinery.

"Got some beer and bottled water in the cooler in the galley. Don't get wasted in case the gods figure out you've left and manage to find us."

I wish. She didn't want to get hammered, but a good buzz would be just about perfect right now. Most of her nerves had faded once he'd agreed to bring her along, and she was almost giddy with the fact that she was finally on her way out of Otherworld. The whole reason she was coming to earth was to feel something other than loneliness unalleviated by boredom and duty.

She walked beneath the pilothouse legs and into the space beneath the metal roof that she'd been standing on earlier. It took her a second to realize that the spartan space *was* the galley. A small stove, a table, a rusty old sink, and a cooler. Height of luxury. About ten feet away was a door that lead into the only enclosed space on the vessel—the bunkhouse, he'd said.

With a sigh, she popped open the top of the cooler and snagged a bottle of beer. It started sweating as soon as it hit the sultry air of the jungle. The bottle was deliciously cool against her fingertips. Damn, the jungle was hot. She closed her eyes and envisioned the tank top and shorts she'd seen Phoebe wear on an episode of *Friends*. She sighed when her heavy leather breastplate and pants were replaced by airy fabric.

"Much better," she said as she headed back to the hammock she'd seen stretched across the port side of the bow. She flicked off the cap of her beer, then plopped into the hammock and leaned back. The water rushed beneath the boat, gentle waves lulling her into a daze as she sipped her beer. She glanced up at Cam in the pilothouse.

He looked competent and manly up there, the way his big hands loosely gripped the wheel and his eyes traced over the water. In his element. But he'd changed so much from the man who'd set her life on this path. And who'd grudgingly agreed to help her now.

She held up a fist in front of her face. He liked boats. She stuck up her thumb.

He ran a company that sold expensive medicine to sick people. She stuck up her forefinger.

He was prickly and bad tempered. Middle finger up. Straight up at him.

A bruiser who fought for fun. She stuck her ring finger up.

But that last one was the strange one. He fought for fun. Joy, or whatever it was he felt from the fights, was an emotion. He'd been a god, so shouldn't he not have those?

But he'd been angry back in the bar. Pretty angry since then too, despite her trying to lighten the atmosphere. All sizzling under the surface, hot enough that she'd burn herself if she touched him. So that was a fifth thing she knew, the fact that he was a god who felt emotion. It was the most dangerous and enlightening of them all. It meant that he really had cared for her back then—it wasn't just a figment of her imagination.

Five things. And that probably wasn't even the start of how he'd changed. She sipped again, musing over all the things she wanted to do now that she was on earth. Sex, drugs, rock 'n roll.

Okay, mostly sex. She shifted uncomfortably in the hammock, struck for the second time that evening by the heat and tingling between her thighs. This always happened when she came to earth. Arousal that she never felt in Otherworld—that she couldn't feel there, she was pretty sure, since there was no sex—would hit her like waves on the beach a few hours after arriving on earth. Here one moment, gone the next, gaining strength like the waves of a storm at sea. Sometimes she acted on it, sometimes not. She blamed it on all the energy and emotion that was present on earth but not in Otherworld.

She sighed and stared up at Cam. Cam, who was alive. Alive when she thought he'd been dead for thousands of years. Cam, whom she'd so briefly been infatuated with. Cam, who'd changed her entire life and was still so damn handsome. Scary handsome. Not so handsome that it was scary. No. Handsome in a scary way.

If she felt fear. Which she didn't. Rugged features that contrasted with ginger hair, enough muscles that he looked like he could snap someone in two.

She didn't like being the weaker one in any situation. Even though she was a god and he was a mystery Mythean of undetermined species, she wouldn't be surprised if he were stronger. He certainly looked it. She scowled, then turned her gaze to the stars.

She might need his help, but nothing else. She'd scratch this itch elsewhere. Getting involved with him had only led to trouble last time, and it would do so again.

CHAPTER FOUR

Southeast Celtic Britain, 13 AD
Territory between the Iceni and Trinovante Kingdoms

"Why are you watching me?" The woman didn't turn as she spoke.

Though Camulos knew her face to be fair and fine boned, the blond curls tumbling down her back and the brown woolen skirt concealing her legs were all he could see from the shadows. Great trees loomed overhead, casting the shade he hid within. It terminated at the edge of a clearing that was blanketed with snow.

How had she sensed him? He'd made a point to stay concealed, to keep to the dark of the forest as she'd practiced her archery in the clearing. Then again, he visited earth so rarely that he was no expert at remaining unseen.

Or perhaps he'd wanted her to see him this time.

"Well?" She spun, gripping her bow loosely at her side. Ire sparked in her green eyes.

She was lovely, though that wasn't what drew him. There were plenty of beautiful gods in Otherworld. No, it was the damnable fact that she made his chest feel strange. Like he knew her, though he was sure he'd never met her.

His foot moved forward. His mind stopped it. Revealing himself to a mortal, especially this mortal... No good could come of it. If he was to kill her, as he should, then it would be better if she didn't see him.

But from the relaxed way she held her bow, she wasn't afraid of him. Or she was confident enough in her speed to think that she could pluck an arrow from her quiver, sight it, and kill him with a shot.

Little did she know.

"You've been watching me for days. I want to know why," she demanded. Her grip on the bow tightened. Nerves?

"Maybe because I want to know how a girl like you can shoot a bow like that." The words were out of his mouth before his mind could stop them.

Her bow was up, arrow sighted, drawn, and fired a mere second before a thudding sound to his left made him glance down. Her arrow vibrated where it pinned the bottom of his cloak to the tree. He raised a brow and nodded.

"You're as skilled as they said." Though they hadn't mentioned how beautiful she was. Or that she had the ability to make a god's chest feel odd.

"Of course I am, but who are *they* that you speak of?"

"The gods," he said, yanking his cloak from the tree and stepping forward. Perhaps it was best that she fear him. The cockiness of her tone made his chest feel even stranger. Was this what emotion felt like?

"The gods." She laughed disbelievingly, but when sunlight hit his face as he walked out of the shadow, she stepped backward, her knuckles whitening around the bow. "Who are you?"

"Camulos." He should make her fear him. It would make it easier to kill her. He'd see the light of panic in her eyes, and she'd be just another mortal.

Her brow creased. "The god of war? Here? In my woods?"

He nodded.

"No, you're not."

"I am." His head drew back. She didn't believe him?

"You can't play me for a fool. The gods don't come to earth. They haven't in centuries. If they ever did at all."

She was right. They'd stopped visiting earth before he was born. There was too much emotion here. The place seethed with it. *He* seethed with it. Because of her? He rubbed his chest.

"You've been watching me for days. But I've never been able to see you, and you've never come close. Why?"

He felt a frown drag at his mouth. He couldn't tell her that he'd come to kill her, but had been stayed by the sight of her practicing with her bow until her fingers bled. Or that the sight of her so diligently training had made his chest tighten.

"I told you," he said, pushing away duty in favor of curiosity. "I want to know why you use the bow. And where did you get your skill? Magic? A spell?"

Her jaw dropped, and his eyes riveted to her parted lips.

"Absolutely not!" she cried.

He arched a brow, almost expecting her to shoot him again. Maybe this time she'd make contact with his flesh. But she'd never answered why she practiced so much with a weapon that the Celts only used for hunting.

Yet she never hunted. She practiced as if she were training for war.

"Well then, let's see it," he said as he raised his bow, notched an arrow, and shot it high into the sky. She mimicked his movements, and her arrow knocked his as it headed back to earth.

She propped a hand on her hip and shot him a smirk. "Why are you so concerned about my skill?"

"The bow is a rare skill among the Celts. It is my skill." Rarely did a mortal's skill match that of a god's. When it did... Well, it was best to kill the mortal. It wasn't unheard of for one of them to usurp a god, though that hadn't happened in centuries.

"Let's see it, then." She shot his words back at him and an arrow high into the air.

He grinned, then scowled at himself, swiftly nocking an arrow and firing. He knocked her arrow with his own.

"You have some talent," she said.

"And you're too arrogant for your own good."

"Not when the arrogance is well earned. As I have earned it." She spun the small bow in her hand, the only movement of her otherwise still form.

He felt his mouth twitch up at the corner. He'd never spoken to a mortal before. Were they all this arrogant? And entertaining? He rubbed his chest again.

When he'd first come to earth several days ago, he'd been determined to find her—kill her, and return to Otherworld. It was the way things were done on the rare occasions a mortal approached godly skill and it should have been a quick job, not unlike hunting deer for dinner.

But then he'd found her, practicing with her bow in a clearing in the woods. And his chest had started to feel odd. His mind as well. She was so interesting that he couldn't look away.

He'd watched her, as the sun had risen and set, for five days. But only when she was in the clearing. He shouldn't be seen by mortals, and with limited time to spend on earth before the other gods noticed his too-prolonged absence, he watched only while she practiced alone with her bow.

"Why do you need to be so good with the bow?" he asked.

"Why not?"

"Haven't you other things to see to? A family? A husband?"

"I shall not marry. I'm from a family of warriors. I shall be a warrior too." She looked proud of the fact, but too slight to bear the burden.

"Female warriors?" The Celts did have some, but a whole family would be extraordinary.

Her lips twitched, almost a frown. "No. I'm the only female."

Ah. That was why she practiced alone; her brothers wouldn't let her join them. Was that why she used the bow? Could she not obtain a sword?

His hand twitched. He should reach for his arrow now. Find it. Shoot it. Kill her.

Before the other gods noticed he hadn't.

There were rules to being a god. Rules that one didn't break without deadly reprisal. Rules that he'd never broken because he'd never cared to. He'd never cared about anything. He'd never even known what it was to care.

But here on earth, things had all started to look a little bit different. A little bit darker back in Otherworld and a little bit brighter when he looked at her.

He should turn, walk away, and shoot her from the shadows. Because he couldn't, he asked, "You've decided that you are a warrior?"

"I'm more than what I am right now, I know that. I'm more than just a girl."

"What's your name?" he asked, then cursed himself. Knowing it would only make killing her harder.

"Andrasta," she said. She wished that her heart would stop racing, but it hadn't stopped since he'd walked out of the shadows. Her eyes were drawn once again to the big hand that gripped his bow and then up to his face. He carried a bow like it was a weapon of war. No one did that. No one except for her.

The damp wind rustled his pale red hair, and she told herself to look away. He was the handsomest man she'd ever seen. Something unfamiliar within her ribs fluttered. He couldn't really be a god, could he?

Most men ignored her. But not this one. He'd watched her for days. Why would a god watch her?

And he was skilled with his bow. Not as skilled as she, of course. But still, quite good.

Good enough to fear? She started to step back, then reminded herself that she feared no one.

Something in his eyes shuttered, and he turned to go.

"Wait." She reached out to stop him. He couldn't leave. She didn't know why, but she'd never felt anything like this before. Excited, nervous, afraid. Danger radiated from him, but not enough to stop her from trying to get his attention.

He turned toward her, and she bit back a sigh of relief.

"Do you use that in war?" She nodded to the bow. "Or just for hunting?"

"Both."

Her heart sped up, pounding in her chest. "And you say you're Camulos, the god of war."

"I *am* Camulos. I don't just say it."

"A competition then." She didn't know if she believed him, but she did believe he used the bow for war. She wanted to believe it. Among her people, no one considered the bow to be a weapon of war. But it was the only weapon she could get her hands on, and if she wanted to be a warrior, she must have a weapon.

He scowled, his eyes darkening, and she swallowed hard, her skin prickling.

She shook her head. She wasn't afraid. Of course not. And she wanted him to stay. His interest made her feel special and fascinating, even if he did make her nervous.

"Between you and me?" he asked.

"Yes." She had to force her voice not to waver. She nodded at the quiver strapped to his back. "I like your arrows. I've never seen feathers of that bright a blue before. If I best you, you'll give me one."

If he really was the god Camulos and she defeated him, his arrow would be proof. It proved that her weapon wasn't just a silly tool for acquiring dinner. It proved that she was capable. To her brothers. To her father. They might not let her wield a sword, but her bow was just as good. The fact that a god used it proved the fact. Now, she had a way to show them.

"One shot," she said, speaking quickly to convince him before he could leave. She pointed to the huge tree upon which she'd carved an X. It was nearly two hundred yards away, but the X was very small. "To that spot on the pine over there."

"And what do I get if I win?" He stepped closer, his big body looming over hers when he stopped only a couple of feet away.

She tilted her head to look up at him. Swallowed again. "What do you want?"

He thought for a moment, his eyes searching her face. "I want to know why you work so hard at this."

He reached out and lifted her hand, gazed at her calloused fingers. Her palm tingled and a shiver ran up her arm. She could feel the heat radiating off of him in the chill air. "I want to know why you've tried to make a weapon of pleasure a weapon of war."

He dropped her hand and she fisted it, but didn't argue his assessment. She nodded, drew a line in the dirt with her toe. "From here. You first."

She admired his form as he stepped up to the line. The broad sweep of his shoulders, the strength of his arms and hands as he drew back the bowstring. His bow was bigger than hers. His arms stronger.

No matter. Speed and accuracy were her signature. But she couldn't help admiring the flex of his muscles as he fired.

His arrow struck the middle of the X. The look he gave her was almost apologetic. But she just grinned and stepped up to the line. In quick succession, she shot two arrows, one after the other, and watched with her heart in her throat as the first split his arrow and the second split her own. She didn't know why she'd been nervous. She hadn't missed a shot in over a year.

She grinned, then turned to him and stuck out her hand for her prize. He didn't hand it over, and there was something she didn't recognize in his eyes.

"We both hit the middle of the X," he said.

"Which is why I hit it twice." She held out her hand again.

He inclined his head, then pulled an arrow out of his quiver and gave it to her. Her palm tingled when she touched it. Could he really be who he said he was?

"Why the bow?" he asked.

"You lost. I don't have to tell you anything."

He removed another arrow from his quiver, held it tightly. She eyed it, debating what he was offering. With only one, she'd have it to show her family, to prove herself. They'd probably take it from her to confirm with their Druid priestess that it was from Camulos. If she had two, she could keep one for herself. She weighed her secrets against her desire.

But her brothers were expecting her home soon, and she wanted to see Camulos again. She said, "Give me the second arrow and return here tomorrow. I'll tell you then."

"If I give it to you now, how will I know you'll return?"

Because I wouldn't miss it for all the arrows in your quiver. Even if he did scare her. But she wanted to see him again more than she wanted the arrow. "Fine. I'll meet you here tomorrow."

His brow wrinkled, as if he were debating something of great import. "All right. Tomorrow."

She ignored the reluctance in his tone and had to stifle her grin.

He nodded, his expression still torn between two things she couldn't identify, then turned to go.

"Wait." He couldn't leave. Not quite yet. She just wanted a minute more.

But he disappeared.

The next day, Camulos waited for Andrasta in the silent, snow-covered forest. He cursed himself for agreeing to return, but he'd lacked the will to resist.

She stepped into the clearing and guilt tugged at him. He had a duty to complete where she was concerned. Force of will made him raise his bow. The bowstring pulled taut beneath his fingers as he sighted the arrow at her.

Let go. When he did, the arrow would pierce Andrasta's skull and this would all be over. *Let go.* He removed one finger. One step closer to killing her. *Let go.*

All he had to do was release the string and his problems would be over. The other gods would be off his back about the upstart mortal who could threaten to take his place with her skill. If she could do it, others might get ideas, and the other gods wouldn't have that.

Let go. The string of the bow cut into his fingers as he watched her practice in the clearing. She used his arrow. Did she realize that he'd given her the ability to kill him? Human arrows couldn't, but his own could. Why had he done it?

He couldn't explain why. Just as he couldn't explain how being on earth, watching her, made him feel. He had no context for the emotions rushing through him. No way to identify them, if that's what they were.

The best he could do was sort the way he felt into *good* and *bad*. The closest thing he had to the feeling of *good* was eating. Or killing. *Bad* was like a nebulous, emotion-ridden version of being stabbed by a sword. The idea of shooting Ana was most closely associated with *bad*. The bow felt like it burned his hands.

"Do it, Camulos. You have to." The voice from behind nearly made his fingers slip from the string.

He lowered the bow and spun to face the other god. "Cernowain. And your boar."

The beast rooted in the snow at the base of the brown cloak of the god of animals.

"Were you sent by the others?" Camulos asked.

"No. I come because I am your friend. I heard the others grumbling, and I wanted to warn you."

Camulos grunted. Cernowain was the closest thing to a friend he had in Otherworld, for whatever it was worth.

"You have to do it. She's a threat." Cernowain nodded to Andrasta.

"No, she's not." She was good, but a threat? No.

"Hafgan was once mortal. His skill with a pike rivaled hers with the bow. If he could replace a god, she could do it too. She could replace you."

"I'd think the other gods would prefer that."

Cernowain inclined his head. "They might, if they weren't so opposed to the idea in the first place."

That was the crux of it. The other gods didn't care if Camulos was replaced. They'd prefer it. He'd grown too powerful. When the mortal kingdom of the Trinovantes had built the city Camulodunum in his honor, he'd gained yet more influence from the power of their worship.

The other gods didn't like that. But then, the other gods could hang. Otherworld could hang, for all he cared. He hated the damned place now. Cold and dead and dull. Everything there, no matter how perfect, was in shades of gray. Earth, with emotion and feeling, was vibrant with color. How could Otherworld be so different? So wrong?

"If you don't want to kill her to protect yourself, do it for her. The other gods might take it into their own hands, and there's every chance she'll end up with a far worse fate than if you had killed her yourself."

"What?"

Cernowain shrugged, a thoughtful frown twisting his mouth. "There's only one reason you would hesitate."

Emotion.

"Emotion." Cernowain almost spat the word.

Was that why his chest tightened when she was near? Why his brain fogged with what he guessed were desire and joy?

"Something is wrong with you, Camulos. As the other gods discover it, they'll do what they can to replace you. Barring that, they'll punish you." He pointed to Andrasta. "Through her. Kill her, Camulos. Give her eternity in Otherworld. Don't leave her alive, at the mercy of the gods when they finally figure out why you're hesitating to do your duty."

Camulos' hand tightened on the bow. There was no question he had to kill her, but how in fate was he going to be able to do it?

"Do it, Camulos. You're running out of time." Cernowain disappeared, aetherwalking back to Otherworld.

Camulos swallowed hard and raised the bow again, sighting Andrasta at the other end of the arrow.

"Are you there again?" Her voice carried through the clearing.

His heart thudded and he jerked his gaze up to meet hers. He lowered the bow, unable to fire, and stepped forward, pulled to her by a force he couldn't fight. She hesitated, her eyes wary, then approached to stand a few feet from him.

Her presence hit him in the chest again. He rubbed his sternum. Why the hell did she make him feel so odd?

Whatever it was, he wanted more of it. His gaze swept her slim form and his breath grew tight.

"Walk with me," he said, hoping for a distraction from his body's reaction to her and from the threat of the gods hanging over their heads.

She nodded and set off on a path around the clearing. He matched his stride to hers.

"Why do you work so hard to be skilled with the bow?" he asked, unable to get the question out of his mind.

"My brothers won't let me use a sword. I can make the bow and arrows myself. They used to take them away, but I'd make another. They don't try anymore, and the bow I have is perfect. I love it." Pride laced her voice, and a smile tugged at the corners of his mouth.

"But why go to so much effort?"

She shrugged, her golden hair glinting in the sun. "I want to be like them. Anyway, what else is there to do? Marry? Tend the home? Not I. I'd rather be like my brothers. They're brave and strong and nothing can get past them. They're a team."

"How many are there?"

"Seven brothers. Seven warriors. I want to be the eighth."

He could hear the need in her voice. Her hands were fisted at her sides, one gripping her bow as if it were her way in.

"You want it badly," he said.

"Yes. Other Celtic women are warriors, why not me? I've been on the outside my whole life, ever since my mother died. But I can prove myself if they'd just give me the chance."

"So you practice alone, hoping to prove your worth."

"It sounds pathetic, doesn't it?" Her morose gaze met his.

"On the contrary. I find it admirable." More than that. Since he'd met her, he'd felt that he recognized her, though he'd never seen her before. Perhaps he recognized himself in her. And perhaps the gods were right. With her talent and her thirst to prove herself, she could be strong enough to take his place. At the very least, she was strong enough to cause problems, should she choose.

He scowled. He'd been avoiding thinking about his duty where she was concerned. It didn't matter that he found her to be intriguing. He had to kill her or the other gods would come for him.

But perhaps he could steal a few more moments with her, though it was stupid and dangerous.

She broke the silence by asking, "Why do *you* use the bow for war?"

"Because I like it. There are a people who live far south of here, across the sea. Greeks. They use bows in war, as do their gods. One of their gods, Apollo, gave me my first bow." He didn't see gods from other religions often, but when he did, he preferred them over his fellow Celtic deities.

"Other gods who use the bow in war? And people, too?"

"Yes."

She smiled, and he realized that the sight made his chest warm almost unbearably.

"I think I would like these people," she said.

He smiled too, then frowned at the unfamiliar sensation of his lips turning upward.

She stopped in the shade of a large oak and asked, "Could I hold your bow?"

His hand tightened briefly on the weapon, but he loosened it and handed it over. A strange bolt of lust shot through him as he watched her hands trace over the fine woodworking.

He stepped toward her, but shock pulled him up short. He wanted to touch a mortal? Not possible. They were a step above animals. But the feelings surging through him now... They were cataclysmic.

"It's beautiful." She gazed up at him. Her eyes could hold him captive if he weren't careful.

It's yours. He barely stopped the words from leaving his mouth. Did she use some type of spell to ensnare him?

If she did, he couldn't bring himself to care.

His hand twitched to reach out and touch her as a thousand unrecognizable feelings and desires surged through him. They made his skin tingle and his cock harden.

Understanding of his desires dawned in her eyes. Her lips parted and she took a step forward.

Unable to help himself, he reached out and palmed her cheek. The contact with her soft skin sent a spike of pleasure through him that was so strong he nearly doubled over. Was this why the Greek gods dallied with mortals so much?

He leaned down and kissed her, an animal noise rising from his throat as her soft lips parted beneath his own. His cock punched against his trousers as she pressed against him, hot and soft and unlike anything he'd ever felt before.

There was nothing like this in Otherworld. He tore away. It was something he couldn't have in Otherworld, and he couldn't have it here either. Contact with mortals was forbidden. The law had been in place since before he was born. He'd never really questioned the details of why because he'd never really cared. But the law was in place, nonetheless.

This was impossible.

A whirlpool of rage sucked him under. There was no way to save his own hide without killing her. Now he desired her too? And admired her for her strength and skill and determination? It was unbearable.

"What's wrong?" Confusion clouded her eyes.

"You," he growled. He had to scare her off, because fate knew he wouldn't be the one to turn away. "Go. Now."

"But—"

He yanked his bow back from her. "I was sent to earth to kill you. I'm terribly close to doing—"

"Andrasta!" A deep male voice called from the forest. Camulos spun toward the voice and nocked an arrow in his bow.

"No!" Desperation laced Andrasta's voice as she tried to pull his arm down. Her strength was that of a fly's.

"Go," he rasped.

Out of the corner of his eye, he caught sight of her desperate gaze. She fled in the direction of the voice.

CHAPTER FIVE

Amazon River Basin, Present Day

The sun was a miserable bitch, shining in her eyes like this. Ana rubbed them and blinked groggily up at Cam, who stood at the wheel. "What time is it?"

Had he not moved all night? He was still grimy from the fight the night before, but looked no more tired. Didn't need much sleep, like a god. But she hadn't thought that she'd be tired enough to doze off. Must be the stress of fleeing Otherworld.

"About seven." His gray eyes flicked over her new clothes, then met hers for a moment before she forced herself to look away. His eyes had been one of the things that had sparked her infatuation when she'd first met him. Better not to let them do so again.

"Do you need me to take over for a while so you can get some rest?"

He laughed, a skeptical sound that let her know what he thought of her taking control of his precious boat.

"Hey, I can drive a boat," she yelled.

"Can you?"

Well, she figured she could. She could do anything she put her mind to. *Had* she driven a boat before? No. Not exactly. So she didn't say anything, just frowned at him.

"That's what I thought. Not a lot of water in Otherworld."

"Is that why you like your boat so much?"

"In part. We're a good distance away from the Caipora's Den, and there's a hidden tributary up here. I'm going to pull into it and tie off. Get a shower and something to eat."

At that, Ana's stomach rumbled, and she watched anxiously as Cam turned the vessel toward a wider section of the river. He steered straight for a section of vines that hung low, and passed under them into the tributary.

"Aren't you worried about running aground?" If they got stuck, they'd be screwed. She couldn't aetherwalk or the gods could track her energy through the aether. And while she could walk through the jungle, she didn't want to.

"No. Shallow draft on the *Clara G.*"

The *Clara G.*? Who was Clara? Something twisted in her stomach, and it felt a bit like jealousy, but she shoved it away.

Cam pulled the boat alongside a rough dock made of logs and hopped down from the pilothouse to tie off to two upright posts near the bow and stern.

"Where does this dock lead?" she asked.

"Nowhere, really. I built it as a place to stop between the Caipora's Den and Havre. Bought a spell from a Bruxa to hide it."

"Bruxa?"

"A witch. Portugese."

"But witches don't sell their spells, not normally."

"Never said I bought it with money." He grinned at her, a rakish smile that opened up his normally closed-off face. She stared, bemused, until it disappeared. Which happened too quickly for her liking.

"I'm going to grab a quick shower," he said. "Keep an eye on shore."

"For what?"

"Whatever might want to come aboard."

"Like?" Jungle cats? Mysterious tribes of tattooed and weapon-laden locals? Angry Mytheans?

He shrugged. "Some local Mytheans know I occasionally carry valuables on board. Jaguars who want a snack."

"Is that—is that a joke?" He was a bigger predator than any jaguar.

"Don't worry. Not likely for anything to bother us." He yanked his tattered t-shirt over his head and turned to walk toward the back of the boat.

She swallowed hard as muscles on his back flexed before her eyes, shifting and rippling beneath the skin. She could make out a scattering of freckles on his shoulders. She wanted to press her lips to each one until she'd accounted for them all. He looked exotic against the lushness of the jungle, his fair skin and red hair a tribute to his Celtic origins. Though those features would be more suited to the misty mountains and rugged hills of their homeland, his feral nature made him fit in out here in the jungle, even as his paleness made him stand out.

She couldn't see the front of him, but she could tell without a doubt that his hands went to the opening of his pants, his triceps flexing enough to draw her eye.

"Keep watch on the jungle, Andrasta, or you'll get an eyeful. And who knows what might sneak up."

Oh. She spun on her heel and faced the trees. Though she wanted to snap something at him about her ability to keep all unwanted visitors away, the idea of him stripping off his pants had ensnared her imagination.

Something soft thudded to the deck, and the quiet hum of a small motor flicked to life. Her brain fogged with images. She had to invent them since she'd never seen him naked, but she was willing to put some creative energy toward the endeavor.

The sound of water droplets pattering on wood and the river's surface echoed in her ears. She tried to focus on the dense greenery in front of her, but no matter how hard she squinted into the forest, she couldn't ignore the images of him flashing through her mind.

"Wouldn't you prefer an indoor shower?" she asked.

"No."

Moody bastard. Sometimes it felt like talking to a wall. But the shortness of his tone did nothing to cool the heat rushing across her skin and through her veins, a heat that coiled between her legs to form a delicious and obnoxious tension.

Damn earth and all its emotions. They were what she'd come here for, but it was annoying to find that they didn't always do what she wanted them to.

Drip, drip, drip. The sound of the outdoor shower wove around her mind like fog, curling tendrils that pulled her head around to peek over her shoulder. She really had no control over it. Truly, anyone would look, so how could she be blamed?

Her breath caught.

She never should have looked.

But now that she had, all the power on earth couldn't drag her gaze away from the sight of a naked Cam standing with his back to her, water sluicing over the defined and flexing muscles of his shoulders to glide over the most spectacular ass and heavy thighs she'd ever seen.

He balanced on a beam that protruded from the side of the boat back out over the water at the stern. A shower contraption powered by a generator poured water over him and the beam, with the excess falling into the river. Clever. But the balancing made the muscles of his legs bulge and flex. She swallowed. Licked her lips.

Oh, hell. She was in for it.

The back of Cam's neck prickled as he scrubbed the soap from his hair. He could fool himself into thinking it was from the cool water pumped through his shower by the generator, a luxury that he'd installed when he'd brought the boat south.

But no.

He'd bet anything that the prickle came from Andrasta's gaze. Fuck. The feel of her eyes—the mere idea that she looked at him—made his cock begin to harden, stiffening and lengthening as he balanced on the sawed-off beam that had once supported the paddle wheel. There was no room for a shower in the bunkhouse, and the idea of installing the plumbing for one was ridiculous.

So the shower was outside. Not a problem when he was alone, as he usually was. It wasn't hard to find an empty patch of river and scrub up quickly. But now, with Andrasta on the boat, the shower had taken on a whole new meaning.

He squeezed his eyes shut. He'd never minded a woman's eyes on him before. But *her* eyes, they were different. Her gaze did something to him. Something more. It always had, even though he'd never fully understood why.

He soaped his chest, then moved his rough hand down, stroking over his tensed abs until he reached the steel length of his cock. He stroked himself under the pretense of washing, but when his hand lingered too long, he knew it was a lie.

She wanted to watch? The idea shot a bolt of lust through him. He gripped his shaft, the soap suds easing the way for his too-hard hand. He imagined it was her fist and pumped it up and down his cock, restraining his hips from moving.

He hadn't planned this when he'd decided to shower. But now that he was here, and she was here, he couldn't seem to stop himself. They'd been denied more all those years ago, and there was no way that they could have it now, but there was no stopping this.

The pleasure streaked too strongly through him, spiking when a soft exclamation sounded from behind him. "*Oh.*"

His hand tightened and he gritted his teeth. Pleasure surged, enough that it broke his haze and snapped him back to reality. He was a second from coming.

Too far. He'd gone too far, standing here with Andrasta's eyes on him. His fist released his cock as a crashing sound echoed from the jungle.

"What the hell?" Andrasta cried.

He spun to see her facing the jungle, her bow drawn and pointed in the direction of the oncoming noise. Cam stepped back on to the boat and yanked on his pants, wincing as the zipper hit his erection.

Fucking idiot.

"Oy, mate, we found it." The rough voice echoed from the jungle just before the enormous demon broke through the trees and onto the shore. Another demon burst from the forest behind him. Both were massive, with inhuman faces and sawed-off horns.

"I've got this," Cam growled, and reached for his sword. He sure as hell wished he had his old bow right now. Bastard Cotra demons always thought he was transporting some kind of treasure. The fact that he sometimes did was irrelevant, because they were never going to get it.

"No." Andrasta's voice had a blade of its own. "It's mine."

Within seconds, an arrow protruded from the skull of each demon. They collapsed to the muddy ground with a thud that made the jungle animals temporarily cease howling and screeching.

"What the hell? I said I had it," he said.

"No, it was my job to watch the shore. They were *my* responsibility." She turned to face him. Something hot and determined burned in her eyes.

He'd seen a shadow of it when he'd met her so many years ago. The desire to prove herself. To do the job she was assigned better than anyone had ever done it before. It was admirable at a time when he didn't want to admire her.

She was a goddess stuck in Otherworld, and he didn't believe there was a hope of her getting out. He was a demigod stuck on earth. There was no way they had a chance and pursuing more would only end in misery.

He shrugged. "Fine. They're back in the hell they came from. It'll be a while before they can bother me again."

As a Mythean, he'd always appreciated knowing that all souls are immortal. Upon their deaths, mortals would go to whatever afterlife they believed in and deserved. Belief was like a window that showed them the road they needed to take to their afterworld. Atheists were a mystery, but they ended up somewhere as well because it took some serious effort to snuff out the energy of a soul. Mytheans, the creatures of myth made real by mortal belief, were aware of the immortality of their souls.

Cam watched the bodies of the demons begin to steam. Within minutes, their earthly forms would sublimate and their souls would return to whatever hell they were from. Eventually they might get out again and come after him, because some Mytheans could cross from afterworlds to earth without death. If they did, he'd deal with them then.

"Where are they from?" Andrasta asked.

"One of the minor hells. Don't know the name. But they like shiny things, and I occasionally carry gold. They're not too smart, but they can recognize the sound of my engine if they're nearby. Good shots with the arrows, by the way."

"Obviously."

The compliment seemed to insult her, like it was beyond obvious that she'd be a good shot and to say so minimized it somehow. But then, he supposed it *was* obvious that she was an excellent shot. It was what had drawn him to her in the first place.

"Enjoy your shower?" she asked, an evil grin on her face.

"Enjoy watching?"

Her grin widened, but she turned away and hopped off the boat. He watched her retrieve her arrows, telling himself to take his stupid fucking eyes off of her. Eventually he did, and returned to the shower to snap off the water.

Hell, what had he been thinking, jerking off in front of her? He never lost his mind like that. The Amazon required constant vigilance, but as soon as he was around her, any brains he had disappeared. It had been like that when he'd first met her, and apparently nothing had changed. Another reason to stay the hell away from her.

"Want something to eat?" he asked. As much as he wanted to chuck her off the boat, it wasn't an option. And he didn't want to starve her. She didn't need to eat as often as a mortal, but she still required sustenance.

"Sure." She was cleaning the demon blood off her arrows and repacking her quiver. The way she stroked the wood as she removed the blood spoke of how much she cared for her weapons and reminded him how much he missed his bow. He shook his head and turned toward the galley.

Quickly he threw together two sandwiches and handed one to her. He ate while untying the lines and casting off. He popped the last bit in his mouth, then climbed up to the pilothouse. It'd be best to get to Havre before nightfall.

"Need any help?" Andrasta called.

His gaze raked across the shore, a green monster encroaching from both sides, unknown dangers lurking within. "Keep an eye on the jungle in case there are more demons."

He'd used the little dock he'd built in this tributary too often. This was the second time they'd found him here. Too many times for it to be coincidence.

"Sure thing." She started to climb the ladder to the pilothouse.

"You can do it from the hammock in the bow."

"I like the roof."

He sighed. "Fine."

She hopped lithely onto the flat roof behind him and paced back and forth. By the time they'd rejoined the main river and were headed toward Havre again, she'd leaned with her back against the wall of the pilothouse, presumably so that she could look out over the stern while he watched over the bow.

It put her so close to him that her scent wrapped around him. She hadn't showered, and yet she still smelled nice? He scowled.

"Anything interesting going on in Havre? Will we be there for a bit?" she asked.

"Keep an eye out on the shore."

"I am. I can talk at the same time, you know. So, back to Havre. Is there a bar? Lots of people?" The hope in her voice was palpable.

"I thought you were looking to escape Otherworld, not find a party."

"That's why I want to escape Otherworld. It's awful there."

"You should be more worried about the gods finding you."

"I am. But do you have any idea what it's like to be out of that place? I can't help it. I've been trapped forever. Alone.

There's no happiness, no friendship, no love, no sex. If I can't get out, and I get dragged back to Otherworld and chained on Blackmoor, then this is all the time I'll have had on earth. I can't help myself. I want to enjoy it." She emphasized *enjoy*, and he wondered how exactly she planned to go about that. If it meant what he thought it did.

Something in his chest twinged. He knew how she felt, even if it was stupidly dangerous.

"You remember what it's like, don't you?" she asked.

He shrugged.

"You do. You're nothing like the other gods. They don't feel anything, so they don't care what it's like. But you know it's awful. Perfectly perfect and perfectly awful. There's no feeling, no emotion, *nothing*. No excitement, joy, anger, lust. Just duty and responsibility to a nearly dead religion. No one feels anything, so no one cares for anyone else. But *I* still feel, and it's the loneliest place in the universe. I'm like a ghost there, and it just feels *wrong*. It's been two thousand years, and it's like I'm wasting away. I can't take it anymore." Heaving breaths escaped her.

His jaw clenched and he realized he was gripping the wheel too tightly. But she was right. Something had been wrong in Otherworld, and he hadn't realized it until he'd met her. Had they never met, he'd probably have turned to living stone like the rest of the gods. As it was, Ana was trapped there, and she was the farthest thing from stone. It must have been suffocatingly lonely for her. Guilt stabbed him like a sword of ice.

He'd done the best he could by her back then, but he never should have spent so much time watching her in that forest. His inability to resist her had brought her to the attention of the gods. He was directly responsible for the terrible years she'd spent there. It didn't matter that he'd been trying to do right by her. He'd still left her in misery in Otherworld.

"But your brothers are there. You have family." He knew he was grasping at straws.

A bitter laugh escaped her. "I wish. They're shadows of their former selves. Automatons. Even Marrek, my favorite brother, hardly recognizes me. It just reminds me of what I've lost."

Shit. She wanted to get out, and he understood that. But escape was nearly impossible. Maybe that's why she wasn't as worried about the gods. She didn't truly believe she would escape, so she wanted to enjoy the attempt.

He pushed empathy aside in favor of practicality. "You shouldn't go into the bar, not if you don't want to leave a trail that the gods could follow. Your glow is unmistakable."

The glow that emitted from a god's skin was modest, unnoticeable to mortals. But Mytheans could pick it out, and they would remember she'd been there if anyone asked about the Celtic god making her way downriver. He'd been grateful to lose his when he'd left Otherworld. It made blending in easier.

"No, it's already fading. Look." A slim arm appeared at his side, stuck out over the half-wall.

He looked down at it, slender but strong. She was right. The glow had begun to fade. He stopped his eyes from following her arm back to the rest of her.

"I've been here nearly a full day. The longer I stay, the more it fades. I think it's because I'm separated from

Otherworld's energy. It'll be fine, really." Her voice vibrated with excitement.

"It's your fate. Go to the bar. I'm not responsible for you. Like I said, you're just tagging along. One hint of the other gods on our tail and I'll drop you." But guilt tugged at him. Did he even mean that anymore?

Ana eyed the taut muscles of Cam's neck as his fists clenched on the steering wheel. She'd annoyed him. She knew that her excitement sometimes did that to people, but it only really bothered her with Cam.

"Anyway," she said, hoping to keep the subject light and unable to keep her enthusiasm tamped down. "Earth is amazing in comparison. I feel like a different person. Like my body is vibrating with all the emotion and life here on earth. Like I'm not alone anymore. I want to experience it all, and I don't want to wait."

"Haven't you come to earth before now?"

"Yes. But usually for only a few hours to visit my friend Esha. I'd stay longer, but then I'd risk the gods knowing I've left. We go out in Edinburgh or hang out at her place. This is the longest I've been on earth since I was mortal, and I've never been to the Amazon. I wouldn't mind meeting some South American men." She grinned.

His head whipped around, and he pinned her with an iron stare.

Her grin slipped away and she squeaked, "What?"

Though his gray eyes darkened with heat, he didn't say anything, just turned back to the wheel.

Huh. He was attracted to her. But jealous also? She shivered. Did he still feel that little twinge of something from the past, like she did? No. The memories of their time together were nothing but dust—bad moments from when her life had gone off the tracks. She'd been wrong.

How could he possibly still be interested in her? She'd blackmailed him into helping her escape Otherworld. Not to mention the arrows she'd put through his chest before she'd become a god. She'd been desperate both times, and he'd been the one to get her out of trouble. He'd also been the one who'd gotten her *in* trouble. So perhaps they were even.

But that thing with the shower... Her hands tightened on the top of the wooden half-wall as several key parts of her heated at the memory. He really had been doing what she'd thought. She shivered again.

Bad idea, bad idea, bad idea. She was grateful the demons had distracted her. Of course she was.

Because the man had secrets. Secrets that had screwed up her life and might screw it up again. She barely knew anything about him—past life or present—and what she did know indicated he was trouble. And she was trouble when she was around him. Together, they were bad news. He'd gotten her stuck in the very place she was trying to escape.

She'd come to earth for a life. For love and adventure and excitement. To be with people who made her happy and pushed out the darkness of the past two thousand years. Not for something complicated that was more than two thousand years in the making. Not for something that had ruined her life last time she'd been on earth.

CHAPTER SIX

Cam heaved a sigh of relief when the little steamboat finally pulled up to the wharf at Havre around dusk. Night animals screeched and howled as darkness descended on the jungle.

Dim yellow lamps shed a sickly glow on the brown river and docks. The jumble of wooden buildings that made up Havre crowded against the wharf and were lit only slightly better, which was fortunate as too good a view of Havre would put one off their visit.

"So, this is it then?" Andrasta asked brightly as she hopped onto the dock. Her bow was still strapped to her back, quiver full, and he figured that she didn't go anywhere without it, even if she was on the hunt for a man rather than a battle. His jaw tightened. As soon as he realized it, he forced it to relax.

Not his business. She could do what she wanted with her body. The fact that he was lusting after it was nothing but stupid.

But he couldn't keep his gaze from following her up the dock, the sway in her step and the fresh scent of her dragging him along like a mutt on a leash. She was a pillar of ivory skin and golden hair that stood out like a beacon of light against the gloomy buildings. He sighed and followed the pull of her.

"Bar is two buildings down on the left," he said to her back.

He stepped onto the shore behind her and followed her down the muddy, deserted street. Ramshackle wooden buildings rose two stories on either side of them, though Cam wouldn't have bet that the second stories were habitable. He made a point to sleep on the *Clara G.* whenever he was in Havre. It wasn't just the accommodation. Being around so many people for an extended time made him antsy.

"Sounds good. Can I buy you a drink? You know, for all the help?" she asked over her shoulder.

"You'll owe me more than a drink."

They'd nearly reached the door to the bar, and she turned to look at him. Her raised brow made him curse.

What kind of more? it said. The wicked tilt to her lips suggested that she had an idea.

He shook his head, trying to force the thoughts away. She shrugged and turned to push into the dirty little bar.

"You do take me to the nicest places," she said out of the corner of her mouth when he joined her in the entryway of the bar. It was twice as big as the Caipora's Den and half as nice, which was saying something.

"Anything for you, sugar," he said, then frowned, not knowing where the joking side of him was coming from.

"Sure."

They approached the long bar together, Cam's shoulders tensing as he took in the heads that swiveled to check out Andrasta. But her glow had faded to a faint luminescence of her skin. The men were looking for a different reason, and though it made something in his brain squeeze hard, he ignored it.

He let her buy him a beer from the unusually friendly bartender, who must be new if she was still so friendly in this hellhole, and then scanned the motley crowd for the person he'd come to meet. He gestured with his beer at the rangy, dark-haired man sitting at the end of the bar. "I've got to go talk to him. Can you keep yourself entertained?"

She grinned at him. "It's what I came here for."

He frowned, then left her to it.

"Harp," he said as he approached the man who was sitting on a barstool looking longingly after the friendly bartender.

Harp, one of his few friends, spun to face him with a smile. "Cam! About time. Did you get it?"

Cam nodded and took a seat on the barstool next to his friend and colleague. He glanced behind him to see Andrasta talking with a hulking bodybuilder of a man. That hadn't taken long.

He frowned and turned back to Harp, pulling a slip of paper from his pocket and handing it over. "Got it off Riley in a fight at the Caipora's Den."

"In the ring?"

He nodded, unconsciously clenching and unclenching his fist at the memory of the fight he'd been in just before Andrasta had shown up. It had felt good to hit the bastard. Better yet to get the name of the man who had the location of the *Rosa McManus* specimen. The rose had proven extraordinarily difficult to track down.

"Find this guy, Harp." He nodded at the slip of paper as he passed it over. "Name's Lorenzo. He knows where the *Rosa McManus* grows. I've got to go out of town for a while and won't be able to do it. Wouldn't go if I didn't have to. But you know how it is."

Harp nodded. "Got a time limit on it?"

"As soon as you can. The *Rosa McManus* sample we had turned out to be as effective as we thought. Before we realized that the bastard who gave us the first sample didn't know where the rest grew, we'd planned to start trials next month for two different drugs. Important ones. Alzheimer's and Crohn's. I've been after those two for years, and our lack of enough *Rosa McManus* is the only thing that stands in the way. Call me once you've found Lorenzo."

"Alzheimer's and Crohn's? Jesus, Cam, if you sold this stuff you could make a mint."

Cam shrugged. "Not about the fucking money. Just find him."

He took a swig of his rapidly warming too-light beer and glanced over his shoulder at Andrasta. Had she just looked away from him? And was that bastard's hand on her ass? He felt a growl rise in his throat.

"Yeah, yeah, I know. I'll find him. When will you be back?" Harp asked.

Cam turned back to Harp and dragged a hand over his face. Fuck, she was making him crazy. "A week? Two, max. But I'm counting on you to find this guy by the time I get back. I've been working on this a long time. Now that we're so close, with the key ingredient isolated, I can almost taste it."

Ana leaned back against the bar, listening with half an ear to Kon, the Incan god of wind and rain, trying to chat her up. A babble of other languages floated through the bar. Mostly, though, she was listening to Cam's conversation.

He was hunting down a cure for Alzheimer's and Crohn's? And it wasn't about the money? She'd underestimated him.

She caught sight of Cam swiveling to look at her and jerked her head up to look into Kon's eyes. He really was handsome. She jumped a bit when she felt his big hand on her ass. A jolt shot up her body, illuminating her nerve endings like lanterns flicked on one by one.

He might not be exactly the man she wanted—as much as she hated to admit it, *that* man was sitting down the bar, talking fancy roses meant to cure diseases—but the arousal that had been riding her hard since she'd gotten to earth was pretty pleased with Kon's advances.

She turned her back to Cam and smiled at Kon. He grinned down at her. He really was much more fun than the Celtic gods. But then, who wasn't?

"Can I get another beer?"

Ana started at the sound of the voice, so rough that it dragged across her skin and made her shiver. Cam. He was standing right behind her. Her skin prickled with goose bumps. Slowly, her heart in her throat, she turned her head to look at him.

But he wasn't looking at her. He had eyes only for the pretty bartender. But if he only had eyes for the bartender, why had he come over to Ana's side of the bar to order his drink? She licked her lips, hoping that he'd turn to look at her.

He didn't, though she swore she could feel the tension radiating from his stiffened muscles and the clenched fists that rested on the bar. Confused and disappointed, she turned back to Kon.

"Thanks," Cam said as his drink was handed to him.

His voice sent a shiver through Ana, a sound that sucked all the noise from the rest of the room until just the echo of it remained in her head, trapping her. Unable to help herself, she glanced over her shoulder to see that he'd walked back to his friend. She felt a twinge of disappointment, then cursed herself for being an idiot.

She'd come here for some company, to make up for all the lost time she'd spent hanging around alone in Otherworld. Cam was too complicated. Being involved with him would get her heart broken again.

She needed a distraction.

"Kiss me." She reached up to grab Kon's big shoulders.

He grinned, a sexy white swath that cut across his tan face. His green eyes sparkled with appreciation as he yanked her toward him and captured her mouth with his own. Hot and hard, he kissed her, and a jolt of lust streaked through her.

Yes. This was what she'd been missing. This was what she needed. Just as she opened her mouth to return his kiss, hard hands gripped her upper arms and lifted her away from Kon.

"Time to be going." Cam's voice, rough before, was gravel at her ear as he all but carried her out of the bar. Kon yelled after them, but he shut up as soon as Cam swung his head around to pin the man with a gaze that promised pain.

"Hey!" she said as the bar door swung closed behind them. "I was having a good time."

"I saw," he growled down at her. "But it's time to go. I'll carry you back if I have to."

The idea made Ana swallow hard as she looked up at him. He towered above her, his huge form cutting out the weak glow of the streetlights so that she couldn't make out his expression. But his anger—that she could feel. It enclosed her as tightly as the humid air of the jungle.

"Come on." He grabbed her hand. His big stride ate up the muddy walkway, and she had to trot to keep up.

"What the hell is your problem?" Though she had to admit that part of her was thrilled he was dragging her out of the bar and that she was holding his hand. He was the one she really wanted. No question. She'd have really regretted it with Kon.

"You're my problem."

They'd reached the boat, and he lifted her by the waist to swing her on board. His hands burned into her skin. He hadn't touched her since last night when she'd found him in the Caipora's Den. He released her too soon and made quick work of untying the boat.

"Where are we going? We're leaving Havre already?" she asked.

He grunted and pointed to some moorings a short way from shore. What a caveman. But her eyes followed him as he climbed quickly into the pilothouse and gunned the engines.

She stood, her breathing too heavy and a faint sweat on her skin as he maneuvered to the moorings. He killed the engines. Silence crashed around them. His speed made her dizzy as he tied off to the two moorings so that the boat wouldn't drift—but then, he was performing a two-man job in the middle of a river.

The lights of Havre gleamed in the distance, fainter now. The little village looked romantic rather than shabby from far away.

She rubbed her arms, looking for a distraction from the heat between her thighs. It'd been too long. And earth was just too much. All the energy of the bar, all the joy and anger and lust that had bombarded her since she'd stepped into Havre, was wreaking havoc with her senses. It was nearly overwhelming.

"Why are we all the way out here?" she asked.

"Safer." He was stomping about the boat, checking lines and the machinery, his movements too jerky and forceful for a normal nighttime routine. With a start, she realized he was as worked up as she was.

CHAPTER SEVEN

Cam threw the last of the lines into the hatch and stood over it, chest heaving. He clenched his fists, staring down into the blackness of the hold as he tried to get himself together.

He'd just dragged her out of the bar. Tossed her on the boat. What the hell had he been thinking?

But as soon as he'd seen that bastard's mouth all over hers, something in him had snapped. It felt like he was only now gaining consciousness, his mind surfacing from the black tar of jealousy and rage that had swamped it.

Damn it, it wasn't his business who she kissed. He stared down at his hands, too big and too strong. Strong enough to do damage. But he'd used them to drag her out of the bar and down the street. He had no idea how gentle he'd been. Probably not enough. It didn't matter that she was immortal and would heal. He shouldn't have done it.

He heaved a disgusted sigh. He was an asshole, and worse, he couldn't seem to help it. He hadn't deserved the affections of someone like her in the past, and he didn't deserve them now.

"Why the hell did you haul me out of there?" Andrasta's voice sent a jolt through him.

He looked up to see her standing only a couple feet from him, her back against the wall of the bunkhouse.

"You don't care about me, so why do you care who I kiss?" she asked.

He shoved his hand through his hair, unsure of how to answer because he didn't understand it himself. He did care about her, damn it, and it felt weird as hell. Gods shouldn't have emotions, yet he had. And still did.

He had them because of her. He'd felt nothing before he'd met her all those years ago. She was brave, skilled, smart, and beautiful. More than that. Yet it wasn't just those qualities that had drawn him to her. They were admirable qualities, but not enough to incite the birth of emotion in him.

The problem was, he had no idea why she had triggered it. It was the damned mystery of his life.

Worse, being with her for the last day and a half had reminded him how much he'd liked her company all those years ago. How much he liked *her*.

It was unnatural. *He* was unnatural. A failed god who felt emotion. It was a mess inside his head that he tried to silence however he could.

Except he couldn't silence it with her.

And now she stood in front of him, tiny and curvy and strong and irresistible, her breath heaving. It shouldn't have sounded louder than the howls of the animals in the jungle, but it did. It reached inside him and squeezed, drawing him to her.

He crowded her, pressed his hands to the wall on either side of her head.

"Cam?" Her voice trembled, but the way she licked her lips, the way her eyes heated, gave him all the clues he needed.

She wanted him. Hell, she was fresh from Otherworld. She wanted anyone. He remembered what it was like to arrive on earth and be sensitive to all the feelings that weren't present in Otherworld. It made one hot as hell in a way that wasn't entirely natural.

The knowledge that she'd have settled for the guy back at the bar didn't deter him. She wanted anyone, and he wanted only her. It made a pang of loneliness shoot through his chest. But it wasn't enough to push him away from her. He'd wanted only her since he'd seen her so many years ago. He'd wanted her enough to ruin her life, to change his.

"Andrasta," he rasped.

Her face tilted up to meet his, desire in her eyes.

"It's Ana," she whispered, gripping his shirt with her small fists. Her cheeks flushed and she licked her lips again. "What are you doing to me?"

He leaned in, close enough to feel her breath. Held himself back with the knowledge that for her, it was just the effect of being on earth, being bombarded by all the feelings that were repressed in Otherworld. It wasn't about him. But he couldn't stop himself from answering. From prolonging this torture.

"Nothing. Ana." He liked the way her name felt on his tongue. Andrasta was from the past. Ana—the same, but so different—was from now. He wanted to do all the things to her that he'd never had a chance to before.

His shaft pressed painfully hard against his fly, and his breath came harshly as he resisted the urge to pull her against him. There were so many reasons not to.

Like the fact that she didn't stand a chance of getting out of Otherworld. Not unless he went back. And there was no way he'd be doing that. The mere idea sent a cold wave over him.

"You're right, Ana. I don't care about you." The words scraped his throat, leaving scars that would stick. It was a bastard thing to say, but it was the only thing that would break the moment between them. "You were making a fucking scene in that bar, and I didn't want to leave anything memorable for the gods to track us with if they followed your signal downriver."

He pushed away from her, steeled his heart against the sight of her shocked and trembling against the wall of the bunkhouse.

He was a bastard. He'd never deserved to be a god, not with his fucked-up wiring, and he certainly didn't deserve someone like Ana. He'd screwed her by getting her stuck in Otherworld. Then he'd run from his responsibilities there and run from her, abandoning her to a miserable fate.

From her perch on the boat's roof, Ana eyed the jaguar lounging on the shore. He blended into the shade of the jungle.

The sound of Cam starting the engines had woken her a few hours ago, and she'd joined him on deck. She'd climbed onto the rooftop to act as lookout while he piloted them downstream. Now that she'd been gone from Otherworld for two nights—the longest she'd ever stayed away—she was sure the other gods knew she was gone. Getting to Druantia first was the only thing that would save her.

The sun beat upon her skin as she peered into the jungle, trying to keep her mind on her task and off of last night.

After Cam had delivered his parting shot and stormed off, she'd lain on the sparse mattress in the bunkhouse, in sheets that smelled of Cam, with the doors and windows open in an attempt to cool off.

The breeze hadn't been nearly enough to douse the fire within her. Despite their past and the fact that he was a moody bastard, she wanted Cam. What she'd gotten was her own hand.

She'd tried to keep quiet, but at a certain point, she just hadn't cared. Cam had been a jerk. Whether he meant what he said or not, she wasn't sure. But she'd gotten off to the thought of him anyway. Like hate-fucking. But solo.

When she'd finally lain exhausted on the bed, with the worst of the damnable tension and arousal gone, she'd decided to pretend that their near-kiss had never happened.

"Why is your boat named the *Clara G.*?" She asked over her shoulder from where she sat on the roof. She couldn't stand the silence or the tension anymore. Had Clara been a woman he'd once loved? She was just curious. Not jealous. There was a difference.

Fates, she was a bad liar, even to herself.

"It's named after the original owner's wife. Clara Goddard. First female pilot on the Yukon River. Bad luck to change a boat's name. And I like the idea of her."

Ana grinned, absentmindedly twirling an arrow in her hand. He liked tough women. No surprise, from such a tough man.

She watched the jungle pass by, enjoying the unfamiliar sight. If she longed for life and excitement, this was the place to get it.

"So your pharmaceutical company is close to a couple big cures?" she asked.

"Yeah. Medicines that could cause remission."

"That's really nice."

"It's fun. I like it down here, and looking for new plants for cures gives me something to do."

"Sure, Mr. President or CEO or whatever you are."

"That's just a title. In reality, I'm just the muscle."

You sure are. But that's not all.

"I've got smart people running operations back in Scotland for me," he said.

"Back in Scotland? At the Immortal University?"

The Immortal University, located outside of Edinburgh, was the educational center and informal governing body of Mytheans in Great Britain. It performed a number of functions, the most important of which was overseeing British Mytheans and keeping them under the radar of mortals.

The university also provided services that Mytheans couldn't get elsewhere, lest mortals figured out that their clients never died. Things like education, a hospital, banking. Everyday stuff, but for supernatural creatures that she'd never dreamed existed when she'd been mortal. The idea that mortal beliefs had willed Mytheans into existence had been a hell of a shock.

"Yeah, some," Cam said, but he seemed unwilling to elucidate.

"You fought that guy in the ring at the Caipora's Den for the identity of some cures?"

"I fought that guy because I like to fight."

"But you got the location of an important rose from him, right?"

"Yeah. That was a benefit."

She had a feeling he was playing up the side of himself that was less admirable, though she had no idea why. "And it's why you're so anxious to get to Druantia and get your cloaking spell reactivated, isn't it?"

"Nailed it. I've been working toward this for decades. Can't let it slip through my fingers now."

"Thought so."

"What do you plan to do about finding someone to take your place?"

"What?"

"The potion isn't going to do you much good without someone to take your place in Otherworld. You knew that."

"What?" Her mind scrambled. "What do you mean, someone to take my place?"

"What it sounds like. Gods can't kill other gods because we're all needed to maintain the balance of power and keep Otherworld running. The only way to leave godhood is the way I did it—with a replacement."

She swallowed hard, fairly certain that her stomach had just dropped to her feet. "But where am I going to find someone to take my place? Can it be anyone?"

Damn it. She'd been so close. She should have realized, but of course she hadn't. She'd jumped headfirst into this like she did with everything, consequences be damned—and she'd learned long ago that the consequences could be very damning. She should know better by now.

"It can't be just anyone." His voice was grim. Like he cared about this. "It's got to be someone of equal skill."

Her heart stopped. She had only one equal in skill.

Him.

CHAPTER EIGHT

Southeast Celtic Britain, 13 AD
Territory between the Iceni and Trinovante Kingdoms

Andrasta raced through the forest toward her home, her mind still alight with memories of Camulos. Her brothers were always worried if she wasn't home by sunset, but she couldn't bring herself to care right now.

It had been hard to make it home before dark this past week. This was the seventh day she'd seen and spoken with Camulos. As ever, he'd waited for her in the shadow of the trees, a scowl on his face that smoothed out when she approached him.

After their kiss a week ago, which had been interrupted by her brother, she hadn't known if Camulos would return. After what he'd threatened, she hadn't been sure if she wanted him to. But he wouldn't actually kill her brother or her, right?

She couldn't believe he would, so she'd returned to the clearing to see him, albeit with her hand on her bow and wariness in her step. Camulos drew her like a fly to honey, and she had a feeling that she did the same to him.

He was hot and cold with her, as if he wanted to be with her but knew he shouldn't. Something dangerous that she didn't understand was at play, but at least she was smart enough to know it hovered over them. He had an agenda she couldn't quite figure out, and he wouldn't speak of it, but it didn't stop her from meeting him every day for long walks through the forest.

Continuing to see him was probably the stupidest thing she'd ever done, but the hope that he'd continue to smile at her and maybe even kiss her again kept her coming back for more.

But he hadn't kissed her again. His desire was so strong it was palpable, but he resisted. As much as she wanted his kisses, his restraint made her trust him. Instead, they walked and talked. They'd shared their pasts and presents, their hopes and dreams. He'd been short on the hopes and dreams, but she'd had plenty to share.

He cared for her. She was certain of it. And she'd grown to care for him even as his statement that he'd been sent to earth to kill her lingered in her mind.

She truly was crazy. But no. He had no reason to kill her that she could see. Even if someone had sent him to do the terrible job, he'd obviously made them change their mind. And who would ever notice her, much less want to kill her?

"Andrasta! You're late again!" Bradan's voice broke through the fog of her thoughts and she realized that she was nearly home.

She looked up to see her second-youngest brother standing in front of the door of their round house, his broad shoulders draped in a brown cloak and his red hair dark in the dim light.

"I'm here, I'm here. The sun has not yet set."

Bradan scowled at the sky. "Close enough."

"I wish you'd trust me to take care of myself!" She could feel her face heating and her blood rushing with the familiar helpless anger that their overprotectiveness engendered in her. Why was it always like this?

"You endanger your own safety. And you're never careful enough to see threats where they really lie." He grabbed her as she tried to slip through the door and pulled her into a hug. Her heart warmed against her will.

"That's not true." Her words were muffled against his chest. But a niggling of doubt crept in. Was he right? She wasn't being entirely smart about Camulos. As much as she cared for him, and sensed that he cared for her, there was something beneath it all that wasn't quite right.

"It's true," Bradan said. "Isn't it, fellows?"

His tone was almost joking—her brothers loved to pick on her—but there was censure beneath it. Six familiar faces in various phases of laughing agreement or annoyance looked up from where they sat on low benches surrounding the hearth in the middle of the room.

She scowled at them all. Each polished his weapon, the symbols of her exclusion. They all looked so similar—such a united front—that her heart pinged with the loneliness of not being included. Ever since their mother had died giving birth to her, it had been just Andrasta and the men in her family. There was no place for her except by their side. As children, they'd played together every day. Countless hours during which she'd been one of them. When their father had died six years ago, they had become an even more cohesive unit.

She'd had the constant companionship of at least one of her brothers until a few years ago, when she'd grown from girl to woman and they'd all grown from boys to warriors. And they'd decided it was too dangerous for her to train and fight with them. A decision made out of love, but one that cut her off from the family she so adored.

She'd never wanted anything like she wanted things to go back to the way they had been. When they'd been a team. The desire was a constant, aching companion that rode on her back as she practiced and practiced and practiced. But they refused to give her an opportunity to prove herself.

Other women were warriors. Why not she? It might be dangerous to fight alongside them, but didn't they know she'd die for them?

She'd tried to get Camulos to show himself to her brothers so she could prove that she wasn't a nobody, that she could shoot her bow as well as a god, but he'd shut her down so quickly that she'd not asked again.

"You need to stop running off to the woods every day. It's dangerous." Bradan settled onto the bench closest to the door and withdrew his sword to polish it as his brothers were doing. "Find a husband. Start a family and give up this dangerous, stupid dream of being a warrior."

A bubbling black tar of rage filled her chest up to her eyes, until her anger and pain blurred her vision.

She yanked one of the blue arrows from her quiver and thrust it toward them. She'd been hoarding it until now, but she could bear their dismissal no longer. "This belonged to Camulos."

Caedmon, her eldest brother, frowned from where he sat in the great chair that their father had occupied before his death. Marrek, the youngest and the one to whom she was closest, eyed it suspiciously.

She stomped her foot and yelled, "I speak the truth. Look at the fletching. I've never seen feathers that blue. I couldn't have made it."

"Ah, come on, little sister. Calm down and have a seat. You're turning red." Caedmon stopped polishing his sword hilt just long enough to indicate a seat on the bench nearest him.

Andrasta almost growled, but she took the seat in front of the popping fire. Its glow illuminated the faces of her brothers, all of whom sat in a circle around the flames. Every night they sat here polishing their weapons before dinner. Every night she sat twirling an arrow. They laughed at the weapon. At her.

"Come now, where did you really find the arrow?" Caedmon's voice was kind. He was kind. They all were, at their hearts, even though they were sometimes mean. They did it to protect her, but it was suffocating.

"I told you," she snapped. *Believe me!* she wanted to shout. *Let me join you.*

Except that her brothers had never let her join them in training or in battle. She was on the outside looking in.

"Here, take it." She thrust the arrow at him so hard he was forced to grasp it. His brows shot up when the arrow made contact with his skin, then dropped as he frowned at it. Her breath caught in her lungs as she watched him inspect it.

"You feel it, don't you?" The vibration of power emitted by the arrow was unmistakable.

His eyes met hers, but he said nothing. He handed it off to Bradan, whose head jerked when he touched it.

"Camulos?" Bradan asked.

She nodded. "He uses the bow for war. Not just hunting."

Marrek frowned at that, but he too stiffened when the arrow was passed his way.

"We had a competition. I beat him."

Caedmon laughed.

"I did. And I'm not little anymore!" This was supposed to convince them. It was supposed to work.

He sighed, then looked around at the other brothers. They'd all touched the arrow now, and met his gaze with heavy stares.

"The arrow isn't from here. And there have been no trade expeditions in months," Bradan said.

"And Andrasta wouldn't keep something like that secret for more than a few minutes."

She scowled at Caedmon, who shrugged at her.

"Ah, gods, you and your little weapon." Bradan groaned.

"It's not just a little weapon!"

"No, no longer. If this"—he raised the arrow—"is what it appears to be, you've brought the god of war down upon your head."

"He said I was skilled."

"You are skilled," Marrek said. He smiled at her.

Warmth filled her chest. She could always count on him to be there for her.

"Too skilled for your own good. This is what we get for leaving you to your antics." Caedmon dragged a hand down his face, leaving a weary expression in its wake.

"Antics? I'm a warrior!" She barely resisted surging to her feet.

"What you are is a menace. All fire and action, but little sense. Always charging forward, not thinking of the consequences or the danger. And you've caught the attention of the warrior to end all warriors, if this arrow is what it appears to be."

"But why?" Marrek asked, concern tightening his brow.

Bradan dropped his head into his hand. "If Camulos is indeed using the bow as a weapon of war, and our little sister has actually become that skilled..." He cursed vilely. "The old stories tell of the gods coming to earth long ago. Hafgan, one of the kings of Otherworld, is said to have once been mortal. He was so skilled with a pike, his weapon of choice, that he defeated the former king of the gods and rose in his stead. He pulled the ladder up behind him, and the gods have been determined to see that no other mortal usurps their power. If Camulos is indeed interested in Andrasta, that's why he's here."

"What?" Fear slithered across her skin; she gripped her bow. So there was a real reason for him to kill her? He hadn't been sent by another, but by himself?

"And they always kill the mortal. It's their law," Caedmon said.

Camulos was resisting killing her. He had to be. For how long could he resist? "What happens if he doesn't kill me?"

Bradan shrugged. "The gods would probably kill him. I don't know. But there's nothing to stay his hand. You're at risk. You can't go to the clearing anymore to practice. He could be there."

He would be there. She swallowed hard.

"He's right," Caedmon, the final voice in the family, said. "You can't go back. No more shooting."

"You can't stop me." But fear tightened her skin until it itched. Did she want them to stop her? She wanted to see Camulos again, and she certainly didn't want to believe he would kill her. But Camulos himself had told her that he had to. Oh gods, what would she do?

"Of course we can." Caedmon plucked her bow from where it sat next to her.

"No! Give it back!" She reached for it, but Bradan gently pushed her back.

"It's for the best. We can't allow you to see him. We love you too much to lose you. Without your bow, you aren't a threat to him. When he forgets about you, we'll give it back."

Panic streaked through her. She'd never been without her bow. "I need my bow!"

No matter how she begged, they wouldn't give it back to her. She'd even cried, which she despised, but she couldn't control herself. Being without her bow made her feel helpless. Worthless.

After a long night of tossing and turning on her pallet without her bow on the floor next to her, she woke to a quiet dawn and grim brothers. The men filed out of the house, silent and stern.

Caedmon, almost the last to leave, turned to her and hugged her. Against the top of her head, he whispered, "I'm sorry. But this is safest for you."

She watched him walk out the door through blurry vision, her throat tight with loss and loneliness.

"Andrasta."

She turned to see Marrek standing behind her.

"I thought you'd gone."

"No, you were just busy staring forlornly after the others."

She gave a watery chuckle, but there was no joy in the sound. He was the youngest, and as such had been with her the longest before he too moved onto training with their brothers. Whenever she was sad, he was usually the one to comfort her.

"Wait a moment." He grinned, then turned and walked to the far side of the room.

Her jaw dropped when she saw him pull one of the huge benches closer to the wall, right beneath the high shelf where they'd stored her bow. She'd never have been able to pull that weight, or reach that high even with the bench.

But Marrek had her bow down before she could fully process what he was doing.

He pushed the bench back in place, then returned and handed the bow to her. "Here. Keep it hidden from the others."

"Thank you, Marrek!"

"You'd just make another eventually. But I know you love this one best. And I'm not saying you can go back to the clearing. I'll break your bow before I let you put yourself in danger like that. But this bow is everything to you, and I respect your judgment. And your skill. So practice near the house. If you see the god again, tell me and I'll stay with you."

Andrasta threw her arms around Marrek. "Thank you, thank you, thank you."

Camulos waited in the forest for Andrasta, his hand clenched around the shaft of his bow. She was late. Hours late. The same fear that had dogged him every other day that he'd waited for her was nipping at his heels.

He was afraid she wouldn't come, because he wanted to see her so damned badly. And he was afraid that she *would* come, because eventually the gods would come down upon their heads.

Every day when he returned to Otherworld, that bastard Cernowain was there, watching him. His eyes asked if Camulos had done it yet. When it was clear he hadn't, Cernowain's expression darkened. Not with anger, because the gods didn't feel anger through their cold logic. And not with sorrow, though if Cernowain had felt emotion, Camulos had a feeling that's what would have been on his face.

Because there was no way for this to continue, not without the death of one of them—or both. Every day, the pressure of the gods' threat weighed upon him. If he didn't fall in line and do what was expected, things would become far worse.

"They've gone to see her." The voice that carried through the trees was masculine, and distinctly unwelcome.

Camulos turned to see Cernowain, who stood with his boar, white snowflakes glinting from the hair of both.

"What?" Camulos asked.

"Hafgan and his close council have gone to see Andrasta. You've run out of time. And so has she."

Helpless rage filled Camulos' chest, pushing at his ribs until he thought they'd break. He'd welcome the pain— anything to distract from this powerlessness.

"Do it, Camulos. If you still have the chance. Send her to Otherworld rather than leave her to face the machinations and tortures of the gods."

"What do they plan?"

"What does it matter? You'll both be dead, lucky if you have your souls to go to Otherworld. They could destroy her. Who knows the whims of gods?" He laughed, bitterness and irony in the sound. "Do it, Camulos."

Cernowain disappeared. Camulos wanted to roar his rage to the sky. Kill her to save her from a worse fate? She'd go to Otherworld to live out her days, but take her from earth to the cold nothingness of their afterworld?

She'd awakened something in him these last days, something he couldn't describe but he couldn't get enough of. As he couldn't get enough of her. And now he had no choice but to take her life from her to save her from something more terrible?

Andrasta paced in front of the doorway to her house, wearing a path through the snow until it was nothing but mud. She shivered and pulled her woolen cloak tighter, fiddling with the bronze pin that held the top closed.

She should go see Camulos in the clearing.

No.

It was too dangerous. She'd been stupid to trust him. What did she know of the goals and desires of gods? He had to have a motivation in continuing to see her. She'd thought he'd liked her. That he'd cared for her, even.

But if what her brothers said was true, then he couldn't possibly. She'd put herself at risk—and worse, far worse, she'd put her brothers at risk.

She continued to pace, weighing the sheer stupidity of going to the clearing against her desire to see Camulos. Maybe he did care for her. Or maybe she was being crazy.

With him, she'd leapt before she'd ever considered looking, just as her brothers always accused her of doing. And even though she regretted the danger she was putting her family in by dallying with a god, she couldn't help but want to keep doing it.

She was too brave to be cowering like this. She gripped her bow tighter and turned toward the clearing. She'd go to him and demand to know his intentions.

She took a step off her well-beaten path, but suddenly four people stood before her.

No. Not people. *Gods.* They'd appeared out of the air and were dressed nothing like Camulos had been. He'd been clothed for battle, whereas these gods, two males and two females, were draped in gold. The torcs around their necks, the sparkling brooches on their cloaks, and the weapons hanging from their belts were all made of the precious metal.

Shock rooted her in place, her breath coming short and fast. Drawing the attention of four gods could only be bad. Her hand tightened around the smooth, comforting wood of her bow.

"Andrasta," the dark-haired goddess said. She was extraordinarily beautiful, with sparkling blue eyes and cream-colored skin. A red cloak finer than any Andrasta had ever seen was draped around her.

Andrasta debated shaking her head. But they were gods. They knew exactly who she was. So she nodded and squared her shoulders, even though they could kill her before she saw it coming.

"You have a problem," the dark-haired goddess said.

Indeed.

"Camulos is going to kill you."

Her heart clutched. So it was most definitely true. "I know. Why are you here?"

"To make an arrangement with you. Camulos should have killed you weeks ago, the first time he saw you. Yet he didn't. We don't know why, but it's dangerous. He's dangerous. He's no longer obeying the rules. Otherworld exists only because of our rules. Without them, we are lost."

"How does this concern me?"

"We want you to kill him."

Andrasta's head snapped back. "What?"

"His behavior is erratic and has become dangerous. He's too powerful. We want him gone."

There was no way she could kill him. Nor was she willing to. "Why can't you kill him?"

"We are forbidden from killing other gods. You aren't. And your skill with the bow matches his. You're the only mortal capable of killing Camulos. When you kill him, we'll raise you to godhood in his stead."

All sound, from the whistling wind to the lowing cows, faded as Andrasta swayed on her feet. *Her*, a goddess? No, that wasn't possible. And not if she had to kill Camulos to become so.

"Why?" The words strangled in her throat.

"We must have a god of war. Merely killing him would create an imbalance. If you defeat him, you will become the goddess of victory, a war goddess."

"You think I'll be weaker than he is. Easier to control." She wasn't stupid. This was a chess game for them and she was but a pawn.

The goddess shrugged elegantly. "True, we've decided that you'll be less trouble than he. You're young, not yet tainted by godhood. And just think." The goddess' voice sweetened. "You'll be the goddess of victory. Far greater than even the warrior you'd hoped to be."

She gripped her bow tighter, recalling the long walks with Camulos. His smile. His kiss. No one had ever been interested in her in such a way. She could finally prove herself as a warrior, but at the expense of Camulos' life.

But if she had to become a goddess to do so, she'd have to leave her brothers. A pang shot through her chest. She didn't want to leave them. She wanted to be one of them. More than she wanted to prove herself, even.

"You don't have a choice in this!" the goddess yelled. "Camulos is dangerous. Eventually he will try to kill you, because he knows that not doing so is against our laws. There will be repercussions for him that he won't want to face. Take your chance. Save yourself from him and receive godhood in exchange."

"He wouldn't hurt me," Andrasta said, certain of it. But was she? He'd threatened her back in the forest a week ago and raised his bow against her brother when he'd come searching for her. She'd known there was something more than what was on the surface between them, something darker. Had it been this fate? "No. I don't believe it."

"Fine." The goddess' voice whipped across her skin, harsh as a blade. "Then we'll slay your family—seven brothers, isn't it?—if you do not do as we tell you."

Her stomach dropped. "What?"

"You'll do this."

The threat, and the command, snapped some of the strength back into her. She gripped her bow and said, "You want to get rid of Camulos because he's trouble. Your threats don't endear you to me. *I* could be trouble."

"You can't play our games." The goddess' voice was harsh. She raised her hands and snow swirled, flying fast on the wind until it was dense white in front of her. Images formed on the snow, and soon her brothers appeared. They practiced at their training field, swords and pikes flying through the air.

"What is this?" she asked, shock at the magic stealing her breath.

"Your brothers," the goddess said. "Look closer and you'll see Hafgan, the god who stood to my left."

Andrasta squinted at the image in the snow and saw the towering form of the god standing at the edge of the field, apparently invisible to her brothers. She glanced away from the image toward where Hafgan had been standing.

He was gone.

"He went there?" Andrasta asked, knowing it was true even as she said it.

"Yes. And he'll kill one of your brothers for every hour you delay."

"No, he can't—" Andrasta cried out when she saw Hafgan throw a short spear at Marrek. The blade pierced Marrek's side and he fell, his blood soaking into the snow. "Stop!"

"When you've done what we've requested," the goddess said. "Do it, or he'll throw another spear."

Andrasta's eyes raced over the image in the snow. Bradan fell to Marrek's side, trying to stanch the bleeding, while the rest of her brothers surrounded them, searching the practice field for the threat.

"They'll never see him coming," the goddess said. "You have an hour before he throws the spear again."

A sob tore free of Andrasta's throat. "Marrek must live!"

"He will. Perhaps. As long as Hafgan doesn't throw another spear."

Andrasta felt the sting of tears freezing on her cheeks as she watched Bradan try to comfort Marrek and keep his life's blood from flowing out.

"Fine." The words were ragged. She met the goddess' eyes. "Promise that they will live if I do this."

The goddess' eyes hardened, but she nodded. "I promise. Do as we tell you and reap the rewards. Otherwise, everything you love will die."

CHAPTER NINE

Amazon Basin, Present Day

"Get the hell up here, Ana! Something's coming!"

Ana's head snapped up at the sound of Cam's roar. She was at the stern of the boat, trying to manage a quick sponge bath and moping over Cam's dire revelation of an hour ago about finding a replacement. She flung the washcloth back into the basin of water and sprinted to the pilothouse.

"What's going on?"

He leaned out, squinting up at the sky. She looked up too.

"Oh, shit," she breathed.

"Yeah. Not normal." Black clouds roiled low on the horizon in front of them, pushing forward across the sky like a clipper at high wind.

"What is it?" she asked.

"Storm. But it's bringing something with it."

A chill wind followed his words, rushing down upon them from the clouds. She shivered; it was the first time she'd been cold since entering the Amazon. The clouds darkened the sky nearly to night.

The screeching and howling of the animals faded. They'd never been silent before. She swallowed hard, then shook herself. She was the goddess of victory. A Celtic war goddess. Nothing scared her.

Keep telling yourself that.

"Get up here," Cam yelled over the wind.

She scrambled up the ladder and onto the roof.

"Watch the forest!" He jerked his head left, indicating the side of the river with the darkest clouds.

Cold rain pinged off of the metal roof, biting into her skin.

She peered into the jungle, appalled to see the previously calm vines and trees whipping about. Raking claws of wind tore leaves from branches, scattering them into the normally calm river. Whitecaps crashed into the bow, splashing over the low guard wall that was meant to protect from such flooding.

Shallow water boat, she thought. Not meant for this kind of weather. Would they sink in the middle of the Amazon, hundreds of miles from their destination?

"What am I looking for?" she shouted, raking her wet hair off her face and peering harder into the forest. Water dripped into her eyes, blurring the jungle to shades of green and black.

"Something Celtic. From Otherworld. I don't know. But this isn't an Amazonian storm."

An unnatural chill broke out over her skin, colder than either the wind or the rain could elicit. She whipped her bow off her back and an arrow from her quiver. Did the gods send something with the storm? Was that how they would get her?

"There!" she yelled, pointing to the forest.

Boar spies. The gods had sent fucking spies after her rather than track her progress themselves.

She raised her bow, sighted an arrow, and shot the ugly gray beast between the eyes. It collapsed, but she looked for more. The gods had conjured the storm to send boar spies, who couldn't aetherwalk, ahead of them. The animals couldn't speak, but they could report back with what they'd seen if Cernowain, god of animals, was there to read their minds.

"Get closer to the north shore!" she yelled.

Cam cursed and piloted the little boat through the waves toward the shore, careful not to let the broad side face the waves. He pulled as close as he could get, and she was grateful that the river was deep here.

Bow drawn, she searched through the trees, now only a dozen feet away. Hanging vines trailed in the water, raking eerily over her shoulders when Cam steered the boat beneath them. At this range, she'd hit anything she could see.

There, another. The arrow flew from her bow and the boar collapsed. But how the hell was she supposed to see them all in such thick cover?

"There!" Cam roared and pointed ahead of the boat.

Another arrow, another downed boar. But the huge storm could carry dozens. How would she see them all and kill them before they returned to Otherworld on another storm with word of their location?

Unless...

She slung the bow over her back and searched for a vine. A perfect one was nearing the bow of the boat as they motored along the shore.

She sucked in a bracing breath, waited for the ideal moment, then took off running across the roof. The vine was thick in her hands, and she prayed that it would take her to shore. Air whistled by her as she sailed through the sky. When it swung her over the shore, she let go and landed in sticky mud.

"Ana!" Cam roared, his rage and worry carrying easily on the wind. "Get back on the damned boat! It's too dangerous!"

She ignored him. The boars would scent her on shore and come to get a closer look. They wouldn't be able to help themselves.

She yanked up her bow and nocked an arrow just before the first boar lumbered toward her. The arrow thudded between its eyes. The mud sucked her feet deep into the bank as she searched the jungle. Three more charged and she shot them in succession. Satisfaction coursed through her when they fell.

"Get back on the damn boat, Ana!" There was real fear in his voice now. Fear for her.

She ignored it and raced along the shore beside the boat, shooting boars as they charged out of the jungle. She counted fifteen before they stopped appearing.

Her arrows had felled them all, but like the demons from the other day, she hadn't killed them. She'd just delayed their return to Otherworld. They would regenerate there, but it would take them longer than if they'd reported back as they were supposed to. At best, she'd bought them some time. How much, she couldn't be sure. Hopefully she and Cam would be long gone from here by the time they regenerated and Cernowain could read their minds.

"Get your ass on the fucking boat!" Cam roared.

She glanced over her shoulder. He'd steered close to shore and looked like he was about to jump off and swing her back to safety. Worry twisted his face, evident even through the rain. Whitecaps still crashed into the boat, and vines dragged at the pilothouse.

There was no time to retrieve her arrows, which were scattered behind her. Mud sucked at her feet as she ran and leapt onto the deck, scrambling to pull herself on board.

She clambered up the ladder to the roof to resume her vigil. But the storm had veered toward normalcy. Pounding rain, but no roiling black clouds.

"They're gone!" she screamed.

She thought Cam growled, and she watched anxiously as he turned the boat into another tributary like the one they'd visited the day before.

He pulled along shore, leapt down from the pilothouse, and tied the boat off to posts stuck into the bank presumably for that purpose.

She climbed down after him, raking the wet hair off her forehead as she hurried toward the bunkhouse to stand beneath its shelter. Rain still pounded down, a cacophony against the tin roof. The din of animals screeching and howling returned, signaling that the threat from Otherworld was gone. She rubbed her arms, wishing that cold and nerves didn't still skitter across her skin.

The gods had already figured out she was gone. It'd only been two days. She'd been sure she'd have at least a few days more, long enough to make it out of the Amazon.

She huddled against the exterior wall of the bunkhouse and waited for Cam to finish securing the boat. He was quick and capable. Rainwater gleamed on his flexing biceps as he yanked on the final line. Satisfied, he dropped it.

Ana started when Cam whirled and stalked to her. He loomed over her and growled, "What the fuck were you thinking?"

"I can protect myself!"

"I know that, damn it! But it doesn't mean I want you to have to. If any of the gods had been with the boars, they could have snatched you and aetherwalked back to Otherworld." He shook her, his rough hands tight on her arms.

Normally cool gray eyes burned down at her, on fire with worry and anger. His lips were tight with rage, his hair plastered against his head, and he looked like he wanted to keep shaking her but never let her go. He was so handsome and so harsh that the sight of him stole her breath, a vise squeezing her lungs.

He'd been afraid for her.

"Damn you, Ana." He crushed his mouth to hers, hot and hard, crowding her against the wall of the bunkhouse.

The heat and hardness of his body, such a contrast to the storm-cold air, forced a small noise through her lips. He thrust his tongue inside, releasing a groan that spoke of pleasure and pain.

Bad idea. Bad idea. Bad idea. But she was unable to stop her wayward, selfish hands from running up the steel muscles of his chest. To test him. To feel him. To know the strength that pressed her into the rough wooden planks of the bunkhouse until they bit into the tender skin of her shoulders.

But the pain only heightened the pleasure. And the fear. He was so big. Big thighs pressing to her own, big chest pinning her to the wall, big hands gripping her waist. So much bigger that she, a goddess, became a rag doll in his hands, his to mold.

"Don't *ever* fucking do that again," he rasped against her lips before claiming her mouth again.

Hard hands traced her sides, his strength and frayed control vibrating through tensed muscles and shaking hands. The fear and anger in his kiss only heightened the aching need that pulled at her.

He thrust one of his big thighs between her own, lifting her easily to set her atop it and drag her against him. His cock pressed into her belly, hot and branding. It was dirty and delicious and stole every rational thought from her mind.

His big hand smoothed up her back to clutch her head, holding her steady for his mouth. His other gripped her ass. A wicked jolt streaked through her when he ground her against his thigh. It was as if he were determined to make her feel every part of him. Every part of his claim on her. Spikes of pleasure shot from her pussy through her body, leaving shivers in their wake.

He growled low in his throat—an actual growl—and it threw propane on the lust and fear and confusion that raged through her blood.

Cam's heart pounded against his ribs, so hard and loud he feared it would drown out the sounds escaping from Ana's lips. Desperate, needy sounds that he couldn't get enough of.

They spurred the same from him—rough, raw noises that sounded like those of an animal.

"Fuck," he rasped, then gripped her ass and ground her against him, working her soft body on his thigh to coax more of those sounds from her throat.

She'd scared the hell out of him when she'd gotten so close to the boars. Fear for her had pushed him over the edge, broken his control where she was concerned.

"I want you," he rasped. "Always have."

More than that, he cared. He couldn't hide from it any longer. All those years ago, she'd given him the gift—and the curse—of emotion, dragging him from the cold existence of the gods. Now, all that emotion and lust and caring that she'd dredged up in him were becoming wrapped up in her. It was stronger than anything he'd ever felt for anyone else, and it confused the hell out of him.

"I care, damn it." The sandpaper words scraped his throat, pulled out of him by a force he couldn't control. He never talked like this. Never *thought* like this. Except with her.

She stiffened in his arms, her hands in his hair going still.

"No." She pushed him away, struggled to get out of his arms. She shook her head, eyes wide and wild. He stepped back, hands clenching to keep from reaching for her. "I don't want this. I didn't come here for this."

"Ana." He reached out to draw her back.

"No." She slipped around him and backed away, shaking her head. "No. Our past is totally fucked up. And now we're the only two who can serve in Otherworld. You won't take my place, and I don't blame you, but starting something again under these circumstances will lead to disaster for both of us. I can't risk that."

Something squeezed his heart until he thought it would pop. She was right. Selfish bastard that he was, she was right. His actions had gotten her stuck in Otherworld, and he couldn't—wouldn't—take her place again. His work needed him here on earth. Millions of people needed him for the good he could do.

But that left Ana out in the cold, trapped in Otherworld.

CHAPTER TEN

He'd have thought it impossible, but Cam was even more grateful to see the wharf at Bruxa's Eye than he had been to see Havre. Being cooped up on a boat with Ana was hell on his mind and his damn emotions. He needed to get a grip.

He kept his sights on the big dock, which swarmed with activity, and brought the *Clara G.* alongside. He leapt down and quickly tied off the bow line.

He made quick work of securing the stern, and as he was brushing his hands off, caught sight of Ana sitting up from the hammock to look around at the bustling port city.

Dusk would fall in another hour, but for now the low sun revealed a town that pushed out of the jungle and onto the shore. Trees had been hacked down to make space for both the wooden buildings and the Mytheans who made their homes or businesses in the largest supernatural town in the Amazon River basin. It was so well hidden by magic that mortals who passed on the river wouldn't even notice it.

Mytheans liked it so much for its secrecy that they moved here from all over the world. He could hear at least half a dozen languages from the people on the docks, and it explained the Portuguese-English mashup of the town's name.

"This is the town with the airport?" Ana asked.

At the sound of her voice, he squeezed his eyes shut. Damn it, he had no idea what to do about her. She roused feelings in him—fucking *feelings*, which had never been an issue before he met her those many years ago—and now that he'd admitted to them... Well, he was fucked.

She'd rejected him. It was smart of her. They were the only two Mytheans qualified to serve in Otherworld as war gods. If she didn't want to be there, he was the only one who could take her place. And he didn't want that, no matter how guilty he felt about sticking her there in the first place.

She didn't want the man whose weakness had brought her to the attention of the gods and then who'd abandoned her to her fate in Otherworld. He didn't blame her. He didn't deserve her.

Yet it didn't stop the sting of her rejection. Which was ridiculous. He wasn't the type who felt those things. Hell, he wasn't the type who felt much of anything.

Yeah, keep telling yourself that.

He turned to her, avoided looking directly at her, and said, "Gotta go check out the flights, see what's available. Nothing 'til tomorrow, probably. And get a hotel room."

"We're not sleeping on the boat?"

He shook his head. "Too unprotected. It's unlikely that anyone can trace you to it, since we killed the boars and haven't seen anyone else, but if the gods do show up, we want a room that's hidden."

"Hidden?"

"Yeah. There are a couple of magically protected hotel rooms in town that are operated by the local witches' guild. Pricey, but worth it. As long as we're in there, any god who shows up in Bruxa's Eye won't be able to find us."

"Okay. Good."

She was silent for a moment, and he realized that they hadn't spoken about her plans for a replacement or if she still wanted to meet Druantia.

But now they had to address it.

"So," he said, feeling like an ass. "What do you want to do about Druantia?"

Her surprised gaze jerked up to meet his. "I still want to meet her. Of course. Maybe there's something else that can be done."

Cam dragged a hand over his face, hoping to wipe away any trace of the grimness he felt. There was nothing else that could be done, but he didn't want to tell her and take away the hope. He nodded, knowing he was delaying an inevitable problem but unable to help himself.

"Right, then. Let's head into town."

She nodded and followed him off the boat. He prayed that there were two rooms available in town. He needed some fucking space to get his head screwed on right.

They joined the bustling crowd on the docks, Mytheans of all shapes and sizes. In mortal cities, they would all look like mortals, even though they were something a bit more.

But here in the jungle, in a city that was specifically built by Mytheans for themselves, you could find all kinds. Demons, shifters who looked more feral than human even in their human form, witches who still favored crone-chic—as his friend Harp called it—and looked like they came from the bad end of a fairy tale.

It took about five minutes to get from the bustling waterfront to the middle of town. The last of the day's heat pounded onto the street as they walked along the wooden boardwalk that harkened back to the days of the Wild West. Better the ancient boardwalk than the mud that caked the streets of Havre.

"In here." He nodded at a two-story wooden building that was as dilapidated as the rest in town.

The interior was nicer, though only slightly. The small room with wooden floors and a single window had a wizened old Bruxa sitting behind the counter on the far wall. Black robes and pointed hat. Broom leaning against the counter.

The corner of Cam's lips twitched. Witches could change their appearance at will, and this one had chosen crone-chic.

He approached. "Hello. We're looking for two rooms for tonight."

"One room only," answered the Bruxa, her eyes narrowed on him.

"Seriously?" he asked.

"Take it or leave it."

"Are there no others in town?" Ana asked her.

So the idea of sharing a room bothered her too? Though in her case, it was because she didn't want him back. Which he shouldn't care about. He raked a hand through his hair. This day was getting better and better.

"Only one in town," Crone-chic said. A fat black cat leapt onto the desk in front of her, eyeing him out of its one good eye. It had another, but that one didn't look up to the task of giving the stink-eye.

"I know, Kitty, he is good-looking," Crone-chic said to the cat. But the cat just turned and stuck a leg in the air to get down to cleaning its business. At least one person in the room thought he was all right.

"We'll take it." He handed over a bundle of Brazilian notes. Crone-chic inspected them and then gave him a toothy grin that was more grin than tooth.

She handed him a key. "Upstairs, last door on the left."

He nodded and led the way, ducking his head to climb the low, narrow staircase. It creaked and groaned under his weight, and the heat became stifling as they reached the top floor.

"No central air, I suppose?" Ana said from behind him.

He chuffed a laugh, then grunted in annoyance with himself. They reached the end of the hall and he pushed open the small door to reveal a little room with two twin beds and a bare light bulb hanging from the ceiling. A chipped enamel sink was pressed into the corner next to a door that presumably led to the toilet.

Ana pushed past him and ran through the little door. "A shower! Oh, thank everything that ever existed, a freaking shower."

He spun toward the exit and dragged a hand over his face. *Gotta get the hell out of here—before she gets naked.*

"I've got some stuff I need to do back at the *Clara G.* And plane tickets. See you in a while."

"Wait, like, a *while* while?" She peeked out of the bathroom.

He weighed it in his mind. A night on the *Clara G.* would be best for him. And for her. But he couldn't sleep there. It was one thing to be working on the boat or out in town, awake and vigilant. Sleeping outside the protection of the hidden room… That was a bad idea.

"A while. I'll be back before it's time to sleep," he said. "You should be fine in the street as long as you're paying attention. You'd know if another god showed up, right?"

One of the few perks of being a Celtic demi-god: he'd feel the change in the aether if a Celtic god popped out of it and into town. She should too.

"Yeah."

"Good. If you feel anything strange when you're out of the room, sneak back here and wait it out. Don't come get me. I can get here on my own." He didn't assume she would. But better for her to be safe in here.

"Okay. Um. Well, see you, I guess."

"Yeah." He made a hasty retreat.

Shoving Ana from his mind, he swung by the small airport and found that there was a flight headed to Miami the next morning. It gave him enough time to rent dock space for the *Clara G.* and batten down the hatches, both literally and figuratively.

But when all the loose odds and ends were stowed and the *Clara G.* was prepared to ride out whatever weather might hit Bruxa's Eye while he was away, he realized he had no idea what to do with himself. He'd pushed himself while cleaning up the boat, hoping that the effort would clear his mind of Ana and what had happened earlier today.

It had, mostly. But hard work meant that the job was finished quickly, and when it was, everything he'd been running from caught up with him. Full dark had fallen, but it was still too early to go back to the room. To Ana.

He looked down at his hands, realized they were clenched tightly on the half-wall of the pilothouse, and finally had a good idea.

A fight. That was what he needed. To turn some of this confusion and lust and fucking hurt into aggression to get it all out of himself.

CHAPTER ELEVEN

Southeast Celtic Britain, 13 AD
Territory between the Iceni and Trinovante Kingdoms

Snowflakes hurtled through the air on a cutting wind, dragging at Andrasta's cloak and pelting her face. The cold numbed her until she couldn't shiver and her fingers froze around the shaft of her bow. Fear tore through her mind, harsher than the wind.

She'd left the gods nearly an hour ago and set off toward the clearing to find Camulos and commit her terrible deed. But the gods hadn't left her.

No, they appeared at the corners of her vision, disappearing just as she turned to look. Her anxiety had become a great clawed beast that tore at her insides to escape. Marrek was bleeding in the snow even now, while Hafgan waited in the wings. Her brothers were strong, but even they couldn't fight a god they couldn't see.

The gods were cowards. But she was their puppet.

She pushed herself harder through snow that rose to her calves. It fell from the sky as a great cloud of white, so thick that she could barely make out the trees on the other side of the clearing. But she didn't see Camulos within the great empty space.

Something flashed out of the corner of her eye. She swung toward it, nearly releasing the string of the bow that she'd drawn.

Nothing. Whatever it was had disappeared. She cursed, turned back to the clearing.

Camulos stood within, the icy wind whipping at his cloak, tossing his hair. Her breath caught at the sight, fear and admiration surging through her. She lowered her bow, unable to help herself.

But he raised his. The breath lodged in her throat like a great boulder, and in her mind's eye she saw Hafgan cutting down her brothers if she didn't accomplish her task.

Fear clinging to her back with demon claws, she swung her bow up, sighted, released. The bow twanged, a sound that she would normally find glory in now turned dark and bitter. The arrow cut through the air, dragging with it her guilt and regret and shame until it punched through his flesh.

At the sight, something pierced her heart. Something sharp and so cold that it froze the organ in place.

Oh, gods, what have I done? No, no, no.

She gasped, then ran toward Camulos' body. The snow dragged at her legs, slowing her until she wanted to scream. Finally, her knees hit the ground in a small puddle of blood that had melted the snow beside him.

"No." The word tore from her throat as she laid a hand on his chest, his cheek. She'd had to do it to save her brothers, but gods, this was terrible. She'd cared for him. Maybe even loved him.

But now his eyes were closed and his skin was so pale. His cheek was cold against her fingertips, somehow colder than even the snow beneath her.

"Wake!" She shook his shoulder as hot tears froze on her cheeks.

She'd had to do it. *She'd had to.*

But her arrow protruded obscenely from his chest, straight through his heart, because her aim was too good to be off-target. The sight made bile rise in her throat.

Done. It was done.

Grief and self-loathing crowded her mind. She'd saved her family. Made herself a god. But at what cost? Was this what the glory of being a god felt like?

She clenched her hand in Camulos' cloak, but she couldn't get a grip on it. His body had begun to shimmer, going clear in places. She watched, mouth agape, as he disappeared, leaving only the red snow in which she knelt. Desperate for him to return and for the horror of what she'd done to be erased, she gripped handfuls of icy snow.

"You've failed." A harsh voice cut through the wind, tearing her from her stupor.

She looked up. The dark-haired goddess loomed over her.

"What?"

"You've killed only his mortal form. Not his godly one." Anger crackled in the goddess' eyes.

"But I—" Andrasta held up a handful of bloody snow. She had no idea what she wanted anymore.

"You didn't use the arrow he gave you. He enabled you to kill him when he gave you one of his own arrows. You, the one mortal with the weapon to kill a god, did not use it. How could you be so stupid?"

"What? I thought—I thought it was my skill that you needed."

The goddess glowered, her hair whipping in the wind. "It was. But the arrow as well."

Hope and horror flared within her chest. She hadn't killed him? *She hadn't killed him.*

"You have to finish."

"What?"

"Kill him, or he will kill your family. Kill you."

No.

"Or *we* will kill your family. He'll know you were sent by other gods. He must be eliminated."

"But—"

"He *must.*"

Heavy gray clouds began to roil above Andrasta's head, rare winter lightning striking trees all around her. The air grew so cold that her blood seemed to freeze in her veins, her knees to the ground. Visions of her brothers dead flashed before her eyes. Even her heart froze in place, fear stopping the beats until she was stone within.

"How?" she whispered.

"Go to Otherworld. Kill him in the land of the gods when he's in his godly form. You'll destroy him permanently if you use his arrow there."

"But only the dead can go to Otherworld. How do I?"

"How do you think?" The goddess tossed a small knife into the snow and disappeared.

Andrasta stared at it, mouth agape, as her vision swam. *This* was what her life had come down to? A blade in the snow?

Tears spilled from her eyes, but from behind them she saw images of Marrek bleeding into the snow. Before she could back out, she grabbed the knife and sliced it along her wrist. She gasped as the pain shot through her, and she fumbled the blade. Her hand shook as she recovered it and tried again. Eventually, enough of her blood poured into the snow that she began to drift away on pain and sorrow.

The throbbing in her wrists faded as soon as she opened her eyes. But the tears still fell, obscuring her vision of an unfamiliar oak forest. When she tried to sniff her tears into submission, she was greeted by the smell of the sea mixed with the green scent of the forest.

She scrubbed her eyes, then inspected her wrists, her stomach clutching at the sight of the long scars. It felt like so long ago that she'd knelt in the snow and dragged the little knife across her flesh. One hand gripped her bow. Of course the gods had allowed her to bring it. She'd need it for her terrible task.

She rose on unsteady feet, her soul feeling pulled to the west. In her heart, she knew that she would find her ancestors there. It took everything in her power to resist. She turned east and away from temptation, determination leading her in search of Camulos.

Andrasta wandered the forest for what felt like days. She felt no hunger, no exhaustion. Nothing but determination to finish what she'd started so that she could save her brothers. The image of Marrek's blood soaking into the snow flashed constantly through her mind, followed shortly after by images of Camulos.

Would she be able to kill him again when she saw him? Would he kill her first? If she wasn't strong, if she didn't remember that she fought for her brothers' lives, she was afraid that she would let him.

"Are you looking for me?" The deep voice came from behind. She stumbled in surprise after so many days alone.

How had she gotten to be so clumsy that he could sneak up on her? She spun to face him, fear leaping in her heart. Relief followed, for he was, in fact, still alive. Her wrist twinged. Perhaps *alive* wasn't exactly the word for it. But here, in the land of the gods, he looked hale, though he lacked the otherworldly quality that he'd had on earth.

Perhaps because I am in his world now. She raised her bow, ashamed to feel her arm quiver. She swallowed, sighted down the shaft of the arrow he had given her.

Why would he not raise his bow? He just stood there, strong and still and calm like an oak.

"Raise your bow." Her voice cracked under the strain. She *had* to kill him.

But she didn't want to. She wanted to go to him and take one of their walks again. To talk and laugh and forget this terrible situation. Her brothers flashed through her mind again.

"Raise it!" *He had to.* She couldn't shoot him if he didn't at least raise his own bow. Something horrible started to rise in her chest, fighting with her determination. She could finish this. She could save her brothers. Her arm shook.

Damn it. She had to pull herself together. But as her breath tore in and out of her lungs, she realized that she...

couldn't. She wanted to scream, to tear at her hair, to return to earth and forget that she had ever met this man.

"Lower your bow, Andrasta." His voice was too kind, his eyes too understanding.

It broke something within her, and her voice rose in a harsh sob. She released the arrow, pulling her bow to the left at the last moment so that the arrow thudded into an oak a dozen feet from him.

She collapsed to her knees as the darkness of what she'd done converged on her. She was here, in Otherworld, with no escape. If she didn't destroy the soul of the man in front of her, her brothers would die. He'd brought her to this, by watching her. But she'd brought herself here too, when she'd confronted him in the forest and then spent so many hours with him that she'd grown to care for him.

Out of the corner of her eye, she saw him sit, prop his arms on his knees, and hang his head between his arms.

"Why didn't you kill me right away?" Her voice broke. Would it have been preferable to this? *Yes.* She gripped her bow tighter, but it did nothing to soothe her.

"I... couldn't."

She looked up to see him staring down at his bow. He chucked it away, disgust and longing etched into his face. She watched the bow slam into a tree and crack in half. Her hand closed reflexively around her own bow.

"Why couldn't you kill me? And why did you do that?"

He met her gaze, but didn't answer her question. "You'll be fine here. You'll find your way. One day, you'll be clever enough to sneak back to earth occasionally."

"What?" Why did it sound like he was rushing to give her last-minute instructions?

116

Regret shone from his eyes as he looked at her. She shifted under his careful regard, under the longing that she thought she saw in his eyes. Confusion raged like a storm around her, buffeting her back and forth as it would a small boat far from sea.

"You cared for me."

His eyes jerked to hers. "I did. I... do."

A smile might have pulled at her lips any other time, but it couldn't now. She'd wanted him to care for her as she'd grown to care for him. But now it didn't matter.

"We're in a mess." He rose.

Her gaze followed him as he walked to the tree where his blue arrow had lodged. He yanked it free and returned to her. He sat again, this time only a few feet from her. The heart that no longer felt like hers fought to be free of her chest.

He reached into his cloak and withdrew a small bottle. Carefully, he unstopped it and poured a few drops of opalescent liquid onto the tip of the arrow. He held it out to her.

"What is that?" she asked.

"Nothing important. For the pain."

Did he lie? But his face brooked no argument, and she was so out of her element that she didn't question.

"Take it," he said when she hesitated.

Swallowing hard, she reached out and curled her fingers around the arrow shaft. So close were their fingers that she swore she felt the heat of his. She looked at the arrow, then back to him.

"What am I supposed to do with this?" Did he not want to kill her? She couldn't let him, fearing that the gods would carry out their vengeance upon her brothers. But how could she stop him when she didn't want to raise her bow against him?

But when she met his eyes again, she realized that he wouldn't be killing her.

"You'll shoot me with it. As you did before. Don't miss," he said.

A tear leaked from her eye, trailing cold and lonely down her cheek. He reached out to wipe it away. The warmth of his hand burned through her. How had she come to be here, in this utterly indecipherable, inescapable, intolerable situation?

"Why?" She wanted to reach out and grab his hand. Instead, she tightened hers on her bow.

"I'd prefer to leave Otherworld on my own terms."

"Leave? You mean, you really won't kill me?"

A chuff of strange laughter escaped him, loaded with so much emotion that she couldn't decipher. His eyes raced over her face, down to the hand that clutched her bow.

"No," he said finally. "I've done enough harm to you."

"Harm to me? But I killed you. I escaped lightly."

"Neither of us has escaped. Spend long enough here, and you'll learn that."

"I would become a god if I do this."

"You wanted to prove yourself."

"Not like this."

He gave a bitter laugh. "It seems you don't have a choice."

"But you want me to destroy you with the arrow, as the gods said?"

"I've lived a long time. I'm not meant for Otherworld. The other gods are determined to see me dead. They've wanted it for a long time, and now they have a way. I could fight them, but at the risk of you and your brothers."

"You'd do that for me?" She searched his handsome face, trying to decipher anything from the gray eyes that watched her so closely.

"For you, for me. For the only way to get out of this disaster on my terms and without your soul being destroyed."

Andrasta shivered. Once a body died on earth, the soul went to Otherworld, the land of the gods. She was proof of that, sitting here in the grass across from Camulos.

It was almost impossible to destroy a soul in Otherworld, however. But she'd killed him on earth, had the permission of the other gods, and had his arrow. That was no ordinary magic. It gave her the power to destroy him. He was a god, which gave him the power to destroy her. It was a power that the other gods possessed as well. There truly was no way out.

As she weighed her miserable options and the trap that she'd built for herself, she looked down at the arrow. Her stomach lurched at the idea of sending it through him.

But there was no other choice. "This is what you want?"

He nodded, and her heart clutched at the resignation in his eyes. He rose. Shaking, she followed suit.

"But first. One thing." He approached her. The breath caught in her lungs at the intensity of his face. "A kiss."

She stared up at him, her voice stolen, lost in the wildness of emotion swirling in his eyes, emotion that wasn't reflected in his still form. Her lips parted in soundless invitation as her lost heart threatened to beat its way out of her chest.

His big hand cupped the side of her head, his heat burning through to her errant heart. Tension vibrated from him as he pressed his mouth to hers, warm and firm and so lovely that her mind stopped. Too soon, he drew away. He closed his eyes, leaned his forehead against hers.

His hand tightened just briefly in her hair as he murmured, "Enough."

He stepped back, and though she wanted to reach for him, the finality in his eyes stilled her. He walked backward from her, his gaze never leaving hers, until he stood ten yards away. So close. Too close for her to put an arrow through his heart. How could he think she'd do this to him?

"Now, Andrasta." His voice was harsh, the emotion in his eyes replaced by determination.

She shook her head, panic beginning to well within her, threatening to flood her brain.

"Now! For your brothers. For yourself. For *me.*" The desperation in his voice, the finality of it, made her raise her bow. Her arms shook and tears spilled from her eyes. She desperately tried to blink them away.

"I—I can't."

"You will. I want this. You want this. Do you want to see your brothers dead? For the gods to destroy their souls? Or yours?" His eyes were stone serious, committed to this path.

She drew in a harsh breath, tried to memorize his face, then let go of the arrow. It flew straight and true, and so fast that her desire to yank it back welled immediately, but not sooner than the arrow pierced his chest. He disappeared, along with the arrow.

On a sob, she collapsed to her knees. He was gone. And she was here. A god. More alone than she'd ever been.

CHAPTER TWELVE

Bruxa's Eye, Present Day

Ana filched the cell phone out of the back pocket of the bruiser leaning on the bar and slipped toward the exit. She'd left the hotel room an hour ago, intent on finding a way to call her friend Esha. She'd called her from Cam's phone the other day, but she wanted to check up and didn't want to have to ask Cam to borrow his phone again. The bar down the street had seemed like the perfect place to find a phone, and the big ugly brute who was currently berating the bartender fit her criteria of people she didn't feel guilty stealing from. And stealing was the only option, considering that pay phones weren't exactly plentiful in the middle of the Amazon.

With the phone clutched in her hand, she pushed through the side door of the bar. The alley outside was narrow and dark, but it was perfect. She didn't feel like company right now, and the quiet would allow her to hear anyone sneaking up on her.

After a bit of cursing and fiddling to make the phone work, she punched in the number of her one and only real friend. And she could really use a friend right now.

"Esha?" she said when the ringing ceased and the line clicked.

"Ana? What the hell are you doing with a phone? Moved up from blenders?"

Ana laughed. Esha thought her obsession with the modern technologies that Otherworld lacked was hilarious. It was the reason she knew Esha's phone number even though she didn't actually have a phone. When Esha had gotten her cell, Ana had insisted on calling it a dozen times from the home line. Thank gods she remembered the number now. "Fates, I miss you!"

"Then come see me!"

"I wish." Normally she aetherwalked to visit Esha, popping in to see her for a few hours whenever she could. "How's Warren?"

"He's good," Esha said. "Says hi."

"Hi back. Anyway, I was wondering if you found out anything about the Druid priestess called Druantia."

"Yeah. She's the top Druid priestess. Most powerful one alive. She's creepy, too, from what I hear. Her magic is legendary, though I think she's fallen on hard times."

"I'm most interested in her location." Though Ana had never met Druantia before, she too knew of her, and everything that Esha was saying was spot on. Druantia had once been extraordinarily powerful, the only mortal capable of contacting the gods directly. She hadn't stayed mortal, though Ana had no idea how she'd made the switch to immortality. But she was grateful for it now. Druantia would be her ticket out of Otherworld. She had to be.

"I don't have that yet," Esha said. "I've asked around and someone will get back to me with something soon, I'm sure. This is about getting out of Otherworld, isn't it?"

"Yeah."

"There's something wrong. What is it?"

"I'm fine."

"Whatever. I can hear it in your voice."

She hesitated, unsure of how to bring up any of the hundred things that were bothering her.

"I found Camulos," she blurted.

"Really?" Nerves tinged Esha's voice. "Are you okay? He doesn't want to kill you, right?"

When she'd first learned that Cam might still be alive, she'd been afraid he'd want to kill her for shooting him with the arrows. Over the years, she'd repressed all the good memories of him and focused on the bad. After the nightmare she'd gone through, she hadn't been able to help herself. But maybe repressing the good hadn't been fair to Cam. "He doesn't. And I'm fine."

"How is Camulos?"

"Um, not bad."

"Not bad? You're holding out on me. What's going on? Come on, 'fess up."

How did she even start? "He's complex."

"Complex?"

"We've got history. You know that."

"You still have feelings for him. I can hear it in your voice."

"You've got great hearing tonight."

"Try morning. It's three AM here in Scotland."

"Damn, sorry about that. I guess with everything that's going on here, I lost track of your time."

"Don't worry about it. Tell me about Camulos. He was your one big love."

"That was a long time ago. And it wasn't love. I was too young for love. And I'm not looking for that, anyway. I want to experience everything I missed out on while I was trapped in Otherworld."

"Maybe you're not picking the right things to make up for. There's something to be said for quality over quantity. What I've got with Warren is incredible. Way better than partying and hookups. I want something like that for you, too."

So do I. To be loved like Esha is would be amazing. Ana started at the thought, then crushed it. "Well, it's not what I want."

"Liar. You just don't know how to cope with strong feelings anymore, after being locked up in Otherworld for so long. You say you want to party and hook up with a bunch of guys, and that's great and all, but I think you're hiding."

She bristled, then fought it back. Esha was just trying to help. But she *wasn't* right about her. "It doesn't matter anyway. For me to be able to escape Otherworld, he would have to go back."

"What?" Esha cried.

Ana relayed what Cam had told her about the power balance in Otherworld requiring a war god of appropriate skill. It made her chest feel heavy and her mind feel cluttered just to think about it.

"There's no way he'd be willing to return?" Esha asked.

"No way. And no surprise. It's utterly awful there."

"Damn. That's just… damn."

"Yeah. Now you see why it doesn't matter if I did want something more. It's impossible when one of us is going to end up in Otherworld."

"Look, if there's anything I can do, let me know," Esha said. "And you know I love you. I think you should have other people who love you too."

Ana's heart thudded with pathetic gratitude to her only real friend. "Thanks."

"Yeah, well, come see me soon."

"I will. We're actually headed that way. We fly out tomorrow."

They said their goodbyes and Ana pressed *End*. She stared down at the phone, wondering if Esha was right about her not being able to cope with real feelings.

No way. She was coming to earth because she missed all that.

And even if the idea of Cam caring for her made her heart ping around inside her chest like a pinball gone mad, it didn't matter because one of them had to end up in Otherworld.

But she wasn't the same girl she'd once been, who'd thirsted for love and approval. She was a goddess, even if she didn't really want to be one, and she was tough and independent and she didn't rely on anyone. She realized that she was pounding her fist into her palm in time to her exclamations and stopped.

Loving someone was the worst way to rely on them. She relied only on herself. That's who she was.

And she was going to go into that bar to pick up a man and prove Esha wrong. She shoved the phone into her pocket and spun, pushing open the door. A blast of noise hit her.

Shit, she was being an idiot. She scowled and let the door swing shut, dropping her back into the quiet dark of the alley. Of course she wasn't going to go in there and pick up some guy while the gods could possibly be on her tail. She should head back. And if she were honest with herself, she didn't really want some other guy.

She huffed, then set off down the alley toward the main street, turning onto the boardwalk toward their hotel. A stumbling pair of drunken shifters lurched in front of her, their tails hanging down behind them as if they'd let their inner animal escape a bit.

The roar of a crowd caught her attention, and she glanced left. There was an empty lot situated between two buildings, a fight ring in the middle, like the one in the Caipora's den. It must have been darkened when she passed by it the first time. Lights now shined down on an empty ring, but from the sound of the cheers, the fighters were making their way to it.

She wanted to step off the boardwalk and wind her way through the crowd toward the ring so that she could feel the action and energy in the air. So that she could feel something other than the angst and desire that Cam dredged up in her. The din of the jeering Mytheans drowned out the howls of the jungle creatures. Maybe it could drown out the howling in her mind.

She'd just turned her head to keep moving toward the hotel when she caught sight of a flash of familiar ginger hair.

Cam was climbing into the ring, his chest bare and his fists wrapped in white.

She stepped off the boardwalk and headed toward the ring. With some threatening glares, she managed to push her way to the front, so close that she could see the dark splotches on the floor of the ring. Blood from previous matches.

Her eyes raked Cam's form, desperately tracing over the muscles that curved and cut across his bare torso. The lights gleamed off of his wide chest and caressed his chiseled arms and shoulders.

Ana dragged her gaze away from Cam to look for his opponent. After a moment, an enormous man climbed into the ring. He looked to be part giant, at least seven and a half feet tall and half as wide. The crowd roared.

"Cam." The whisper slipped through her lips before she could stop herself.

He looked toward her as if he'd heard her, his gaze finding hers across the night. His eyes flashed. He turned to face his opponent.

Her heart clutched. She glanced nervously at the giant. But Cam was big too. Probably only a foot shorter than his opponent. All gods were bigger than the average mortal. Except her, the formerly mortal halfling.

He stood in his corner, as relaxed as if he was on the beach, and watched the other fighter. His slate eyes were calm, his pale skin and red hair gleaming in the light. He lived out here in the jungle, all northern warrior in the southern heat.

He would be fine. Just fine. But she clutched her bow all the same, seeking what little comfort she could.

The screech of a whistle cut through the night, and Cam strolled to the center of the ring to face his opponent. The fight started too soon, before she could brace herself for the smack of fists on flesh.

Cam took the first punch, an anvil to his shoulder that sent him back a step. He grinned. They circled each other, and Ana's heart lodged itself uncomfortably in her throat.

Cam landed a punch to the giant's right cheek, another to his midsection. He was more than holding his own in the fight, despite their difference in size, and Ana found lust competing with her fear. His face looked mean, ready to hurt, and a different kind of fear crept along her nerve endings. The good kind.

She shivered, drawn unconsciously toward the ring. He was so big. So dangerous. So everything. Her hand tightened in a fist of want.

She was so screwed.

Cam's muscles sang and sweat dripped into his eyes as he delivered the punch he was sure would end the fight. The big bastard across from him reeled on his feet, suspended almost comically, and then crashed to the ground. Cam stood over him, breath sawing in and out of his lungs.

This hadn't cleared his mind as he'd hoped it would. It might have worked, if he hadn't seen Ana standing outside of the ring.

"Round goes to Cam!" a deep voice hollered from the corner of the ring.

It was time to get the hell out of there and away from this crowd. Away from Ana. He climbed between the ropes just as his opponent was dragged beneath them. He grabbed his shirt from where he'd left it draped over one of the lower ropes and pushed his way through the crowd so that Ana couldn't catch him if she followed.

The aggression of the fight, the bloodlust, still rode him hard. Combined with everything he was still feeling, he needed a few more minutes before he saw her again. He was starting to lose control where she was concerned. Combined with his high from the fight, it was a dangerous combination.

He unwound the wrapping on his hands as his long strides ate up the street. The tiny hotel lobby was empty and he slipped up the stairs. When he finally made it to the shower, he groaned as the water poured down over him. He shouldn't feel old. But he did. His shoulder and jaw ached where his opponent had popped him, and his brain felt beaten up from the ride he'd taken it on these last couple days with Ana.

"Cam?"

At the sound of Ana's voice, Cam dropped his head back beneath the spray and squeezed his eyes shut. She was back already. Damn it, he would have to go out there and keep his hands off of her. He dragged a hand through his hair, shook his head violently.

There was nowhere else to go, so he stepped out of the shower and dragged his dirty jeans back on, ignoring the shirt that was too streaked with sweat and boat grease to consider wearing. He'd been in such a damn rush he'd left his change of clothes on the bed.

He walked into the room to see her sitting on the bed. She rose from her seat on one of the beds and looked at him with big eyes that raced over his body, searching for wounds from the fight. The dim bulb that hung in the center of the room cast a soft glow on her shining golden hair.

Her gaze snapped to the side of his face and she approached him, standing so close he could smell the fresh scent of her. She reached up with a tentative hand to stroke his injured cheek. He stood, his muscles tense and his breath stuck in his lungs.

He ducked his head and hissed at the contact.

"I'm sorry," she said. "You're hurt."

It wasn't pain that forced the noise from him. It was the touch of her skin on his. The heat of her so close.

His eyes met hers, and what he saw within had his blood pressure spiking and his fists clenching.

She wanted him. He'd seen it in the eyes of all the women who approached him after a match, wanting to see what a man like him was really like. This time, though, it felt different. There was a desperation and a heat in her eyes that wasn't entirely normal. She wanted him, yes. But her body was still reacting to earth. She wanted anybody. Needed anybody.

He wanted to be that anybody. Even if just for tonight. Even if she was too good for him. The thought made a spike of pleasure shoot through him. It took everything he had not to reach out to her. To touch. To taste.

To take.

He spun from her. "Go to sleep, Ana."

He stalked to small sink, bent over it, and gripped the enameled metal so hard he feared he'd crush it. He prayed to gods he'd never worshiped that she'd go to sleep. That she'd stop looking at him with hungry eyes.

He didn't hear her footsteps, and after a moment he couldn't help but let his gaze be dragged around to her. She still stood in the center of the room, one hand rubbing her arm absentmindedly while she stared at him with her bottom lip bit between her teeth.

"Fuck," he rasped.

What she wanted was plain on her face. What *he* wanted was plain on her face.

Pulled by the magnet of her, he strode to her, reached out and yanked her to him. Hard. He delighted in the gasp that escaped her lips just before he claimed them with his own.

His kiss was rough, lacking any finesse. It was made of the want and frustration and anger that propelled him toward her, made him desperate to feel her with his hands, his lips, his cock.

Her moan feathered over his lips and her hands fisted in his hair so hard it stung, which only propelled him farther down the rabbit hole of his complex desires. If he made this just about her, it wouldn't matter if he didn't deserve her.

CHAPTER THIRTEEN

"Wait." Ana tore her mouth from Cam's, mourning that last delicious taste of him. She panted, trying to get hold of her mind as his hard, rough hands ran down her body. "This is—is a bad idea."

She knew it was, deep inside, but all her arguments were starting to sound really frail.

"Shh." His raspy voice at her ear made her knees tremble and her skin prickle. He held her head still in his big hand and bit her earlobe, sending a shiver down her spine. "You need this. I know that you need this."

Fates, she did. She wanted him. Cam, the man who had screwed up her life and stuck her in Otherworld. But more than that, she was burning up inside from the unholy lust that had gradually been building since she'd come to earth, stoked by the heat of Cam's hot looks and touch. Trying to slake it with other men had only left her with a sour taste in her mouth. Now it felt like a live thing within her body, demanding to be fed.

"We can't get involved. This will only end badly. One of us will end up in Otherworld. If this becomes something…"

"Bullshit," he rasped. "This isn't a thing."

He didn't sound like he believed his own words. He leaned his forehead against hers. His chest rose and fell in deep bellows, pressing in tantalizing rhythm against her chest. She did this to him? Made him want her so bad? *Shiver.*

He felt as big and as intimidating as before. But his immense body was strung taut with desire for *her.* The idea made her so hot that she swore her pussy vibrated with it.

"This isn't an us," he said. "It's one night, nothing past it. This is just me, doing something for you. Let me make you feel good." He dragged his teeth down her neck, a spike of pleasure-pain that made her shudder. "No reciprocation required, and we'll worry about the future when it comes."

"Out of the goodness of your heart?" Her laugh was a little desperate and a lot wanting. And could she really ignore all that the future held?

If it meant a night with him, then *yes.*

"The goodness of my heart's got nothing to do with it. 'Cause I can't take your needy looks anymore. The heat in your eyes. The way you smell when you get hot. It's driving me up the fucking wall."

A low moan rose in her throat; she forced it down. To make this big, hard, scary man feel all that?

"Just let me touch you. Make you feel good. Then we walk away. Tomorrow is normal."

"Nothing for you?" Did he really mean he didn't want her to see to his pleasure too? Did she even want that? To just take from him?

"Oh, there'll be something in it for me." His hands bit into her hips, almost too hard. But hard enough to tell her he was going over a ledge.

Go over. Don't make me ask you for this terrible thing.

"I'll make you feel good," he said. "Real good. And when you come back down, that fucking lust will be out of your eyes and the want will be out of the rolling of your hips when you walk and I can get some fucking peace."

Whoa.

He ran his hard hands down to her hips and pulled them flush against the erection that burned through the heat of their clothes. He made her feel what she did to him, and she liked it.

"Say yes, Ana." His voice was the roughest, most delicious sandpaper against her skin, lightly dragging until goose bumps appeared in its wake.

She moaned, her stupid arguments long fled from her mind, and hoped he'd take it for an assent without her having to verbalize her fall into idiocy.

"I gotta hear the word," he growled into her ear, punctuating the statement with a thrust of hips.

Evil man. Don't make me say it. Just do it so I don't have to feel complicit in my own stupid decisions.

"Last call." He bit her shoulder, hard enough to threaten, to hurt. It only made her desire flare higher. To know what he offered. What he promised.

"Yes." The word was high, reedy with want.

He growled his satisfaction—a low, terrifying, hellishly arousing sound—and scooped her off her feet and tossed her on the bed.

The mattress bounced beneath her, too thin and as cheap as the rest of the seedy hotel room. He towered above her, broad chest heaving and muscles tensed. Desire and need shone on his face and a shiver raced through her.

She'd had plenty of partners—she was two thousand years old, after all. But never one as big or powerful or commanding as the one towering over her and sliding the belt from his jeans.

She swallowed nervously and scooted back on the bed, unable to deny that fear spurred the heat racing through her brain. He wouldn't hurt her.

But he looked like he could. And it made something flare inside of her.

"Lie down." His voice was harsh, hot. Like he had a job to see to.

She did, unable to resist and not caring that she was a goddess who did whatever the hell she pleased. Apparently, whatever the hell she pleased was following this man's brusque orders.

"Hands above your head."

They shot above her head as if of their own volition. The cold metal bars of the spare headboard brushed her wrists, making her realize that she'd thrust her hands through the spaces between the bars.

The bed dipped under his weight when he knelt by her hip. His scent—shampoo and the heady deliciousness of his arousal—enthralled her as he leaned over her, chest hovering above her face. His heat and size surrounded her, made her feel smaller than she ever had.

Something—his fingertips, probably—brushed gently against the scars on the insides of her wrists. His face was so close to them. *Seeing* them.

"Don't," she whispered. They were the physical evidence of all that had gone wrong between them. Of her mistakes.

He stopped, silent, and then the bite of warm leather wrapping around her wrists made her gasp. "What are you doing?"

He didn't answer, just continued to wrap the leather until he could buckle it. Relief over the distraction from her scars fought her nerves over being bound. She yanked, grew cold and hot at once when she felt no give. He edged down the mattress until his breath was at her ear. "So you can't touch. Lay a finger on me and I'd lose my mind. And this isn't about me."

Liar. Cam looked down at Ana. His goal might be her pleasure, not his own, so that she'd quit sending *fuck me* vibes at him. But that didn't mean he wasn't getting something he wanted. The sight of her, bound to the bed and wide eyed with excitement and nerves, made his heart pound so hard he felt like it would pulverize his ribs.

The belt wasn't to keep her tied down. She could break free if she wanted. She was a goddess, after all, with inhuman strength.

No, the belt reminded him that he was in control. *Responsible.* It would keep him in check. He couldn't lose himself if she was bound. Couldn't let his mind go foggy with want until he yanked off her clothes and sank his painfully hard cock into the heat of her pussy. Couldn't take the things he shouldn't have if he wanted to walk away from this tomorrow.

He licked his lower lip. Bit it. Studied her. Then had to squeeze his eyes closed to get it together. After a long moment, he opened them and looked down at her.

"You want this?" His voice was gravel leaving his throat.

She hesitated, so slight he might not have noticed. Then nodded.

"Say it." He wanted to hear it on her lips.

"I want it."

He wanted to peel off all her clothes, trace every inch of her skin with his eyes and hands and mouth. To hear all the noises she made when he did something she liked. He was desperate to make her feel him. Desperate to make her want him. To be the best she'd ever have, even if they could never have this again. Especially if they could never have this again.

He thrust the tender thoughts away and focused on what this was supposed to be about. Not seduction. Not connection. It was about getting her off. Keeping his mind and his wants and his heart out of this.

He reached down to drag her shorts and underwear from her hips, knowing that the sight of her curls and the pink flesh between her thighs would put his mind where it needed to be.

"Beautiful," he rasped, then leaned down over her so that his face hovered above hers and his hand brushed against what he most desired.

He cupped her pussy, something inside him jerking at the inappropriate possessiveness that bolted through him. Her hips lurched and she cried out, wide eyes meeting his.

Though he wanted to kiss her, he didn't. He didn't want to make this more than it was, while something dark within him wanted it to be as raw as possible.

Subtle changes flashed in her eyes as his fingers parted her softness and dipped into the wetness that scented the air. He thrummed her clitoris, grinned when she gasped, and pushed a finger inside her, desperate to know all of her.

With a start, he realized that his hand trembled. He hoped she didn't notice. "I am going to make you come so hard that you forget your own name."

She whimpered, but held his gaze.

"But you won't forget *my* name," he said. "You'll scream it when you come."

Her eyes widened, lids fluttered, then locked with his again, full of desperation and want and things he didn't recognize. He realized then that it was a terrible idea to make her say his name when she came. Realized too that he'd still do it.

He lowered his lips to her ear, barely held himself back from tracing the shell of it with his tongue, and rasped, "I'm going to taste you now."

She shivered. He moved down the bed and yanked her legs wide, set his mouth upon her without warning, a broad sweep of his tongue that allowed him to taste her and feel her and revel in her.

He grinned, pinning her hips to the bed while he repeated the motion. From the way she moved and cried out, it pushed her hard and high and fast.

"Fuck, you taste good," he muttered against her flesh, and swirled his tongue around her clitoris, wanting to feel her move beneath him. He was rewarded by her thighs clamping about his head, by her broken moan echoing through the room.

"Say my name," he rasped, looking up to see her clutching the bars of the headboard and panting, her pink lips parted so seductively that his cock jerked.

She shook her head, and he wasn't sure why she resisted—maybe because she sensed that this was all a dark game, a way to get a taste of what he wanted while holding her at arm's length.

He was a selfish bastard.

"Say it," he growled, pushing a finger into her and curving it upward to make her *want* to say his name.

"Cam." High and needy and desperate.

He watched her lips form his name and realized that her voice was the only thing he could hear. As if he were in a vacuum, with nothing except her. Even the forest had quieted, so cacophonous before, now drowned out by the blood pounding through his limbs and ears and cock.

He set his mouth upon her ravenously, wanting to feel her come, shake, clench beneath him. He pushed another finger inside her, moaning at the feeling of her gripping him.

"Cam!" Her legs trembled. She was close.

Though he wanted to taste her orgasm on his tongue, he realized he wanted to see her face, her eyes, as she lost herself in what he could give her.

It was fucked up, saying this was a selfless act when he did it for his own pleasure. He was getting in deeper than was wise, wanting to see her face. But he couldn't help it. His cock throbbed against his pants, demanding. But it was his mind that he couldn't disobey.

She whimpered and jerked at her bonds when he drew his mouth away. He rose swiftly up her body, rubbing her clitoris with his thumb while continuing to thrust his fingers inside her.

He watched her as pleasure clouded her eyes, occasionally dragging his gaze down to watch his big hand working between her white thighs.

Unable to help himself, he ground his cock against her thigh, helpless to stifle the groan that rose in his throat.

"You want this?" he growled, partially to remind himself that this was about her. But also to hear it from her lips.

"Yes," she said on a breath, her eyes locked with his. Desperation flared in their depths.

Someone pounded on the door. Cam froze, then picked up his pace again.

"Cam!" Ana cried in alarm.

"Come for me, Ana," he rasped.

The pounding continued. *No, damn it.* He would have this. She would have this.

"Ignore it. Come for me, Ana. Let me feel you."

His words pushed her over the edge. Her pussy gripped his fingers in delicious spasms, her hips flexing and her arms straining against the bonds. He couldn't look away, kept trying to coax her higher with his fingers as his eyes raced over her face.

The pounding came again, this time harder and faster.

"A minute, damn it," he yelled.

He watched as the strained pleasure faded from her face, then he gently removed his hand.

"Hurry!" a voice yelled from the other side of the door.

"Fuck." Cam undid the belt around Ana's wrists, took one last look at her, and went to the damned door.

CHAPTER FOURTEEN

Cam swung open the door, ready to tear the head off of whoever had interrupted them.

"Someone's after you!" Crone-chic cried, her fat black cat on her heels. It danced anxiously in place on too-small paws while Crone-chic waved her hands.

"How the hell?"

"Get dressed, get dressed! A man stopped by the desk, asking about someone like your woman. They had magic. Strong enough to sense the protections here. I can't guarantee they'll hold, not against one like him. You've got to get out."

"Shit!" He turned back to Ana, who now leaned on her elbows, shorts tugged haphazardly about her hips. She stared at him, eyes wide.

"Cernowain," she whispered.

Fuck. She had to be right. God of animals. He felt it then, like the snap of a rubber band against skin.

"Someone else is here," Ana hissed.

Someone had come through the aether from Otherworld. Someone *else*, if Crone-chic was to be believed about Cernowain. Which she was. The witches prided themselves on the security of their hidden rooms. Protecting their guests when the spells broke was protecting their own reputation.

Cam cursed himself for being so caught up in Ana that he hadn't felt Cernowain's arrival. He dragged on his shirt, not caring that it was filthy, and turned to see Ana ready to go, dressed and with her bow strapped across her back.

"Hurry!" Crone-chic cried from the doorway, her cat meowing its agreement. "Just because I sent them away doesn't mean they won't be back!"

Cam grabbed his bag from the corner and followed Ana out into the hall, leaving behind an empty room and the heat that had so recently engulfed them.

"We need a flight out," he said to Crone-chic. "Now."

"Well, um—" Crone-chic waved her hands some more while the cat continued to hop around, nervous energy radiating from its spiked black fur and one good eye. Not good under pressure, these two. "There's nothing 'til tomorrow, but my nephew can get you out." A crafty gleam entered her black eyes. "But it'll cost you."

Cam sighed. "Of course it will. Take us to him."

They followed Crone-chic down the stairs and into the back alley, eyes alert for their pursuers. Though he and Ana could feel the arrival of someone from Otherworld, knowing that person's exact location was beyond their ability. He could only tell that they were nearby. Which could be in this very alleyway.

Cam kept his gaze alert, constantly scanning the darkened passage for any sign of movement. The night was black and still, the animals quieter than usual.

"Here, here," Crone-chic whispered and pointed to a small door. "Inside."

Cam ducked under the little doorway behind Crone-chic and Ana, surprised by the modern kitchen within.

"Wait here."

She returned within a few minutes, a sleepy and disgruntled man of about twenty following her down the stairs.

"This is Paolo. He'll fly you inland."

"Inland? We don't have that kind of time. We need to get to the coast. To an airport big enough to get us to London."

"Take it or leave it, man," Paolo grumbled. "I got cargo to deliver. For you and your money, I'll leave early. You can catch another flight from there."

Cam considered their options and realized that they didn't have any. "Fine."

It took them five tense minutes to sneak across town to the tiny airport, thirty more for Paolo to prep the plane—all of which were fraught with anxiety—and finally they were airborne.

"Fates," Ana muttered, shifting to find a comfortable place on the floor of the plane as it headed toward its cruising altitude. Cargo boxes full of who knew what teetered in piles surrounding her. "Finally."

Cam just nodded at her, then settled back against his crate and folded his arms over his chest. He closed his eyes, pretending to doze.

So that's how he was going to play this? Tie her up, give her a crazy orgasm, and then ignore her?

Fine by her. She shouldn't have done it in the first place and maybe now she'd have a chance to pretend she never had. All the reasons she'd had for not getting involved with him — like the fact that one of them was going to end up in Otherworld — were just as relevant now.

More so, considering the fact that Cam in bed was something she could get used to. The memory of him, all tensely coiled muscle and harsh face hovering over her, was enough to send her over the edge. She shook her head. *Forget it.*

"So, what are we going to do now?" she asked.

"What Paolo said. Land, hope the gods haven't followed us, and find the first flight out."

"Oh. Okay." Shit. Now she couldn't think of anything else to say. And she wasn't sure if she wanted to. Listening to his rough voice just dredged up memories of earlier tonight.

The rumbling of the landing gear woke her sometime later—seconds or hours, she had no idea.

"What?" She rubbed her eyes and looked around blearily. "How long has it been?"

"Hour."

The plane pulled to a stop and Cam rose, having to duck in the small space. She followed suit, and soon they were hopping down onto the tarmac. It was narrow, set right into the jungle, which was as black as the night sky. Runway lights provided the only illumination. Animals rustled and shrieked within the forest.

Paolo shut the plane door behind them and said, "Got some time 'til the sun comes up. You're in luck, the weekly plane out of here leaves just after sunrise. It's a six seater, so maybe there'll be room."

"Will your aunt tell anyone where this plane landed?" Cam asked him.

"No. If your pursuers knew to ask, she wouldn't say anything."

"But she'll be in danger!" Ana hadn't thought of this before. Ugly guilt oozed through her at the thought of leaving the little old woman behind to face Cernowain.

Paolo laughed. "Not likely."

Ana's eyebrows rose. *Must be some witch to stand up to gods.* But there were beings more powerful than the Celtic gods, and Ana figured the Bruxa might as easily be one of them as anyone else.

Paolo led them across the abandoned tarmac to a little building set into the jungle. He unlocked the door to reveal a single room with a desk that was presumably for tickets, a big scale, chairs, and a tiny cafe that was nothing more than a counter and a few tables.

A door in the back of the room opened, and Ana was grateful to see a man in an apron walk through.

"An airport this small has a cafe?" Ana asked, nodding at the aproned man.

Paolo shrugged. "Only place to eat in town, if you want to call it a town. Just happens this building had space. Luis will feed you if you ask nicely."

Ana vowed to ask very nicely. She could eat a water buffalo right now.

Cam paid Paolo, handing over a fat stack of bills that made the man's white smile cut across his tanned face. Twenty minutes later, they were tucking into a breakfast that was the best thing Ana had ever tasted. It'd been so long since she'd eaten that she'd have enjoyed almost anything.

Cam hadn't said anything to her since they'd landed, just kept his eyes trained on the ticket table for when someone showed up to sell them a ticket. She peeked at him whenever she could. He looked more solemn than she'd ever seen him, his mouth pressed in a grim line and his eyes shuttered.

It was going to be harder than she'd thought to pretend last night hadn't happened. Impossible, most likely. She chewed her eggs, realizing that they'd gone tasteless in her mouth.

Cam shoved up from his seat and she jumped. A relieved sigh escaped her when she saw the ticket attendant. Or rather, the woman shuffling papers at the little desk who she assumed was the ticket agent. Hard to tell.

Cam returned a few minutes later. "That was the pilot. I got us a ride out on the next flight. Leaves in an hour." He didn't bother looking at her, just tucked back into his breakfast.

Ana frowned, bothered despite herself. He'd been so intense last night. And now he wouldn't look at her. *Not that you want him to!*

But she was a liar. And an idiot. Actually, she wasn't just an idiot. She was the world's biggest idiot. Because she was falling for the only person qualified to take her place in Otherworld.

CHAPTER FIFTEEN

A day after fleeing Bruxa's Eye on Paulo's small plane, Ana sat next to Cam on the biggest airplane she'd ever seen.

"You all right?"

Cam's voice sounded like it was pushing its way through water to get to her. She jerked her head. It was the first question he'd asked her, and some of the very few words he'd spoken to her since they'd fled Bruxa's Eye. They'd made it to a bigger city on the coast, gotten two hidden hotel rooms for the night, then caught this monster of a plane that was supposed to take them to London.

Cam had barely spoken to her since *that thing they did*, but she'd caught him looking at her dozens of times as if he didn't know how to deal with her. Good, because she didn't know how to deal with him.

She jumped when she felt his warm, hard palm cover hers on the plastic arm rest. She twitched, but didn't loosen her grip. Couldn't loosen it, even though this was the first time he'd touched her since the other night.

"You weren't afraid on the other planes," he said. His low, concerned voice soothed her, if only a bit. "Remember that you can aetherwalk to safety if something goes wrong."

Though huge, the plane was nearly empty. The only other passengers sat several rows ahead. The lights had been dimmed for anyone who wanted to sleep, according to the announcement made by a dark-haired woman in a red suit with matching lipstick. Ana had kept her eyes glued to the red scarf tied right below the beautiful woman's chin.

"I'm not afraid." Her voice almost cracked, and it horrified her.

He squeezed her hand, then pried it off the arm rest to grip in his own.

"Why are you being so nice?" she asked.

"I'm not. You're terrified. I'm simply not being an asshole about it."

A grin tried and failed to pull at her lips.

"Why, Ana?"

Some of their walls had broken down over the last days, it seemed. She drew in a ragged breath. "My bow. I've never been away from it."

"Shit." Realization tinged his voice.

Unlike the two tiny Mythean planes they'd taken, this stupid, gigantic ocean-crossing plane required that she pack her bow in the hold because the airline was run by mortals. For the first time in thousands of years, Ana had been parted from her bow. It was her protection, her friend, her past.

They'd been pretty sure the gods hadn't followed them to Sao Luis, the city where they'd caught this plane, so there was no reason to think the gods could find them and send the plane into the sea. But if something *did* go wrong, she'd have to aetherwalk and leave her bow.

Leave her bow. She shuddered. It would be as good as gone; she had no idea how to get it back from the hold. Didn't even know where such a place would be on such a big plane.

"I've seen how you hold it," he said. "You clutch it when you're nervous. I noticed that back when I first met you."

That made her turn her head to look at him. The aloofness had faded from his eyes. The gray was warm with memory, his lovely mouth slightly upturned in his harshly beautiful face.

"Really?" she asked.

"In the forest. I've seen you do it recently, too."

He'd noticed that about her? Her bow was more than just a thing to her. It defined her—restrung thousands of times, imbued with magic to make the wood last. It was her safety blanket, as stupid as it sounded.

"I know how it feels," he said. "Giving up my bow after godhood was one of the worst things I've ever had to do. Took a hell of a long time to get used to."

She couldn't even imagine. "This is the first you've really spoken to me in almost two days."

"Been thinking."

"About what?"

"About a lot of things. About how to help you get out of Otherworld." Cam's eyes met hers. Hers looked a little less panicked, he noted with relief.

Her jaw slackened. "Wow. Thanks. Does this have anything to do with what happened when you tied me up?"

"Maybe." But he'd been headed toward this decision for longer than that. If anything, the night in Bruxa's Eye had tipped him over the edge. He'd backed away from Ana since that night because the things he was starting to feel freaked him the hell out. But he couldn't avoid it any longer.

"Well, whatever the reason, thanks for the help."

"Sure. Don't know what the hell we're going to do though, because I'm not too keen on going back." The idea made a muscle at the corner of his eye twitch as memories of Otherworld surfaced. He wasn't cut out to be a god. When he'd been young, he'd assumed he was destined for greatness. How could he not, having been born into such power?

He'd been wrong. As the years had passed, he'd grown to hate Otherworld and the other gods. He'd been the only one to feel emotion, that lowly element that separated the mortals from the gods. Becoming enamored with Ana all those years ago had led him to fuck everything up. No matter what he'd thought as a kid, he wasn't destined for greatness. Certainly not as a god.

"We're going to the university first, right? I called my friend Esha to see if she knows anything about Druantia. Hopefully she'll learn her location or something else useful."

"If she discovers something, we can stop by." For someone on the run from gods, it was safer than anywhere else in Scotland. Gods who hadn't been granted permission to be on campus couldn't trespass on the grounds.

"Good."

"You're really friends with a soulceress?" Creepy and dangerous, they were.

"She's not as bad as everyone thinks. She gets a bad rap for stealing people's power, but she doesn't mean to."

Perhaps not, but Cam didn't fancy having the strength of his immortal soul sucked out of him. But he stayed silent, not wanting to insult her friend. He closed his eyes and tried to ignore how good it felt to hold her hand.

Just as he was debating letting go, her voice broke the silence. "Do you think about Otherworld at all?"

He shrugged. Of course he'd thought of it. If you escaped prison, how could you stop thinking of it?

"So you don't miss anything about godhood?" she asked.

"Parts of it, sure. Aetherwalking. My bow. Miss that a hell of a lot. Having a role and a job that's valuable." Though he'd been shit at being a stone cold god after he'd met Ana, he'd been a damn good god of war. He'd kept the battles even—for the most part—and the casualties not overwhelming.

Her eyes caught his, her brow scrunched. "Is that why your drug company is non-profit?"

He twitched. She'd always been insightful, but it was annoying when she caught something he felt weird talking about. At her unwavering stare, he said, "Yeah, I suppose so. I guess I got used to making a difference in Otherworld, doing something important. The company is my way of doing that here on earth." *And of making amends for everything that I screwed up by sticking you in an awful fucking afterworld.*

"Interesting choice. Most Mytheans wouldn't care about helping mortals."

"Yeah, but I started out as a god. That's our job. Doing that on earth, albeit in a different way, just made sense to me. Though it took me some time to figure it out."

"It suits you, running all over the Amazon looking for fancy plants. Fighting in bars at night. Making out with nymphs."

The word *nymphs* made him flinch, though he didn't know why. But she was right, the life did fit him. Adjusting to life on earth had taken centuries. The more fun he'd had, finally free of responsibility and with access to the lowlier pleasures earth offered, the guiltier he'd felt about ditching godhood. He'd run from his problems and was probably still running from them. He shook the thought away.

"Yeah," he said. "The Amazon works for me. No rules, not too many mortals to worry about."

Plenty of things to keep his mind occupied. So what if the nights in places like the Caipora's Den had started to get lonely? He still liked the fights, if only as a way to temporarily clear his head, and the women were nice. But even variety got old once you'd had enough of it.

"And you're doing good work there, with your cures," Ana said.

"Yeah. The work has taken decades. For the two cures to be available at the same time, because of the same plant... Huge deal. We had a sample of the plant, *Rosa McManus*. We just have to find the source of it now."

It was the main reason he could never even consider going back to Otherworld.

Cam blinked. Consider going back to Otherworld? *He'd never had that thought before.* Was he really considering it? Fuck, 'course not.

But he looked down at Ana, the one who was suffering in his place there. He rubbed his chest absently. Shit.

CHAPTER SIXTEEN

Ana was screwed. No doubt about it, she was falling hard for the man sitting next to her in the plush seat of the small private jet. She could believe he'd agreed to help her get out of Otherworld—that's just the kind of guy he was. He'd tried to protect her so many years ago by letting her take his place in Otherworld. It might suck up there, but it was better than being an automaton or having her soul obliterated. He even understood what it was like for her to be away from her bow. He was like Marrek, in the way he understood her.

If he kept this understanding, protective business up, she'd be a goner.

"You good?" he asked her.

She nodded, gratefully eying her bow, which leaned against the wall next to her.

They'd arrived in London earlier that morning. She'd never truly appreciated aetherwalking until she'd had to wait at a baggage claim for her bow. There were definitely some aspects of being a god that rocked. At least Cam had the contacts to get her a fake passport.

"Thanks for getting the private charter to Edinburgh," Ana said.

Talking to Cam on the last flight had helped her forget most of her anxiety, but she was glad that his thoughtfulness—and deep pockets—kept her from having to go through that again. Not to mention the fact that she was grateful for the hotel room he'd rented them in the airport while the jet was prepared for takeoff. The quick shower made her feel a million times better, not to mention the clean clothes she'd conjured that were more appropriate to the cooler weather. They'd both studiously avoided looking at the bed.

"Traveling as a mortal takes a decade," she said as the plane hurtled into the air. By her calculations, they'd been on about three hundred planes in the last few days. Exhaustion should haunt her, but she'd gotten some decent sleep on the last plane.

He laughed, low and husky, and squeezed her hand briefly. Her mouth kicked up at the corner.

Yep, she was screwed.

She shot him a look out of the corner of her eye. Though he'd changed into clean clothes in the hotel, he still looked out of place on the plane, just as he had when striding through the London airport. He should fit in here, with his Celtic coloring.

But he didn't. He was made for the jungle. Out of his element, the contrast made him more intimidating, more deadly. His eyes and mouth were too hard, too wary. His body too tall and dangerous. No doubt there were places in London where he would fit in, but it wasn't the airport

Hilton. Maybe that was one of the reasons he hung out in the jungle. He looked like a mortal, but didn't quite pass for one.

She shifted in her seat. The memory of what he'd looked like in the ring, fighting like an animal, flashed in front of her eyes.

She could warn herself away from him all she wanted, but it didn't seem to be working.

Her eyes trailed down his chest to the long legs that stretched out toward the seat in front of him. She glanced at the door leading to the cockpit. It was visible over the top of the chairs in front of theirs. If one of the pilots came out, she'd be able to see Cam's head but not much else. There was no flight attendant on this flight.

Ana gripped the arm rest of her chair, debating. Then grinned. She wanted to live dangerously, right?

Swiftly, she unbuckled her seatbelt, climbed out of her chair and onto Cam's lap.

"What are you—"

She cut off his question with her mouth and ran her hands up to his shoulders. She waited for him to give assent. It'd been days since they'd touched like this, both of them warily circling each other, and it was torture not to touch all of him.

He groaned, and she felt his big hands grip her waist. Reveling in the strength of him, she smoothed her palms along his strong chest. She'd admired it on the boat and then again in the hotel room in Bruxa's Eye.

But this was the first time that she'd actually gotten to touch, to feel all the hard muscles that could do so much damage.

His hands tightened briefly on her hips and he dragged his mouth away from hers. "Ana, this is—"

She pressed a finger against his mouth while she ran her teeth along a straining muscle at his throat. He groaned and his head dropped back.

His skin tasted amazing, fresh and clean with the faintest bite of salt.

It made her wonder what the rest of him would taste like. She slid off of him until the hard floor bit into her knees.

He looked down at her, brows arched and lips parted.

"Ana, you know this is a bad idea." His voice was rough, sandpaper once again, and she shivered.

It was a bad idea. She'd been telling herself that since she first saw him in the Caipora's Den. But he turned her brain to mush.

"I want to return the favor." She reached for the fly of his jeans. "Anyway, it's just sex, right? Don't overthink it." She didn't believe it even as she said it.

His hand gripped hers where she'd started to unbuckle his belt, so she slipped the other one up to cup the bulge in his jeans. Heat bloomed between her thighs. She wanted this. Wanted to taste him. Wanted to hear the sounds he made in his pleasure.

Cam met Ana's eyes as she massaged his cock through his jeans.

"Come on, Cam, I'm just returning the favor." She licked her lips, and his hand tightened on the arm rest. He barely remembered not to crush the small fist he still held in his other hand. "I won't kiss you anywhere else. Same as what you did for me."

Fuck. He dropped his head back against the seat. He got where she was going with this. Less intimacy from less kissing and touching. But hell, what her eyes promised... That was intimacy enough.

"You need this, Cam. I can feel it."

Hell, of course she could. But by her logic, he'd needed it from the first time he saw her at the Caipora's Den.

Deftly, she slipped her hand from his and pulled at his belt. He gripped the arm rests and stared at the door to the cockpit. What the fuck was he doing?

Something he couldn't stop. He didn't want to. She tugged his jeans down to free his cock. His eyes darted down to see her small hands gripping him. The dusky head of his cock flared above her pale hand.

She stroked him and his breath caught in his throat.

The sight of her pink tongue darting out to lick the head made his shaft twitch. The silken glide forced a strangled groan from his throat. He stifled a shout when she took him into the heat of her mouth. She stroked him and sucked until his mind fogged.

His chest heaved as he watched her. He prayed she'd let him come in her mouth. Not because it was hot, which it was. Because he didn't think he could recover from it if she wanted to hold his gaze with her own while he came in her fist. A direct parallel to the night in Bruxa's Eye when he'd wanted to hold her gaze with his own.

She looked up at him and withdrew her mouth. His heart clutched.

"Show me what you like." Her lips were shiny and her cheeks flushed.

Comprehension and lust hit him hard when she picked up one of his hands and put it to her head. Her eyes told him to add the other as well.

His eyebrows rose. Seriously?

"I'm a goddess, Cam. I don't need to breathe. *Show me* what you like." Her voice was firm, husky with arousal.

He groaned, fisted his hands in her silken hair, and lowered her head until the heat of her mouth enveloped his cock.

"*Fuck*, Ana." He gritted his teeth, fought to control himself and his movements.

He set an easy pace, the mere sight of his hands pressing her mouth down onto his cock enough to make his thighs tremble.

Her low moan vibrated around his cock, and he realized that her hips were unconsciously moving as if she was as turned on as he was by this act. He heaved out a shaky breath, trying to make this last, knowing it wouldn't.

Eventually, she seemed to realize that he wasn't going to put much force behind moving her head. She cradled his balls and took him deeper into her mouth than he'd dared press. Pleasure spiked through him and his hips jerked uncontrollably.

"Fuck, I'm sorry," he rasped.

She didn't pause and continued to fuck him with her mouth. Soon it became too much—the heat of her, the smell of her, the sounds of her. Heat suffused him and pressure rose in his shaft.

"Ana, I'm close." He tugged lightly on her head, but she sped up, heat and wetness and friction working his cock.

He groaned deep in his throat, well past caring where he was. The orgasm blasted through him, so strong it was almost painful, and it took everything he had not to lose control of his hips and thrust uncontrollably into her mouth.

When he finally recovered enough to focus again, he looked down to see Ana panting, collapsed back on her heels and watching his face. At some point during the orgasm he'd apparently let go of her head to squeeze the seat's arm rests. A good thing, considering the grip that he had on them.

He heaved out a sigh, still shaky from the pleasure.

"Thanks." His voice was raspy, as if unused for a thousand years. He reached out to rub a thumb across her cheek.

She grinned. "No problem."

He zipped his fly while she stood and headed back toward the lavatory. His head turned to follow her, disappointed. He'd wanted to kiss her.

He dropped his head back into the seat, squeezed his eyes closed. Damn it. He was a goner.

Ana's hands trembled as she struggled to shove the lock into place in the tiny airplane bathroom. She turned toward the sink, gripped the plastic edge and leaned over it, gasping.

What the hell had she done? She'd totally wanted that, no doubt. Wanted it so bad that she'd told herself it was just sex and it didn't matter. Fates, she was actually bullshitting herself and falling for it. The shaking breath that she drew in did little to fill her lungs. Which made sense. Her brain wasn't working, so why should her lungs?

Not to mention her heart. She pinched the bridge of her nose. She should *not* be thinking about her heart. That was ridiculous. But of its own volition, her hand moved from her head to her chest, rubbed absently. Ugh, this was awful.

When she'd decided to escape Otherworld permanently, she'd wanted all the feelings and emotions to be had on earth. To live and feel and enjoy. But this? This was not what she'd signed up for. This was too much.

Had she ever felt like this when she was mortal? Like there was a wild thing scrabbling around in her chest, desperate and anxious for something? For him? She had no idea how to deal with it. How to deal with him. Their past was a pit of snakes that she was trying to cross on a tightrope. And now he was the only person who could take her place in Otherworld. And idiot that she was, her chest was going crazy over him. For the man who was probably going to leave her stranded on the tightrope.

CHAPTER SEVENTEEN

"Do you come back to Scotland often?" Ana asked Cam. It was the first she'd spoken since they'd departed the Edinburgh airport twenty minutes ago in one of his company's cars.

"No. I don't like it here."

"Why not?" she asked from the passenger seat.

Apparently neither one of them wanted to talk about what had happened on the plane. It was fine with him. That conversation couldn't go anywhere good, considering that one of them would end up back in Otherworld at the end of this.

"I just prefer the jungle. And since I've been lying low, it's safer there. The company has staff that deals with things here, like testing and grant writing. And they have excellent research facilities that we partner with. The operation is too big to not be involved with the university. We need staff, and most prefer to live here around other Mytheans. Company meetings usually happen in Rio. That way, I can stay in the jungle."

But Scotland, and his past, had managed to creep into the jungle all the same. In the form of Ana. Amazing Ana, who did amazing things with her mouth. She turned his flat world round. It was totally fucked up, but everything that he was doing, the good that he was trying to do with his company, was starting to take a back seat to her. To the feelings that bubbled up whenever he thought of her or looked at her.

He'd thought he had a handle on it all.

She proved that he didn't.

"So your company arranges for the car like they did the plane?" Ana asked.

He nodded, grateful for the distraction from his thoughts. "They would have picked us up. But I like to drive."

"Yeah, you're a bit of a control freak."

His head whipped toward her. "I'm not."

"Kinda."

"Fine. You ever come to Edinburgh?" Better to talk about her than about him.

"Whenever I can. Literally. Whenever there's a chance to sneak away unnoticed, I do."

Cam nodded. Before he'd met her, he'd had no reason or desire to go to earth. The other gods were the same. Earth was a mess of mortal emotions, unappealing to the gods. Most even believed that their presence was required in Otherworld to keep it operational.

But then he'd found her in the forest all those years ago and changed the entire course of his life. And hers. Guilt tugged at him. It clung to him like the barnacles to the hull of a ship.

"Why do you come to Edinburgh when you could go anywhere else?" Cam asked as he turned the car onto the less-crowded country road that would take them out to the university.

"My friend Esha lives here. She works for the university."

"You don't mind it when she drains your power?"

"No, I like it. Makes me feel mortal again."

He supposed it would. "It's dangerous to be weakened like that."

"Don't get me wrong, I like having the strength and abilities of a god. But sometimes it's just nice to feel a bit different. And the world isn't as bad as it used to be, especially if Esha and I stick to mortal places."

She had a point. The university, which was more than just an educational institution, kept tabs on the Mytheans who were too violent or likely to reveal their existence to mortals. Only law-abiding Mytheans were permitted to live in cities. The rest were sent back to their afterworlds when they became a threat to the secrecy of all Mytheans. The university had a department that dealt specifically with keeping track of such things. As a result, Edinburgh was safer for the law-abiding Mytheans than it had been in the past.

All the dangerous ones were pushed into the fringes, like the jungle, with him. Which was how he liked it.

"What mortal places do you and Esha visit?" Every minute he spent with her, he wanted to know more about her. Dangerous is what that was.

"Depends. Bars and clubs if it's night. Crazy stuff in the day. Scuba diving, skydiving, skiing. Anything exciting. Anything I can't do in Otherworld."

"Makes sense. You've lived a long time. Lots of Mytheans seek out thrills."

She sighed, and he caught sight of her fiddling with her bow out of the corner of his eye. "It's not that, really. Being in Otherworld is like being in a coma. It feels like time passes more quickly there. Enough that I feel like I haven't really lived. I guess I just want to make up for that on earth. All the fun stuff I miss out on when I'm stuck there."

The car suddenly felt very quiet and small. The longer he spent with Ana, the more aware he became of what exactly he'd done to her in their past. He'd been a selfish son of a bitch when he'd stalked her in the forest. He should have left her alone. Instead, he'd brought her to the attention of the gods. It was getting harder and harder to ignore that.

Being around her brought into sharp focus how much she loved life—how curious and intelligent and passionate she was—and how he'd truly screwed her by getting her stuck in Otherworld. He'd done the best he could in a shit situation, but she'd still gotten screwed. The more he realized how much he liked her, the more he realized how much he didn't deserve to even be near her. He was a bastard.

So lost in recriminations was he that he nearly missed the turn for the university. He stomped on the brakes and turned onto the road that was hidden from mortal eyes. The car hurtled through oak trees that were just an illusion until an enormous wrought iron gate loomed before them. It swung open silently, and Cam drove them down the lane toward the cluster of ornate stone buildings in the middle of fields scattered with hardwoods.

It was beautiful, he supposed, but he didn't care for it. Too civilized or something. He couldn't pinpoint what was wrong with it, but he didn't care.

"I love this place," Ana said as they pulled up to the ancient buildings that loomed over the main part of campus. She pointed to a gray stone building on the other side of the cobblestone courtyard. "Fiona's office is in there, I think."

She'd called Esha when they'd landed to let her know they'd arrived and to see if she'd learned anything more about Druantia. Esha had told her to go see an Acquirer in the Department of Magical Devices, Fiona Blackwood. Acquirers were like archaeologists who were magically inclined to find artifacts.

Cam parked in one of the cobblestone parking lots in the middle of a group of stone buildings, one of which held Fiona's office. Ana climbed out of the car and looked around, taking in the monstrous stone edifices that rose all around. She set off across rain-damp cobbles. They gleamed in the yellow light of the old-fashioned street lamps.

"Ana!" A feminine voice echoed across the parking lot.

Ana whirled to see her friend Esha running down the wide stone steps of the biggest building in the square, her scruffy black cat at her heels. Her familiar, Chairman Meow, never left her side, though sometimes it pained him to have to keep up with her. The Chairman liked a nice fire and a tuna steak more than anything in the world, and if he didn't have both in front of him, he was a bit of a grump.

"Esha!" Ana cried and threw her arms around her friend. Esha's long black hair tickled her nose.

She heaved a sigh of relief when much of her power drained away. She'd always felt like the power of being a god never fit quite right on her shoulders. Sure, it gave her extra strength, immortality, and the ability to aetherwalk, all of which came in handy. But it also made her feel tense and strange, probably because she'd started out mortal.

And there wasn't much to worry about as long as they were on the university campus. By law and by magic, the gods weren't allowed on the campus except by invitation. It better allowed the university staff to manage relations between the afterworlds if they were protected from the wrath of any gods who might not agree with their diplomacy. Ana had a standing invitation from Esha, which got her around the rules and allowed her to see her friend.

Ana pulled away from Esha and grinned up at her. Esha's smile reached her amber eyes.

"Is that guy—" Esha stopped abruptly, presumably at the sight of Cam.

Ana glanced over her shoulder. Yep. Cam stood behind her with a *You've been talking about me?* expression. Ana turned back to Esha.

"That's him," she mouthed. "What are you doing here?" she asked in a normal tone. Esha's black hair matched that of her familiar, who now sat at her heels staring combatively at Cam. Chairman Meow was the suspicious sort.

"Visiting Warren. His office is in that building. You're on your way to see Fiona?"

"Yeah, thanks for setting that up. She's in that one?" Ana pointed to a smaller building at the edge of the lot, and Esha nodded.

"Yeah. And no problem about arranging it. I asked around after you called and she's the person to talk to. Come to my place after." Esha's amber eyes lit up with excitement. "Warren will be working all night. We'll stay in my tower."

Cam stepped forward. "Actually—"

"Seriously. Come up after you talk Fiona," Esha said.

Ana turned to face Cam, wondering if her face showed how much she wanted to stay with her friend. There were guest quarters they could stay at, but it would be so good to see Esha, especially with everything else in her life going crazy. Apparently her face did show something, because Cam nodded.

"Ana, we should go see Fiona," Cam said.

He shifted on his feet, and she realized that Esha was probably pulling power from him as well, only he didn't like it. Ana was the only one who really did; other Mytheans gave Esha a wide berth. She and Esha were both outcasts, which might have been one of the reasons they bonded so well.

"Great," Ana said. "We'll be over in a bit."

"Brilliant." Esha headed into the night, her black cat a silent shadow on her heels.

"All right, let's figure out where this priestess is," Ana said, and strode across the cobblestone lot.

A few minutes later, after passing through gleaming wooden corridors and beneath the eyes of ancient portraits, she knocked on Fiona's door.

"Come in!" The voice echoed through the door and Cam and Ana stepped into a cluttered little office. It was almost a broom closet, but instead of brooms, there was a tiny desk, a chair, and a beat-up laptop. A dark-haired woman turned away from a bookshelf she'd been trying to squeeze a book into and smiled.

"You must be Andrasta and Camulos. Come in. Enjoy the ambiance of my office." She swept her hand around the space. Her eyes welcomed them from behind glasses. A little black cat peered over the edge of the top shelf on the bookcase. It was a ball of fluff that blinked big yellow eyes at her from where it perched three feet above her head.

"Oh, don't worry about Fluffy Black. She comes to the office on Tuesdays. That's her nap spot."

"Okay." Ana looked around for a place to put herself. With Fiona occupying the space in front of the bookshelf that stood behind the desk, and the cat on the top shelf, the only space available was to lean against the desk. Ana and Cam squeezed in.

"It's cozy," Ana said.

"Sure, like a grave. But whatever. You're here to ask me about Druantia, the Druid priestess."

"Exactly," Ana said. "How'd you find her?"

"I didn't find her, exactly. I found her boyfriend."

"Boyfriend?" Ana had not been expecting that.

"Boyfriend, lover, whatever. The man she's currently boning. Who, by the way—and this is crazy—is *the* Logan Laufeyson."

"What?" Cam's voice was sharp, disbelieving.

"I know," Fiona said. "I was shocked too. Everyone thought he was dead. But he's not."

"Wait—explain, please," Ana said.

"Oh, sorry." Fiona squished her face into what Ana always thought of as an *apology face*. "For hundreds of years, Logan Laufeyson was a renowned mercenary whose skill was the bow. He sold his services all over southern Europe. He was the absolute best in the world. But he fell off everyone's radar about three hundred years ago. We thought he was dead—until he popped up and stole an artifact from us. An ancient bow and a set of arrows that belonged to a great queen of the Britons. No one else in my department thinks it's worth the effort or the money to go after it, so they dropped the recovery effort. But I know it's important. I'm sure of it."

"Why do you care?" Ana asked.

"Ah, well. I care for history's sake. The artifact should be in a museum. But, on a more personal note, these fabulous accommodations of mine"—she swept her hand around the office—"are the result of a bit of a mix-up with a very important artifact a few years ago. Basically, I fucked up bad. Real bad. I was demoted from field Acquirer to record keeper in this purgatory."

"I'm sorry," Ana said. Fiona gave off the vibe of someone who'd been stuck in her surroundings too long, desperate to get out.

"You're wondering why this is all relevant, I'm sure. Simply put, I'm trying to win my old job back by finding the artifact that I lost, as well as any others that have been stolen. That's how I came across Logan. I found him living with a woman in Inverness—Druantia, your Druid priestess."

"Holy shit," Cam breathed.

"Crazy, right? I found the info about a week ago. I was going to go up there on my week off to find him and retrieve the artifact."

"Isn't that dangerous?" Ana asked, glancing around the office. If the woman was used to spending her days in a place like this, was she really qualified to go up against one of the greatest warriors the world had ever known?

"I'm *not* a desk jockey. I'm a field Acquirer. I'm just being punished here in the stacks. Anyway, I'm not going to challenge him or anything. He's dangerous as hell. I was going to try to sneak in and steal it. You'd be surprised how often that works."

"Did you learn anything about Druantia?" Ana said.

"I did some digging when Esha told me you were interested. She's still acting as a Druid priestess—though with a lesser following than in years past, of course. For the last two hundred years or so, she's had a shop that sells magics and trinkets."

"Excellent, thank you."

"No problem." She turned and grabbed a notebook off the shelf. With a quick hand, she flipped it open and transcribed an address on a page, then tore it out and handed it to Ana. "Here you go. Don't scare off Logan. I want that bow."

"Sure. Thank you again. Really."

"Not a problem. I know what it's like to want something badly. Glad I could help."

The cat above her head peered down and meowed a tiny *meep*, as if it agreed with Fiona.

"That's right, Fluffy. Way to be hospitable."

Ana huffed out a small laugh, then said her goodbyes with Cam and departed.

Cam's head buzzed with possibility as they walked across the rolling green lawn toward Esha's tower at the far edge of the campus. The night was so silent compared to the jungle that it made his skin itch. A pale moon illuminated the damp green grass, and it made him ache for the Amazon.

"So, what do you think?" Ana asked, nearly hopping in her excitement.

"I know what you're thinking. But I don't know. I doubt he's powerful enough."

It'd be the perfect conclusion to this. Someone to take both their places in Otherworld. But it was unlikely. He wasn't being cocky. Being a war god took an extraordinary strength of will and a desire to succeed above all else. And skill in war. In all his years as a god, he'd only ever met one person who had what it took.

Ana.

"But it's Logan Laufeyson," Ana said. "You heard how she talked about him."

"Yeah. And though I've never met him, I have heard of him. Centuries ago when I was living in northern Canada."

"News traveled all the way up there?"

"Some news. I listened particularly for news like that. Even I was impressed with what I heard. But he'd have to agree to become a god."

She sighed, and they trudged along. "I'm operating under the assumption that we're going to convince this guy to take my place, okay?"

He nodded. He doubted it would work—when had anything been that easy?—but even he couldn't fully crush the hope that had started squatting in his chest as soon as Fiona had mentioned the man. From what Cam remembered, if anyone on earth was qualified, it was Logan Laufeyson. Lucky as hell he wasn't dead.

They arrived at the base of the round stone tower that sat near the forest a few hundred yards from the rest of the campus buildings. Cam pushed opened the door for Ana, his eyes following her inside. Christ, he liked looking at her.

"Oh, chivalry," she teased as she climbed the spiral stair to her friend's apartment.

He followed behind her, not particularly excited to be spending the night in the home of a soulceress. It was an eerie feeling, having his strength drained away like that. All Mytheans had something extra in their souls, a power that gave them immortality and whatever other strengths were inherent to their species. Esha fed upon that power. And there was nothing he could do about it, which he despised.

But Ana trusted her, and the flat was one of the safest places in the world. Not only was it on the university campus, no Mythean would come to a place where their immortality was drained away by the resident. Even the gods would be affected here.

They reached the top of the stairs and Ana burst through the door without knocking. She leapt over the scruffy black cat sprawled in front of the door. Cam followed suit with a less excited step.

"Gods, I'm so glad you're here!" Esha said from where she stood in the kitchen of her open-plan flat. She eyed Cam suspiciously, which he figured was par for the course. People didn't normally take to him easily.

"Gods damn it, this stupid thing isn't working!" a feminine voice exclaimed.

Cam glanced toward the living room to see a small woman who was all shades of gold—skin, hair, eyes—sitting on the floor in front of the couch, glaring at the glowing screen of a tablet. Her short hair stuck out at all angles, like she'd been shoving her hand through it.

"Hey, Aurora," Ana said to the woman.

"Huh?" Aurora jerked her head up. After a moment, her eyes cleared. "Hi, Ana. Sorry, I was so distracted I barely even noticed you come in. This stupid tablet is giving me hell."

"Tablet? I've never seen one." Ana's voice brightened and she veered toward Aurora. "Show me."

Aurora handed over the device and explained the problem while Ana ran her fingers over it, fascination evident on her face.

"You should have seen them last month," Esha said. "They were playing with a flashlight like it was the most advanced technology on earth."

A grin tugged at Cam's mouth. Ana really did love technology. Probably because there was nothing like it in Otherworld. Her happiness and fascination were magnetic. He glanced at the other woman whose golden eyes were so like Esha's.

"Your sister?" he asked.

Esha nodded.

"Here." Ana handed the tablet back to Aurora, reluctance in her voice.

"Thanks. Hey, Esha? I'm going back to my place. I left the instruction manual over there. I'll see you tomorrow." After saying goodbye to Ana and looking at Cam questioningly, she departed.

Ana looked at Esha. "I'm going to get a shower, okay?"

"Sure. Hang on a sec." Esha turned and rummaged through her fridge, then spun back around and handed over a bottle with a grin. "Here's a beer."

"Score. Shower beer is the best."

"True story. Sorry I don't have any donuts or we'd have the perfect dinner."

"Well, I saw you've got the *Die Hard* movies on your shelf, so we could still have the perfect night." Ana waggled her eyebrows.

"That I do. We can watch one when you're out."

"Awesome." Ana shot Esha a grin over her shoulder that hit Cam in the chest, punched through his ribs, and yanked on his heart. Seeing her at ease, in her element with her friends. Shit, it did something to him. Something dangerous. She took so much joy in life and in other people. He loved that about her, but it gave him the strangest empty feeling. Like loneliness. He shook the thought away. He might be a loner, and his life might lack the joy Ana felt at being with her friend, but he wasn't *lonely*. That was ridiculous.

"Can I get you something, Cam?" Esha's voice cooled when she addressed him.

He turned to catch her still eyeing him suspiciously, then caught sight of the cat doing the same, his citrine eyes offering threats along with distrust. He was big, with a tomcat face and disheveled fur.

"Ah, beer. Thanks. Mind if I take a seat?" Cam shifted on his feet, feeling eerily like he'd stepped into the den of some kind of predator.

"Sure." She snagged a beer out of the fridge and handed it to him. The sound of water singing through the pipes emitted from the bathroom. Esha sprawled in the chair across from him, but it wasn't hard to see that the sprawl was an act. "So you and my friend have a history."

Here it comes. He sipped his drink. Nodded.

"A fucked-up history, from what I've heard."

He nodded again and she gave him an appraising look.

"Hmm. Didn't expect you to admit it," she said.

"Well, you're right. It's fucked up."

"You gonna unfuck it up?"

"What do you mean?" But shit, he knew what she meant. Exactly what he'd been fearing since Ana showed up on his river.

Esha's amber eyes now glowed with the same aggression that shone from her eerie cat. "Get her the fuck out of Otherworld. She hates it. No." She shook her head and gestured. "She doesn't just hate it. It's killing her, from the inside out. She was a fucking mortal. Skilled and driven and strong enough to be a god, but not built for it. Not inside. She's so lonely in Otherworld that her soul is withering."

Cam's grip tightened on the beer bottle as some invisible force squeezed his ribs. At first he thought it was her magic, just a hit to convince him she was serious. *No need, lady.*

But then he realized it was him, because he was fucking agreeing with her. Guilt was a live thing in his chest, filling him up until he nearly strangled on it. He was responsible for what had happened to Ana. For all the loneliness and misery in her life.

He'd made the decision before he'd ever set foot in Esha's tower, but only now was he accepting it. He'd go back to Otherworld to save her. No question. He could hardly live with himself now, knowing how lonely she'd been in Otherworld. She was too bright and fun and lively to be in a place like that.

But the idea of going back, to that place where he'd tried and failed, made him sweat. He prayed that Logan Laufeyson was strong enough for the task and wanted the job, because if he wasn't, Cam's own life was about to get a hell of a lot more miserable.

Going back to Otherworld—well, shit. He supposed he'd been headed in this direction, he just hadn't wanted to acknowledge it.

"I'll fix this," he said.

Esha seemed to see the truth in his eyes and she relaxed. The cat didn't, and Cam had a feeling that the bruiser would be glaring at him all night. It hissed, like it could read his thoughts, and he glared back.

"The Chairman likes you," Esha said.

He raised a brow.

"Yeah, just fucking with you. He'd eat you if he were big enough. But I trust you to take care of this. Because if you don't…"

Then he did feel something squeeze around his chest. And his legs, arms, head. His vision temporarily blacked out, and claws of panic pierced his heart while his muscles strained to break free. When the pressure finally released and he opened his eyes, he had to force himself not to gasp in front of her.

"So we're on the same page." Esha gave an eerie but genuine smile. "Can I get you another beer?"

CHAPTER EIGHTEEN

Keane Hotel, Inverness, Scotland, Present Day

"I can't believe she wasn't there," Ana said as she crossed the street with Cam toward their Inverness hotel. A cold drizzle exacerbated her pissy mood.

"She'll be there tomorrow." He held open the door of the hotel for her.

"Yeah. It's just so anticlimactic. We're so close, and we came up empty." After waking late at Esha's—Cam on the couch and Ana in Esha's bed with her friend and the space hog of a cat—they'd driven north all afternoon until they'd reached Inverness.

"Tomorrow," Cam said.

Ana looked around the lobby of the hotel. She'd never have guessed it was another Mythean hotel, complete with protections, from the look of the place. A shining wood registration desk and plush couches decorated the space. It looked like any other mortal hotel in the city.

"Let's head to the pub," Cam said after they'd checked in.

"What, you've got business down there?"

"No, just thought you'd like to go out. Live a little."

Her head swung toward him and she took in his not-quite-casual stance. "Just for fun?"

He nodded.

Huh. He'd really been listening when she'd talked about her trips to earth and wanting to live as much as she could. A smile tugged at the corner of her mouth.

"They've got some local whiskeys I'll bet you've never tried. But no getting drunk." He smiled. "One glass only, so we stay alert."

It felt warm and fuzzy and strange to do something so normal with him. But maybe that was the point. They had no idea what was coming tomorrow. She knew what she hoped for. But there was no guarantee. One last night—the only night—when they wouldn't think about what was coming.

She smiled. "Yeah, all right."

They walked into the crowded pub in the basement of the hotel a few minutes later and managed to find a seat by the old wooden bar. The beauty of the hotel's protection charm was that if someone sought out another with ill intent, he wouldn't be able to find them. Not even if they were standing right in front of his face. The place was dark and low ceilinged, all wood and leather, dingy in the way of a beloved old pub that hadn't needed to change to keep its clientele coming.

Clientele which, she noted while looking around, were quite strange. Most were human-passing Mytheans, but more than a couple looked like creepy movie extras. But then, it was the only Mythean watering hole in town, so if they wanted a drink, this was it.

When she finally turned back to the bar, Cam was holding out a heavy glass of golden liquid. One corner of his mouth was kicked up in a sexy grin. She swallowed hard and reminded herself that she had the control of a saint.

Sure.

"Thanks." She raised her glass to his, caught his eyes and then her breath, and finally found the focus to take a sip. "It's good."

He nodded, and they sat on the barstools with their backs to the bar so that they could people watch.

"Not too different from your jungle bars, is it?" she asked.

"Nah. Just needs a fight ring out back to be perfect. A few of these fellows could stand to work out some of their aggression." He gestured to a group roaring over a football match on the telly.

"Work out something else, more like," Ana said as she caught sight of a couple groping each other in a darkened corner. A flash of jealous heat streaked through her. She glanced at Cam. Her state of mind was contagious, and the dark heat in his gaze made her turn away from him and sip her whiskey to get control of herself.

But when had alcohol ever made one wiser or less prone to their baser instincts?

A man stepped up next to her on the side away from Cam. He caught her eye and grinned. He was handsome, and nearly as big as Cam. But he left her cold.

"Buy you a drink when that's finished?" he asked.

Cam made a low noise in his throat, but didn't intervene. He didn't treat her like property that the other man was encroaching upon, and she liked it a hell of a lot.

"No, I'm good," she said.

"Come on. One drink won't hurt." He put his hand on her back, and her skin prickled uncomfortably. Didn't this moron understand *no*? Or that she was with Cam?

A low noise, like a growl, sounded from her side. It was Cam. She caught sight of his fists on the bar, the knuckles whitened.

"Seriously, I'm not interested." She scowled up at the man, who hovered too close.

"Come on, bird."

That's it. She set down her whiskey tumbler and shoved the man so hard that he flew across the room and slammed against the wall. She grinned darkly. Being a god might suck, but the strength was a real bonus.

The man righted himself and surged toward her, his scowl-twisted face red as a sunset. "You bitch."

She stood, but before she could face him, Cam slipped around her side and collided with the man. He lifted him up by his shirt collar, and Ana caught sight of Cam's face in a mirror on the wall. Pent-up aggression twisted his features. She hadn't seen him in a fight ring in a while, but the fighter was still there.

He shook the man, and Ana swore she heard teeth rattle.

"You sure you don't want to rethink your approach?" Cam growled.

Ana moved to stand next to Cam, unsure of whether or not she wanted to kick her annoying suitor or save him from possible death. "I can handle my own fights!"

181

Cam glanced down at her and growled, "No doubt. But I'd like to help."

Warmth spread within her. She liked to handle her own battles, but something about having Cam fight for her was undeniably appealing. She wanted him, more than she'd ever wanted anyone else. All it took was a glance from him, much less a fight on her behalf, to send her toward the deep end. Anything else—anybody else—was just fleeing from the very real thing that was developing between them.

"I think we're done with him," Ana said, nodding at the man, who had gone limp in submission.

Cam dropped him and turned to her. The man caught his balance and scrambled away.

"I didn't like seeing you with him," he growled. Something like jealousy or desire glinted in his eyes. Maybe both.

"Then with who?"

CHAPTER NINETEEN

"Me." Cam stepped forward until he'd caged her against the bar. He wanted to grab hold of her and never let her go. He'd tried to resist. He didn't deserve her, but even that couldn't stop him now. With every passing day, he was reminded of all the reasons he'd grown to care for her in the past. Seeing that bastard come at her with violence in his eyes had thrown his situation into sharp relief.

He cared for her more than he cared for himself.

"You?" Ana was breathing so quickly he could see the pulse flutter in her throat.

"Yeah. What we have is better than anything you'll find anywhere else." He knew that for sure now. Knew that everything in their past hadn't been a fluke.

"Maybe that's not what I'm looking for." She didn't sound like she believed her words.

"You're looking to run away, that's what you're looking for." He pulled her toward him, his hands on her waist. "I remember what it was like when I first left Otherworld and came to earth. Getting close to anyone was strange as hell, even if I didn't feel things quite as strongly as mortals."

She nodded slowly, her eyes wide.

He leaned down to her ear. "Didn't you say you wanted to live dangerously?"

"Yes," she whispered.

His hand engulfed hers and he pulled her down a darkened hallway in the back of the pub to an alcove off the end. Probably once used for storage, it was now empty and dark.

"What?" she gasped as he pressed her against the wall and cupped the back of her head.

"You said you wanted excitement," he said against her lips. And he didn't know if he could wait to get back to the room.

"I—" she panted. "I was joking."

He kissed her, reveling in her sweetness, and the high-pitched moan that escaped her mouth when he pushed up her shirt belied her words.

"I don't think so. I think you like this." He cupped her small breast, circling his thumb around her nipple until she arched into his hand.

She gripped his shoulders and he pressed himself hard against her, to keep her upright but also to feel the heat and softness of her belly pressed against his cock. He stifled a groan when she rubbed against him.

The sound of revelers in the pub a mere ten yards away clashed with his harsh breathing and her low whimpers.

He pressed his mouth to hers, parting her lips and tasting the bite of whiskey on her tongue. Desperate to feel more of her, he ran his hand down her stomach to her shorts. He unsnapped them and slid his hand inside, easing into her underwear until his fingers dipped into her heat.

She made an animal noise in her throat, tore her mouth from his. "We could be caught."

Her breath was coming hard and fast, the lightest tinge of fear to it, but she arched into his touch. Her hands ran over the muscles of his chest and arms, squeezing and petting and making him feel like he could move mountains.

"Maybe." He parted her sex and pushed two fingers inside her, his cock twitching jealously as her muscles closed around him. He moved his thumb in small circles around her clitoris. Damn, she was soft.

"I want you inside of me." Need was thick in her voice, as was fear. But the edge of excitement to it had him fucking her more slowly with his fingers as he rubbed her clitoris.

"Fuck, I want to kiss every inch of you. Taste you." His voice was scratchy.

"Cam, hurry." Her hand ran down his abs to the fly of his jeans. But her fingers were uncoordinated, fumbling with the buttons.

Footsteps and raised voices sounded from the entrance to the hallway. Someone was coming. Cam started to withdraw, but Ana stiffened, then moaned. Her pussy clenched on his fingers.

"That gets you hot," he said, and her whimper confirmed it. He thrust his fingers harder, making her moans come faster and closer together until her fingers failed on his jeans and her hands fluttered to her sides.

The voices faded away as the revelers changed direction, but Ana was already close to the edge.

"Come for me, Ana. Let me feel you." He watched her head drop back against the wall as her hands gripped his shirt. Her lips had parted and her body was tensed for that final flight into oblivion.

His cock twitched as he felt her inner muscles begin to clench around his fingers. So *good*.

She pressed the back of her hand to her mouth to stifle her moans and he caught sight of the scar striping down her wrist. He didn't think, just grabbed her hand and raised her wrist to his mouth. He'd barely pressed his lips to the surface before she jerked her arm away.

"No." She tensed in his arms, the flutters of her impending orgasm fading away. Her eyes were intense on his, another type of desperation all together. "Fuck me. Fuck me now."

Shit. He'd blown it with his careless kiss, a reminder of all that stood between them. But he wanted this. Wanted her. Too much to stop even when they should.

"You're on something?" he rasped against her lips. Disease couldn't affect immortals, but pregnancy was another matter.

She nodded frantically, reaching between them to free his cock. The feel of her hands on him made his knees weaken.

Keep it together.

They were still in a pub, he reminded himself. He struggled to keep an ear out for anyone approaching while she stroked him. Roughly, like the situation called for and how he liked.

He pushed her shorts to her ankles. They slipped off easily when he yanked her into his arms. Her legs wrapped around his waist, and he inhaled deeply of her arousal.

186

"Fuck, you smell good."

"Hurry, Cam." She rubbed against him.

He squeezed his arm between her and the bite of the stone wall, then slipped his other hand between them, yanking aside her underwear and inhaling deeply of her scent.

"Fuck, you're wet," he growled.

"Now, Cam."

He wanted to look at her, to make this last and make it important. But he couldn't. Not with Otherworld standing between them. He'd chosen the dark hallway for this because he thought she'd like it, and because it wouldn't allow the intimacy that would suck him under and make this all harder when it was over.

"Please, Cam."

He obeyed, sliding into her. She was tight and hot and wet and so good that his mind blanked out from the pleasure. She buried her face against his neck and keened long and low against him as he fitted himself inside her. He didn't move, not yet, taking a too-brief moment to revel in the feel of her before his body took over.

"I need you," he muttered. He thrust, slow and deep, savoring the feel of her, the sound of her, the smell of her.

He slipped a hand between them to find her clitoris, an awkward maneuver that was made worth it when she stiffened in his arms. The crook of his neck stung where her teeth bit into him to stifle her cries, though he couldn't have given less of a fuck if she screamed the house down and brought the Pope in.

A low growl, animalistic in its intensity, was dragged from his throat when she spasmed around him, squeezing his cock as he thrust into her. He tried not to focus on how good it felt to have her shivering in his arms, or his desire to see her face, and finally withdrew his hand when the spasms faded.

He gripped her hips and thrust hard enough that he forced a noise from her throat each time he seated himself so deeply within her. *Yes. More.*

It must have driven her up again, because she whimpered, "Fuck me, fuck me, fuck me," against his neck, a desperate mantra that broke the last threads of his control.

His hands bit into her hips as his thrusts lost coordination. Roaring need made him heave over her, lost in the feel of her pussy squeezing him. Hard and fast and frantic, he went over the edge with her in an orgasm that reached within him and twisted with outrageous pleasure.

Later that night, Ana lay in the small bed next to Cam. They didn't cuddle or kiss, which was good, because she didn't think she could handle it. After stumbling up from the pub, they'd both fallen into bed exhausted. Physically, and for her, emotionally as well. Tomorrow he would have his charm. And he'd go on his way.

She glanced at Cam to see him asleep on his back, his brow drawn as if he were having a vaguely miserable nightmare. The yellow glow of the streetlights gleamed in his hair and highlighted the harsh planes and angles of his face. She reached out to touch his shoulder, but drew her hand back. *Damn.*

That hadn't been nothing. Just scratching an itch? Yeah right.

CHAPTER TWENTY

Highlands of Celtic Scotland, 634 BC
Long before Andrasta met Camulos

Druantia stood on the hill, the howling wind whipping her hair and cloak behind her, and surveyed the bloody chaos in the valley below, where two Celtic kingdoms collided. Blood spilled into the grass, the screams of men and horses drowned out the clash of iron, and the dead lay scattered. But her side would prevail. She'd made sure.

"High Priestess, the king has sent a message from the front." The voice of Alban, one of the lesser Druids, broke through her concentration.

"What?" She glared at him. She'd worked long and hard for this moment, rising from the lowliest ranks to High Priestess of her people.

"He wants to cease fighting. They are outmanned." Alban cowered at her feet and she barely resisted kicking him.

"Do not cease." Her voice, low and hard, carried on the wind. "I have ensured our success with Camulos, god of war." For she was *gutuatri*, one who spoke to the gods.

"Yes, mistress." Alban bowed his head, once, twice, then spun away to run down the hill and into the fray. King Suibhne would heed her, for while he was king, she ensured his victory in all respects. Were she ever to feel the need, she would replace him. But in good time.

She stood on the hill, impervious to the cold and the wind, and watched as the battle turned in favor of her people. Soon, the last of the enemy fled over the horizon. Rough cheers rang up from the battlefield, male and female warriors alike surging to take the heads from the bodies of their bravest foes. An honor, for her people believed that the soul resided in the head.

She swept down from the hill, heedless of the blood and mud that stuck to her shoes as she strode through the chaos. The women who had not fought ran from their vantage points on a nearby hill, bringing torches to light the now-darkening sky.

A cheer rose up from the warriors as she neared the center of the grisly scene. Men and women, covered in their blood and the blood of others, waved their swords in victory and cheered her name. Power and pleasure surged through her. Some of her disciples said that her power went to her head.

They were wrong. She, Druantia, caused victories such as this. Druids all over their great isle were revered for their power and wisdom. But she—she was their leader.

She stopped in front of King Suibhne, her gaze flashing over the victorious scene. He bowed to her, his eyes cast down, and a smile curved over her face. His second-in-command brought her the head of their bravest foe, slain not an hour past.

She nodded. "Take it to the altar." It would sit there, to honor the warrior's bravery and skill. For one day his people would be hers as well.

A woman handed her a torch and Druantia grasped it, thrusting it into the sky. She yelled, "It is I, Druantia, who have brought you this victory."

They cheered, their cries filling her body with everything she craved. "Gather the heads of the greatest fallen. They will line the walls of my temple! We will take their strength into us."

The crowd—warriors, their families, children—all had come to praise her for their victory. As they should. Their cheers rose on the air, first wordless, then coalescing to form her name. She raised the torch higher, pleasure surging through her at their adulation.

A crack of thunder broke through the night, so strong that it shook the ground beneath her feet. Before it had faded, a man appeared.

No, a god. Camulos stood before her, god of war, and rage lined his face. She stepped back instinctively, then caught herself, horrified by her weakness.

She was Druantia, High Priestess of the Druids. She didn't cower from anyone. Not even a god.

"Cease," Camulos roared, his gaze cutting across the people.

Their cries died as they caught sight of him, larger and more powerful than any mortal and with a gods' rage all but vibrating from him. Whispers passed through the crowd that a god was among them. A rare occurrence, but not unheard of.

"I am Camulos, god of war! Your success on this battlefield was granted at *my* will. You fought fellow Celts. Yet *I alone* decreed that your kingdom should be victorious over theirs." He swung his arm out, pointing at her. "Not this woman."

She fell to her knees, propelled by his power until the wet ground soaked through her dress and the rocks bit into her flesh.

"She is but a priestess, bound to do my will as I see fit. Nothing more!" His arrogance cut through the night.

Rage such as Druantia had never experienced engulfed her, made all the worse by her impotence. She could do *nothing.* No matter how she struggled, she was pinned, kneeling in the mud. In front of her people. Their faces all turned to her, confusion turning to disdain. *No!*

"Your tributes are to me!" Thunder followed his bellow, the elements urged on by his fury. Rain poured from the sky, turning the mud and the blood of war into a foul swamp that soaked through Druantia's clothes. "Gather the heads of your greatest foes and bring them here."

Druantia, trembling in her rage and humiliation, watched as *her* people brought the heads forth and piled them in front of Camulos. Their faces were awed, glowing with admiration in the light of the torches.

The god of war watched, satisfaction and arrogance glowing from his face, until the heads were piled high, a gruesome tribute to his power and glory. The gods were known for their passions and jealousy, but never had it been turned against her. The heads were meant for her temple, so that she might benefit from the power of their souls. But no, they went to him. And such pleasure he took in it that it burned her.

From his outstretched hand, Camulos shot a blast of godly fire that immolated the tribute, the flames rising high despite the pouring rain. The souls of the fallen, what would have been her tribute, poured forth from the flame, rising to Otherworld in his name.

And worse, worst of all, the people cheered.

Camulos, they yelled. Over and over and over until Druantia was certain that the refrain would never leave her head. Did they not know that it was her, Druantia, who had bartered for their victory? Assured it?

The last of the flames died down until there was nothing but ash, and without hesitation, the god of war departed for Otherworld, disappearing before her eyes.

Finally, his hold on her disappeared. Trembling, she rose to her feet. Her people spared not a glance for her.

Something dark within her surged. Camulos might be a god, but she was the High Priestess of the Druids. And he treated her *like a servant*. She was but a tool to him, a thing to cast aside.

He would regret this night, she vowed. All the gods would regret this night.

CHAPTER TWENTY-ONE

"You know, I really thought she'd live in a tree or something," Ana said as they crossed the street toward Druantia's shop, an ornate stone building that rose three stories above a bustling city street in the heart of Inverness.

"A tree?" He arched a brow.

"Well, a big one. Or at least in a copse of trees. In the forest. You know, very Druidy."

"The old days."

"Well, this building is creepy."

"She's strange, but she's a valuable tool with valuable skills." He led her around the building to a side entrance in the alley and pushed open the wooden door that lead into a shop.

Ana stepped in behind him, and her eyes took a minute to adjust to the light. It was nice enough, full of books and crystals and tiny statues all piled on shelves and tables. Dim light filtered in through small windows, glinting off dust motes and glass. All the sorts of things mortals would buy from a witchy type.

"Times have changed," Cam murmured.

"Indeed they have." A husky, feminine voice came from an archway in the back of the store. Surprise lit her green eyes when she saw them, and a strange smile twisted her lips. "Camulos. Times really have changed. It's been nearly two thousand years since I've seen you last, hasn't it? And now you're in my shop and I'm consigned to peddling trinkets to the mortals and the occasional spell to Mytheans. The good old days are long gone."

Ana assumed she meant back when Druidry was still the dominant religion in Britain and she'd held an enormous amount of power as the intermediary between mortals and the gods. Ana shrugged mentally. Tough tits—it happened to all the old religions.

"Druantia," Cam said. "We've need of your talents."

No salutation, Ana noticed, and his voice was different. Businesslike and brusque. Far from how he spoke to her. Druantia took it in stride, with only the barest tightening of her lips.

"And who might this be?" Druantia asked, looking at her appraisingly.

"Andrasta, Goddess of Victory."

The briefest flash of something like shock crossed Druantia's face, there and gone. Had it existed at all?

"Her glow has faded," Druantia said.

"I've been on earth a while," Ana said.

"What can I do for you?" Druantia asked.

Ana listened as Cam explained his lost protection charm, but she focused her attention on the store, hoping to see Logan Laufeyson lurking amongst the shelves.

"Aye, I can replace it," Druantia said when he finished. "But it will cost you."

"Not a problem. We can do it now?"

She nodded.

"Could I get one, too?" Ana asked. She didn't know why she hadn't thought of this before. It would solve all her problems.

"No. It doesn't work on gods," Druantia said.

"Oh." Ana suddenly felt as collapsed as a pile of dead leaves.

"Come on back." Druantia waved a hand and turned to walk under the archway that led to a back room.

Ana glanced at Cam expectantly, the question in her eyes. He nodded and she followed, weaving around the little tables and shelves until she passed through the arch. A zip of magic sang across her skin when she stepped over the threshold. She must have just entered the Mythean part of the store, protected from mortal eyes and ears.

"Sit down." Druantia nodded to a big wooden chair in the corner of the room.

There wasn't much other than bookshelves and a few chairs. Not as creepy as Ana had been expecting. Then she felt like a bitch for assuming the worst of the spell peddler.

Cam sat in the chair and stripped off his shirt, revealing the hard planes of muscles that always gave Ana dry mouth. He was pale and huge in the cozy room, and suddenly her breath became a little harder to drag into her lungs.

Druantia strolled to a bookshelf and picked up a black curved wand-type thing that had a pointy end like a pen. Cam's face tensed as she neared.

"Wait, what are you going to do to him?" Ana asked, suddenly nervous. The thing in Druantia's hand did look very pointy.

"Protection tattoo," Druantia said, and waved the pen-wand.

"He doesn't have a tattoo from the last one."

"Aye, he does. It's invisible. Magic inked into the skin." She stepped close to his side and Cam looked up at her.

"Add her name," he said. "So she can see me."

Druantia nodded and set the tip of the pen-wand on the meatiest part of his shoulder. Cam didn't flinch, but Ana was pretty sure she saw faint lines form at the corners of his eyes. She wanted to ask what he'd meant by seeing him.

Ana held her breath as Druantia began to draw. Fine red lines appeared in the wake of the pen-wand, glowing for a moment until they disappeared. Ana's eyes darted back and forth between Cam's glowing shoulder and the harsh set of his lips and eyes. A drop of sweat trickled from his temple.

It all made Ana vaguely ill, and though she was desperate to ask if it was almost over, she held her tongue. Causing Druantia to slip up could only be bad.

"Right. You're done." Druantia stepped back, and Cam's face finally relaxed.

Ana let out the breath she hadn't realized she'd been holding.

He stood, flexed his arm and shoulder, nodded appreciatively, then dragged his shirt on.

They walked to the front of the store, where Cam settled his bill with a wad of cash she didn't realize he'd been carrying. How did he make his money if his company was non-profit? She shook her head. Not her business.

"We'd like to speak to Logan Laufeyson. Is he here?" Cam asked.

Druantia's brows drew together. "I'm sorry, he's not."

"Do you know where he is?" Cam asked.

"No. He walked out a few weeks ago and didn't leave a note or anything." A grimace twisted her features.

Ana's breath rushed out of her lungs, disappointment filling up her body like an overflowing jug left out in the rain. *Shit.*

She winced when her hand started to hurt and looked down to see that she had a death grip on her bow. The sound of Cam requesting the now-worthless potion that he'd used to Fall from Otherworld echoed through the fog in her brain. Why would they even need it if they couldn't find Logan?

At the request, Druantia's eyes widened, then her features went blank. "Of course. I have a bit that I could sell you."

Cam paid for the potion—because Ana couldn't seem to function—and turned to leave. Ana snapped back to attention and turned to face Druantia.

"Is there any other way for a god to Fall from Otherworld? Without a replacement?"

Druantia looked at her thoughtfully and Ana's heart thudded with hope.

"No," Druantia finally said. "To my knowledge, there isn't."

"Not a spell or a potion or anything? Something to hide me from the eyes of other gods, at least? Like a version of Cam's tattoo?"

Druantia shook her head, the thoughtful gleam still in her eye. "No. I'm sorry. Gods follow different laws than other Mytheans. Most of my magic won't work on you."

A low buzzing sounded in Ana's head and her vision blurred. This was it. There was no way out. As if from outside of herself, Ana felt Cam's hand at the small of her back as he nudged her toward the exit.

They stepped out into the alley and were hit with a downpour. *Damn it.* Just her fucking luck. Her hair was soaked and clingy in seconds, her clothes not far behind.

"Come on." Cam hustled her to the car.

She scrambled into the seat and sat with her bow pulled up to her chest. Eyes squeezed shut, she counted to five while he rounded the car to get into the driver's side.

By the time she'd opened her eyes, she'd gotten rid of the worst of the knot strangling her throat and the burn in her sinuses. She wouldn't cry. She wouldn't.

"So, you've got your charm." She tried to inject a note of cheerfulness into her voice and came out sounding half deranged.

"Yes."

"When do you head back to the jungle?" Her grip tightened on the bow. Now that he was going back, she realized how much she'd started to care for him. More than care for him. Real, scary, horrible feelings that scrabbled around inside her chest like a wild animal. How could he possibly feel the same? It was insane.

"What?" Cam turned to look at Ana. He hadn't even considered leaving, he realized. Technically, he'd done what he'd come for—gotten his charm renewed. So he should be heading back soon. "I'm not leaving. I told you I'd help you."

Her overly bright eyes—tears, he just now noticed—widened. A fist closed around his heart and squeezed. He cared for her, too much and not enough.

"You thought I'd leave you?" That pissed him the hell off, actually.

"Well, I—"

"Let's get something straight, Ana. Shit's complicated between us. That's true enough. But I said I'd help you get out of Otherworld. I owe you and I fucking care for you. We're going to figure this out together."

A shuddery breath escaped her lips, and her fist relaxed infinitesimally on her bow. He dropped his head back on the seat and stared at the ceiling. Shit, he was in deep.

"We don't know where the hell this bloke is, so I'm going to call Fiona," he said.

"You think she'll be able to find him again?"

"Don't know unless we try. And she's got a stake in finding him too. If I offer to retrieve the amulet for her, it might grease the wheels. It's our only resource right now."

CHAPTER TWENTY-TWO

"We've got a little while until Fiona calls back with something," Cam said to Ana when she walked out of the bathroom wrapped in the hotel robe.

The clouds had finally parted and sunlight streamed through the window to glint off her blond hair. They'd checked back into the hotel because it was the safest place to be while they sorted out their next move.

"You reached her?" Ana asked.

"Yeah. Took a while to convince her to share any info she finds, but she really wants that bow. I promised to try to retrieve it. She's going to call in a favor with the witches, which I'll have to pay, but they should be able to locate him. We'll wait here until then."

"Okay." Ana grabbed her clothes from where she'd set them on the chair, upsetting her quiver of arrows in the process. It tumbled to the floor and several arrows slid out. A flash of blue caught his eye, and he swooped down to pick up the quiver.

He reached in to withdraw an old arrow that he hadn't seen in millennia. He stared at it for a second, an odd feeling welling in his chest. Ana was watching him when he looked up. "You kept it?"

She nodded.

"Why?"

She looked away, tightening the robe around her throat, then shrugged.

"Why'd you save this for two thousand years?" He found that the answer had suddenly become very important to him.

Her eyes met his, exasperated. "What was I going to do? Shoot a god's arrow? The god of war?"

He gently grabbed the front of her robe and drew her to him. Her wide eyes met his as he said, "You're that god now."

She shook her head, suddenly looking smaller than she ever had. "I wasn't, Cam. I wanted to prove myself as a warrior, but not like that. You were the war god—I am a placeholder."

Placeholder. Because he'd run.

"You did a good job," he said, trying to imbue his words with enough truth that she'd believe him.

She smiled. "I know. I'm good at whatever I put my mind to. I just wasn't meant to be a goddess. I'm not cut out for that life."

He heaved a sigh, shook his head. "Neither was I."

"Sure you were." She dragged him toward the bed and sat next to him, turning herself so that her knees pressed into his thigh. She reached out and stroked his cheek, and somehow that touch meant more than what they'd done in the darkened pub last night.

"Maybe at first," he said. "When I still acted like a god. But then I saw you. And everything changed. I became... different. I *felt* things."

"Maybe that's not so bad."

He laughed, low and bitter. "It puts me halfway between god and mortal. I'm neither one, not fully."

Not as emotionless and stalwart as a god, capable of seeing things through without being swayed by emotion. It was a shitty way to live, but it was their way. Nor could he feel as strongly as mortals seemed to. Except where Ana was concerned.

He had the suspicion that what he felt for her now, if he were mortal, would be something like what they called love. Yet it was just out of his reach.

"What'd it feel like when you were a god? Just... nothing?" she asked.

He frowned, his brow scrunched. "Before I met you, it's like the world was in gray. Crisp and clear, so that I knew exactly what was going on and what I should do about it. Yet victory was hollow, so I never fully understood why I was the god of war. Then I saw you. Everything was in color suddenly, but blurred." He could still remember how strange his chest had felt. As if his heart had actually registered something, though it was physiologically impossible.

"Why do you think I was the one who made you feel emotion?"

He dragged a hand through his hair, frowned. He'd barely known her then, but had seen something in her, something that drew him to her still.

"I don't know, but it's what I've learned about you now, in the present, that has me feeling like I'm walking backward on a tightrope, desperately trying to reach the other side. Where you are." And that the tightrope might snap at any moment, dropping him into the mess that they'd created of their lives.

"I fucked up, Cam." Her voice was raw. "Back then. I didn't know what was going on. My confusion and fear all lead me to Otherworld. I'm sorry about that, for the position it put you in."

He picked up her wrist, and when she tried to jerk it free, he didn't let go. He didn't touch her scar or look at it, but he didn't let go.

"The other gods led you to Otherworld," Cam said.

Ana shivered. "They'd have killed my family. Going to Otherworld, as awful it was, saved them. They lived long lives, even if I didn't get to see them. Now they're in Otherworld, and they're different. A shadow of their former selves. Like the gods. Emotionless."

"But at least they had their lives," Cam said.

Ana pushed the thought of her brothers away. It hurt too much to contemplate for very long. Instead, she asked, "What kind of Mythean did you become?"

"When I realized that I couldn't kill you, I knew I wasn't fit for Otherworld. So I went to Druantia for the potion that turned me into a demigod."

"So you're a demigod."

"Yeah. Not quite as strong as I was, but not dead either. The catch being that I could no longer use my bow. Which I hate like hell."

She nodded. That would have sucked. "But you must have loved earth when you arrived."

He frowned. "I didn't know what to expect, and it was more than I ever could have imagined. I knew that something was wrong in Otherworld, and I ran. I did it to try to save you, but at the end of the day, I was running."

"I don't—"

"No, Ana. I was born with all the power of a god, and I ran. I could have stayed, tried to figure another way around our problem and done what I was born to do. But I didn't. I haven't lived the life I was supposed to."

"You came to earth, where you've done an enormous amount of good with your company."

"We're *trying* to do an enormous amount of good. We haven't actually done it yet. There's a difference."

"Maybe not yet with this company, but you've been on earth two thousand years. This can't be your first attempt."

He sighed. "It's not. But they're substitutes for what I should have been doing. I realize that now."

"No, you've done good here. We all have our paths to tread."

"And I didn't tread mine. I should have stayed in Otherworld, served my time." His eyes met hers, intensity shining within. "If we don't find Logan Laufeyson, I'll take your place."

"No, Cam—"

"I care for you, damn it. I'll not leave you to the fate I should have saved you from. After the half-life I've lead, after the fate I consigned you to in Otherworld, I don't deserve you. The least I can do is save you from the fate I doomed you to."

"This fate *did* save me. Otherwise, I'd be like my family right now." The thought of them sent a pang of pain through her chest. So old now, but still there. Their shadows haunted both Otherworld and her heart.

"And you'll have earth back, no matter how it has to happen," he said.

"No, Cam. I've grown pretty fond of you, too." Understatement of the century. "Ditch me now and I don't know what I'll do."

He yanked her to him and kissed her hard, the press of his lips against hers making her head spin. The thought made her shudder. He'd be trapped in Otherworld, allowed to escape only a few times a year for an hour here or there. But it could be *her* fate.

CHAPTER TWENTY-THREE

Highlands of Celtic Scotland, 634 BC
Long before Camulos met Andrasta

Anticipation sang through Druantia's veins as she watched her disciples, the lesser Druids, prepare for the feast ahead. They laid out fruits and wine, turned great haunches of meat on spits, and hung the sacred mistletoe from oaks surrounding the clearing. Spirits were high, for such a party had never before been thrown in the mortal world.

The sun would set within the hour, and then the gods would arrive. She shivered with excitement. But not with nerves. No, there was no reason to be afraid, for they would never anticipate what she had planned. Not a mere servant such as herself, she thought bitterly.

"High Priestess, the nymphs are here," Alban said from behind her.

Finally, they'd arrived. Druantia turned to see a bevy of beautiful young women and men. Tree nymphs, specifically of oak trees, called Dryads. And as such, they were under her direction. They came because their presence was requested. They'd do as she commanded because she willed it.

"The gods will be joining us for our great feast this eve," she said to them. She gestured to the food and wine behind her and glanced at the bodies of the beautiful Dryads. "We will welcome them to the earth, to taste of our bounty. Tonight there will be revelry such as they have never known."

And they would come. All of them. For the gods never could resist a pleasure. Ruled by their emotions, they were. Joy, greed, pride, jealousy.

Tonight they would see all that she was capable of.

"Go now." She gestured to the clearing. "For they will be here soon, and we must be ready to welcome them."

The Dryads nodded, though not all their faces showed pleasure at the idea of what was to come. No matter. They would do as she commanded, because as the gods had control over her, she had control over the Dryads.

When the last rays of the sun sank behind the horizon, the first god arrived from Otherworld. Cernowain, along with his boar. Before long, dozens of gods littered the clearing. Then three hundred of them, perhaps more. All the Celtic gods, even the ones worshiped by people from lands far away across the sea.

They drank and ate and sang and caroused. Wine flowed as freely as rain, the scent of roasted meat filled the air, and the sound of revelry rang through the night.

"You make amends." The deep voice from behind sent a chill down her spine. Her hands and face stiffened to iron, but she forced herself to breathe deeply. To soften her features into repentance and docility.

She turned to face Camulos. "But of course, god of war. For you are great and wise, and I wish for you to partake of all that the earth has to offer you."

He nodded, drank from the mug of wine, and surveyed the revelry. The energy in the air had grown frantic, joyous and sultry. It affected even her.

"There are many pleasures to be had in our woods," Druantia said. She pointed to a tree, under which sat a Dryad who wasn't carousing as she should be. "There, she waits for you."

Camulos grinned, arrogant as ever, and walked off toward the Dryad, a pale thing with shining blond hair. Quite pretty, as they all were.

With something dark boiling in her chest, Druantia watched him go. When he walked off into the forest with the Dryad, she turned to survey the rest of the festivities.

Clothes had scattered, wine and food spilled all over the tables set in the clearing, and gods and Dryads danced to music played by a band of mortals from her village. A select few of the lesser Druids were here to see to the occasion. No doubt they thought she was actually making amends with the feast.

She smiled. And waited. And watched. And as the dark grew deeper and the night grew later, the revelry became frantic and frenzied and wild. The energy that swirled in the air from the gods' joy was palpable, throbbing to the beat of the drums that played faster and faster.

They took such joy in this night. Such joy in their godhood, in their power. They loved and laughed and raged and fought. Were ruled by emotion, lived by it. So she would take from them that which they loved most.

Their joy. And every other emotion that went with it. For humiliating her, for treating her like she was nothing, she would take from them. For lording their power over her, she would trap them in Otherworld. She'd instill in them the belief that if they were to leave, their home wouldn't survive. They thought so highly of themselves, it wouldn't take much of a spell to convince them that Otherworld's very essence depended upon their presence. And with the gods stuck in Otherworld, she would truly be the only intermediary between gods and mortals. A true *gutuatri*, one who spoke to gods.

She would be the *only* one to speak to the gods. And then only if she chose. The most powerful Druid to ever live.

All with a single spell. And yet she was not stupid. One didn't rise to the heights that she had by being stupid. No. She could not cast a spell upon the gods. For the only ones who could cast a spell upon the gods were the gods themselves. So she would make them cast a spell upon themselves.

Druantia watched as the festivities reached a fevered pitch, as the wine and food and music went to the gods' heads. She watched as the Dryads began to disrobe, to dance and touch and kiss the gods. Until the clearing floor and the forest beyond were covered in bodies rolling and sweating and rutting—until every earthly pleasure that could be had created such a wealth of emotion and joy and lust in the gods that it became a physical thing that swirled upon the air.

A thing that she could manipulate into something darker and to her purposes. When it reached such heights that it became magic worthy of the spell, she reached into her bag and withdrew a hare, that most sacred animal to their people. Never should one harm a hare.

Without a glance, she dragged a knife across its throat until blood sprayed onto the ground and onto the nearest god, rutting atop a Dryad.

The energy changed. From lust and joy to dark and dire. The god rose up and tore the Dryad limb from limb, his passion and rage contagious. The other gods followed suit, until the clearing ran red with Dryad blood.

Druantia watched as their joy and rage turned to nothing. To motion, not emotion. The blood of the Dryads soaking the ground, a sacrifice that sealed the spell. When they all lay dead, Dryad, Druid, and mortal—all except her and the gods—the night went silent.

As if in a trance, the gods looked into the sky and around at each other. But they saw nothing. Nor did they remember. Not the party, not their past. Not ever feeling emotion. One by one, they disappeared to return to Otherworld.

Druantia stood in the clearing, panting and exhilarated, as the blood of the Dryads soaked into the ground and the bones grew into great oak trees that created a canopy over the forest floor. They drank up the blood and sprouted leaves. A dark forest formed, imbued with the memory and the emotion and the life force of the gods.

It flowed into Druantia, imbuing her with power such as she had never known. Into herself she took the immortality of gods. Their emotion, their passion, their joy all became hers. They would live in Otherworld, continue on with their duties and their titles. Yet for Camulos victory would become hollow, for Scathach prophecy would become rote, for Carlin the night of Samhain would become dull. As it would be for all the gods, because they had dared to cast her aside.

CHAPTER TWENTY-FOUR

Highlands of Scotland, Present Day

"Pull over," Ana said. "I think I see it."

Cam pulled the car to a stop on a gravel patch at the side of the road. Ana climbed out, shivering under the cloudy sky in the chill winter wind. They were in a valley with mountains sweeping up on either side of them. Snowflakes fluttered around them as dusk turned the white mountains gray.

"Do you think that's it?" Ana asked, pointing to a small cottage nestled in the deepest part of the valley. Fiona had called back a few hours ago with the supposed location of Logan Laufeyson and they'd set out immediately, driving into the Highlands.

Cam walked to her side of the car and peered into the distance.

"Could be," Cam said, turning to meet her eyes. "Fits the description and location, so it's—"

Ana jerked when she felt the familiar rubber-band snap of another god appearing from Otherworld. She spun in tandem with Cam and drew her bow. Silence. Snow fell more thickly, obscuring her vision.

Suddenly, a boar broke over the top of a nearby hill and charged them. Ana aimed and fired. The boar fell, but another had appeared in its place. Within seconds, there were a dozen. She fired off arrows as fast as she could.

"Cernowain," Cam said as he flung a dagger at a boar and felled it.

"But where?" She downed another boar, but more had appeared. She couldn't see Cernowain anywhere. Were there other gods as well? She blinked snow out of her eyes and fired again.

Cam sprinted to retrieve his dagger and flung it again. His invisibility to the other gods gave them an advantage, and for now, they were just barely holding off the—

Ana screamed as arms grasped her from behind. Her bow clattered to the ground as the grip tightened. She struggled, fighting the pull from the aether that tore at her insides. He was trying to aetherwalk with her! She'd be dragged back to Otherworld.

The arms dropped her and she stumbled to her knees. She jerked around to see Cam throw Cernowain onto his back. The god's brown cloak fluttered in the wind.

"What is this magic?" he bellowed.

Of course. He couldn't see Cam. When he surged to his feet, Cam punched him so hard in the face that he flew backwards.

"How did you find me?" she yelled. Had the boar spies found them during the storm in Inverness? Would Cernowain really have sent the boars into the city?

"I had help," Cernowain ground out through broken teeth as he started toward her, eyes darting for the unseen threat. "You're coming back."

Cam hit him again, compounding the damage to his broken face. Cernowain crashed to the ground.

"Fuck." Cernowain's words gurgled through the blood he spat out.

"I'm never coming back," Ana said. She grabbed her bow from the ground and fired, sending an arrow through Cernowain's leg. Then another through the heart of a boar that had gotten too close. She turned back to Cernowain and shot his other thigh.

"Fuck!" Cernowain glared at her, his gaze as black as the night creeping over the mountains, then disappeared. The boars followed. The rubber band snapped against her skin and she was sure he was gone.

Ana slumped. "Shit. He'll bring the other gods back."

Cam ran to her and pulled her against him. She shook all over, feeling colder in her bones than her skin, despite the wind that picked up speed. No matter how hard she sucked the cold air into her lungs, it didn't seem to fill them.

"Come on," Cam said, rubbing her arms and pulling her toward the car. "We don't have long before he can gather enough gods to force you back. He'll want to heal up before he faces them. We have a few hours at most."

"Yeah, let's go."

Cam looked at the sky and a frown stretched across his face. "Let's find Logan before this snow turns the roads to shit and we get stuck."

She hurried into the car, and Cam engaged the four-wheel drive for the last few miles to what she hoped was

Logan Laufeyson's house. It was slow going, with big fat flakes hitting the windshield and turning the road white.

"What will you say when you meet him?" Cam asked, his eyes intent on the road ahead of them.

"Um—hi, do you want to be a god?" Honestly, she was so freaked out from having seen Cernowain that she'd be proud to be that eloquent.

"Subtle."

"I'm not exactly at my mental best. And it's got to be appealing to some people, right?" As long as they didn't know what Otherworld was really like. She felt a twinge of guilt. But if one were power hungry enough, it would be a decent trade-off.

"To some, sure. I think it's as good as anything. So long as he doesn't shoot us on sight. Just lay it all out."

Not being shot on sight would be good. And she liked the idea of laying it all out. It would ease her conscience. She wanted Logan to agree so badly that she couldn't imagine it not happening. It was poor logic, but she couldn't help it. Nervous, she gripped her seat's arm rest as they rumbled down the drive to the cottage.

"The lights aren't on," she said, her gaze darting around the exterior of the cottage. Small, only a couple rooms. No footsteps in the snow. "Are you sure this is it?"

"No. All Fiona said was that it's a small cottage in the Cairngorm mountains off of the A939, south of the village of Tomintoul. This could be it, or it could be down the road a bit."

Ana nodded, peering hard into the darkened windows of the cottage as Cam parked in the small drive. *He had to be here. He had to.*

CHAPTER TWENTY-FIVE

Cam followed Ana to the door, his eyes alert for any movement in or around the house. Fat snowflakes glinted in the light of the car's headlights. They stepped onto the stoop, and Cam glanced down at Ana. She nodded, so he knocked. Waited. Knocked again. The wind picked up, and with it the snow.

"This sucks," Ana said, rubbing her arms.

Cam knocked again, but by now didn't expect an answer. He glanced behind him to see the drive to the house now blanketed with snow. What had started as fat white flakes had turned into a storm that was whiting out the night.

Ana hopped off the stoop and walked to one of the windows to peer in.

"I think it's empty," she said, moving on to the next window.

Fuck. Disappointment dropped Cam's heart to his feet. As much as he felt like a worthless bastard for abandoning his post in Otherworld, he wanted to stay with Ana far more than he wanted to live out that destiny. He hadn't realized how much hope he'd had riding on finding Logan Laufeyson and getting him to take Ana's place.

"Let's try the back," he said, and trekked through the snow to the rear of the cottage. It was just as dark on this side, but when he tried the back door, he found it unlocked.

"What do you think?" Ana whispered.

"It's worth a check to see if we're in the right place. And we're not going to get back up that road until this storm lets up."

"Good. I'm freezing. Let's go in."

They scraped their shoes on the mat and stepped inside, careful not to drip too much water. Better not piss off their host when they wanted something from him. They crept silently through the cottage, determining within a minute that it was empty.

"Must be a rental," Ana said, tapping the small binder of brochures and house directions on the counter. Sturdy, generic furniture and the lack of photos corroborated the theory. "Do you think he's staying here?"

"Could be. If so, he's changing his hermit ways." Cam swung open the fridge to reveal a six pack of Tennant's Lager and some ham and bread. He went back into the bedroom, drew the curtains, flipped on the light. The closet revealed a bag containing a few changes of men's clothing and a passport at the bottom. He flipped the passport open and peered down at the face of a man who looked to be in his mid-thirties, though he was far older.

He frowned at the name next to the picture. *Conrad Allen.*

"What'd you find?" Ana asked as she walked into the room and stopped at his side.

He tilted the passport to her.

"Could be fake," she said.

"That's what I'm thinking. He wouldn't leave his real name lying around." With that thought, Cam slipped a cell phone out of his back pocket and dialed Fiona.

"It's Cam," he said when she picked up the line.

"I bet you have another question that's going to be a pain to answer," Fiona said.

"Probably. Do you know what Logan Laufeyson looks like?"

"Sort of. I've got a description from the Acquirer who saw him steal the bow and arrow. It's one of the ways I tracked him."

Cam looked down at the passport. "Has he got real pale skin, a thin scar along his jaw, longish black hair, and"—he squinted at the picture— "black eyes?"

"That scar sounds right, as does the rest."

"Good. Do you have any record of him going by the name Conrad Allen?"

"No, but I'd buy it. I'll do some research, add it to my records. But I'd bet it's him. The witches pinpointed him to that valley, and almost no one lives there. And that description fits."

"Good. How would he feel if he came back to his rental and found two squatters waiting for him? The snow's coming down hard and we won't make it out of here 'til it clears."

"I have no idea. But there's no record of him being insane. A rental isn't like your own house, you know? So just leave the lights on and wait in the living room. It'll probably be fine."

Cam didn't love the sound of that, but he also didn't love the sound of waiting in the car. It'd be damn hard to defend them while he was sitting. And lurking outside was too threatening.

"I see. One last thing. What is he? Can he aetherwalk?"

"Don't quite know what he is, but he is Mythean. And I've never heard of him aetherwalking."

"Thanks. I appreciate it." He hung up when the line went dead.

"It's him?" Ana asked.

"Think so. Come on. Let's go in the living room so that when he arrives we're not shifting around through his stuff. He probably doesn't aetherwalk, so we'll have to hear his car come up the drive."

He flipped off the light and glanced back to make sure the room looked the same as when they'd entered. When they reached the tiny room with its overstuffed couch, Ana went straight to the window and peered out into the darkness.

"It's a mess out there. Really coming down now," she said.

Cam flipped on two of the lamps so that a low glow would shine out the window and stepped up behind her to look out into the night.

"Damn. It'll be a while before he's back," he said, trying to focus on the view rather than the heat of her back pressed against him. The memory of last night in the pub made him shift behind her, drawing his hips away. Now was not the time for a fucking hard-on.

She slipped her quiver from her back, let it slip to the floor, and leaned back against him. He couldn't stifle the sigh that escaped him. He wrapped an arm about her middle and pulled her back to rest against him.

"It's barely seven. We might as well keep a lookout," she said, resting her head against his chest.

He nodded and reached over to turn off the closest lamp so that they could see out. There was still enough light to alert Logan when he came home, and their shadows in the window would be a big clue.

"Do you really think Cernowain used the rain in Inverness to send his boars to find us?" Ana asked, idly running her hand up and down the arm Cam had wrapped around her waist. Her other hand hung at her hip, gripping her bow so that it rested against his thigh. He swore he could feel her all over his body, and he had to shake his head to focus.

"I don't know. Seems odd. But I suppose. They're determined to have you back."

"It's not my destiny."

"No. It was mine."

"But you hated Otherworld. And your destiny."

"True. But it's hard not to feel like I ran from something that felt wrong without even trying to fix it."

"Part of you wants to go back, doesn't it?" Her voice wavered, so slightly that he could barely hear it.

It shot a pang through his heart even as that same heart leapt at the idea that she would miss him. He spun her to face him, vaguely registering her bow hitting the carpet and her hands coming up to grip his shirt.

"Yes, but I have important work to do here, back in the jungle. I *can't* leave it. But more than that, I'd rather be here with you. A thousand times over." He'd realized it as soon as Druantia had told him that Logan wasn't there. With the safety net that Logan provided gone, the likelihood that he might have to go in order to save Ana had hit him hard. He'd realized without a doubt that he didn't want to leave her, not even to fulfill the destiny that he'd been running from.

A tremulous smile stretched across her face. "Good." She reached up to yank his head down to hers. The press of her lips drove any thought of liking or loving from his brain, and he gripped her tighter to him.

The feel of her body, hot and soft and curved, drew his hands, desperate to touch as much of her as he could in the few seconds they had to spare before common sense returned. The shadow of all that weighed on them hovered at the corner of his mind as he bit her bottom lip and tugged with his teeth. When she moaned, he slipped his tongue inside her mouth, stroking and tasting and wishing it could go on but knowing it couldn't.

He broke the kiss, his chest heaving, and leaned his forehead against hers while his hands gripped her hips. "Ana, the things I feel with you."

She clutched his shirt. "Don't leave me. Logan will agree to go, and it'll be fine. It'll be fine." There was the barest crazed edge to her voice, but she spun quickly and put her hands against the window to peer out.

He stepped up behind her and reached for her hand. After a few minutes, she relaxed enough to lean back against his chest. They watched out the window for nearly an hour, hypnotized by the falling snow. Finally, it started to lighten.

"If he's been waiting this out in the village, he should be heading back soon," Cam said.

Ana nodded, her gaze still intent on the outside. It was another hour before headlights came down the drive. Ana stiffened in his arms.

"Wow. I can't believe this is happening," Ana said. She bent down to pick up her quiver.

"Leave it." He touched her arm and she straightened. "Close enough that you can get to it if you need it. But he knows we're here. I'm a fast draw, and we don't want him to feel threatened if he sees us armed."

Ana watched the man climb out of a Range Rover. Her eyes met his through the window and a chill raced across her skin on tiny mouse feet. Suspicion stretched across his face at the sight of her in his house, but she didn't see anger or fear.

No, it didn't look like anything would frighten this man. He was tall, with a lean strength that couldn't be concealed by his black winter coat. His strides ate up the ground too quickly as he headed toward the house.

The front door creaked as it opened, the sound ominous in the silence. A rush of cold air followed Logan inside, but Ana couldn't really feel it. She was too focused on the man who stepped into the living room. He was eerily beautiful, with inky hair and eyes that only emphasized his pale skin.

He had more than just dark color in his eyes. He had dark thoughts as well. They made him a type of scary handsome. But not like Cam, who looked as if he could beat the shit out of anyone with his fists without breaking a sweat. No, this man was another kind of frightening, a kind she wasn't familiar with because she hadn't felt fear in a very long time. She swallowed hard.

"Visitors?" His raspy voice carried a sarcastic twist.

"Um, no," Ana said, unsure of how to start now that he was here and pinning her with his black gaze. No, not her. Cam, who was standing behind her. Was he looking at Cam strangely? "I'm Ana, Celtic goddess of victory. This is Cam, a Celtic demigod."

There. She saw it. A light of recognition in his eyes. She looked behind her to see suspicion in Cam's gaze. Did he recognize him? She tried to catch Cam's eyes, but his were glued to Logan.

Fates, this was already going poorly. She'd expected this to be awkward; they were sitting in this man's living room, after all. But something was off, something that made her heart climb into her throat and beat like a moth trying to escape a jar.

"Why are you here?" Logan asked.

She rushed to make her offer before the suspense made her pass out. "You see, I don't want to be a god anymore. And we heard that you're an incredible archer. Strong enough to maybe take my place if you wanted to. Be a Celtic war god, that is."

A sardonic smile twisted his lips, and a chill raced down her spine. "That's an interesting offer."

"It's a lot of prestige." The words tumbled from Ana's lips. *He had to agree. He had to.*

"Ana," Cam said, warning in his voice.

But she ignored him, her tongue running away from her mind in her desperation to convince him. This was her last, her only, chance. "It's not the most exciting place in the universe, but Otherworld is lovely. And you'd be a god. The respect and fear people show you is great." He had to agree it was a good deal.

"Being a god does sound good," he said, that strange smile still cutting across his face. "But I'm —"

The rubber-band snap of many gods appearing in the living room made Ana's knees weaken. They filled the space, a dozen or more of the most powerful gods in Otherworld crowded into the room. Their eyes found her before she could count them all, and every expression was darker than the last. Logan looked on with interest, and she remembered that he was the only person besides her who could see Cam.

Her heart almost burst from her chest when she caught sight of Hafgan and Arawn, the kings of Otherworld. Their eyes zeroed in on her and they stalked toward her.

"Ana, your time is up," Hafgan said, his voice carrying the low roll of thunder. "You're coming back to Otherworld, to Blackmoor, where you'll live out your punishment."

The tor. Where she'd be chained to the granite in the wind and the rain and the snow to fully realize her stupidity and pride. As the thought flashed in her mind, she felt Cam back away from her. The cold slick of sweat broke out on her skin and she spun to face him.

Her jaw dropped when he plucked the blue-fletched arrow out of her quiver. The one they'd already anointed with the demigod potion.

"Cam, no!" She reached out to stop him.

So fast that she could barely follow the motion of his hands, Cam plucked her bow off the ground and nocked the arrow. *She was staring down the shaft of her own arrow.*

He shot. Pain exploded in her chest where the arrow struck, and his face, twisted with determination and horror, was the last thing she saw before she collapsed.

The sticky warmth of her blood pooled beneath her back as her vision went black. Unidentifiable noises echoed in her ears, but she couldn't decipher words. She felt her power leaving like a physical thing, draining out with her blood. Was someone touching her? She tried to move her hand but couldn't.

Cam? Her last thoughts raced across her mind as the chill spread out from her chest. Cam had chosen Otherworld over her, or for her. So hard to tell, the way her thoughts tumbled in her mind, each grappling to be the truth. Fears and hopes, all worthless now. But one thing stood clear in her fading mind. With all her options taken away, she realized that what she really wanted, more than life on earth or any of the exciting things she'd longed for, was him.

And now he would be trapped in Otherworld, chained to a tor on Blackmoor.

CHAPTER TWENTY-SIX

Seconds slowed to hours as the room erupted into shouts and chaos. An invisible hand squeezed Cam's throat as his gaze locked on Ana's body. She seemed to fall in slow motion, the blue-fletched arrow protruding from her chest and her eyes wide with surprise. The bow that had felt so natural and wonderful in his hands now felt unfamiliar. Foreign and evil.

The thud of her body hitting the ground spurred him into action. He was at her side in moments, his hands tangled in her hair, his chest and mind on fire. Her mouth was slack, her eyes half closed. Not dead. Not yet. And thus the gods couldn't see him. The sight of the blood that pooled beneath her body struck his mind like a blow and wrapped his heart in barbed wire.

Familiar. He'd done it to save her, but that didn't take away the horror of watching her die. Or the eerie feeling that he'd watched her die before. He blinked the vision away.

She went still barely a second later, and the uproar in the room swelled. Hands yanked him back, away from Ana.

"Camulos." The booming voice echoed through the room, but he could barely hear it. His gaze was still glued to Ana. Movement surged toward him as the gods closed in. Another pair of hands jerked him roughly, and he realized that he'd be dragged to Otherworld any moment.

He panicked. His gaze jerked around the room until it landed on the only other person who didn't have a reason to hurt Ana. *Take care of her*, he pleaded with his eyes.

The other gods ignored her now, assuming her soul would arrive in Otherworld, as his had after he'd been shot so many years ago. She'd be safe, as long as they didn't know about the potion that would turn her into a demigod.

But Logan's face was blank, and before he received a response, Cam felt the jerk of being forced through the aether and back to Otherworld. It had been centuries since he'd aetherwalked—demigods were some of the Mytheans who lacked the ability—and the light head and queasy stomach sent him to his knees when he felt the ground beneath his feet again.

His head spun as he tried to focus his gaze on the gods surrounding him. They'd taken him directly to Blackmoor, to endure the fate they'd had planned for Ana. She'd only tried to escape. He actually had. And they could see that he was a god again. If anyone deserved to be imprisoned in Otherworld's most desolate moor, windswept and miserable, it was he.

But even in the worst part of Otherworld, he realized how wrong he'd been to run. Power surged through his veins, singing along his nerve endings and clearing his mind. He was meant for this. No matter how wrong Otherworld felt to him, being restored to godhood felt as natural as breathing.

"Camulos. You ran from Otherworld."

Cam's eyes jerked to the god who possessed the booming voice. Hafgan. King of the Otherworld, with Arawn, the other king, standing next to him. Large black birds of all sorts circled in the sky above, flying low beneath the heavy clouds and buffeted by the roaring winds. Freezing rain would come soon, and here, even a god was susceptible to the misery.

Hafgan glared at him, clearly awaiting a response. He was an enormous man, all wild red hair that was a darker, more vibrant shade than Cam's. A rough brown cloak swirled about him, and the gold of the torc around his neck gleamed. The other gods were garbed similarly, given that they almost never left Otherworld for earth. They all glared at him. All except Aerten, the goddess of fate, who hung back, a strange expression on her face.

Cam's gaze returned to Hafgan and he jerked his chin up. "Fuck you, Hafgan."

Hafgan's mouth hardened. "Is that all you have to say in your defense?"

Cam laughed, then jerked at the hands that pressed on his shoulders. They were firm as iron. So he was stuck kneeling in front of these assholes. "What the fuck do you want me to say? That these jackoffs"—he nodded to the cluster of gods who had coerced Ana into coming to Otherworld to kill him all those years ago—"plotted to have me killed? What the hell were they thinking, that Ana could possibly have killed me?"

Now that he was thinking about the past, it made the long-repressed rage push at the edges of the cage he'd used to trap it. And their arrival had fucked things up with Ana in the future, as well.

"What kind of fucking trap was that, you fuckers?" he demanded, his breath heaving. He struggled against the hands holding him. Iron.

"A test." Thunder boomed as Hafgan answered. "You should have killed her when you found her, as we do with mortals whose skills match our own. Yet *you* acted mortal."

He'd known that his hesitation all those years ago had signed his death warrant. Hafgan was right—he had acted like a mortal. But the way he felt now, how right it felt to be a god again, made him realize that he'd been wrong to think emotion made him lesser.

"Fuck that. I acted as a god." He spat out the words. "Something's wrong here in Otherworld. Why do we feel fucking nothing when all the other gods—Roman, Greek, Norse, Mayan, you name it—have feelings as the mortals do?"

"We're superior to the other religions." Hafgan crossed his arms over his chest, but the eyes of the other gods shifted.

"Sure, tell yourself that when you jerk off. But it's not the fucking truth." The afterworlds were all equal, none more powerful than any other. It was the truth of their worlds. The mortal world was where the power lay, for it was mortals' belief that made the afterworlds exist. Maintaining that equality, and making sure none of the gods made a stupid power play, was of the utmost importance to peace and one of the primary purposes of the Immortal University.

Hafgan ignored his statement. "You've run once. And with no defense worthy of a reprieve, you're sentenced to a thousand years on the tor."

Fuck. Cam heaved against his captors, his muscles straining. But the gods had finished their trial. Two others joined the gods restraining him and dragged him to the nearest tor, a great granite pile of rocks that punched through the earth and rose toward the sky.

"You're just looking to punish someone, aren't you? You're making a fucking mistake," Cam roared. Thunder boomed in the distance, echoing his rage.

His captors climbed, dragging him along. Freezing rain heaved down from the heavens, making the granite slippery. The gods trudged on.

"Chain him." Hafgan's voice carried from the ground, and the lesser gods followed his command.

They grappled and struggled, but soon they forced Cam to lie atop the great rock. Gofannon, god of metalworking, brought forth unbreakable chains and threw them across Cam. He grunted when they crushed his ribs.

Of their own volition, the chains wrapped about his body, drawing bone-crushingly tight, then thrust their length through the granite to hold him. The rain had turned to hail, giant fist-sized chunks that shattered upon hitting the tor but not upon hitting Cam's body. No, those merely bounced off after leaving a cracked rib or a crushed kidney. Rain blurred his vision and all he felt was pain.

He heard the gods scramble off the tor, returning to the scrubby ground, which was covered in dead heather.

They said nothing—finished with him for the next thousand years—and disappeared. The wind howled louder in their absence. Cam struggled against the chains, muscles bunching and straining, sweat breaking out on his cold brow. The iron cut more fiercely into his skin with every twitch of his muscles, driving deeper into the granite until no matter how hard he pulled, he couldn't move an inch.

His mind felt as trapped as his body. Worse, for all the horrors that it could envision. Had Ana awoken? The memory of the blood seeping through her shirt and out from under her punched into his mind again. *Familiar.*

Spurred on by the memory of her covered in blood and dead at his feet, his mind was sucked back into a past that he had forgotten.

The birds of prey circled above, cawing and shrieking, their black bodies ominous against the dark clouds.

Consciousness came in fits and spurts. First, Ana's hearing buzzed in and out, then her vision faded from blurry shadow to black and back again. Eventually, she realized that the plushness beneath her was a bed.

Groggily, she dragged a hand to her face and tried to rub her eyes, but her arm weighed a million pounds and the hand against her face didn't feel like it belonged to her. A moan almost escaped her throat, but she stifled it at the last minute, unsure if she was in a place safe enough to make noise.

"Calm down. You're safe." The rough voice was unfamiliar. Despite the words, a chill broke out on her skin.

She forced herself to stay perfectly still, inanely thinking that if she didn't move, he couldn't see her. Eventually, she blinked until the room came into focus. A bedroom. A flash of movement out of the corner of her eye made her turn her head.

"Logan," she rasped, then coughed through a throat lined with sandpaper. The sight of him brought back everything that had happened and she doubled over, grief spearing her stomach. *Cam.*

"Hang on." He walked out of the room and returned holding a cup of water. "Here."

She moaned, then struggled to sit. Wallowing in her own pain would do Cam no good. She forced her body, so heavy and slow, to straighten and accept its fate. Her hand closed around the water glass he handed her and she gulped the water down. Dying hurt.

"What happened? Where's Cam?" She struggled to get out of bed, managed only a sitting position. Shit, how long would it take to get back her strength?

"Dragged to Otherworld by the other gods. I didn't realize he was invisible to them until they lost their shit when you finally died on my floor. Then they could see him and all hell broke loose."

Of course it had. Druantia had said the tattoo wouldn't work on gods. When he'd taken Ana's godhood, his tattoo had ceased working.

Logan crossed his arms over his chest, his face hard. "You're a miserable houseguest."

"Sorry." But she didn't feel sorry. She felt pissed. Pissed that she hadn't had time to convince him to take her place.

"No, you're not," he said. "But you wanted out of your godhood. You'd have done anything to get that. I understand."

"Yeah?" The bitterness rang in her voice. She'd gone from being so close to having everything that she wanted to being a broken mess in this stranger's bed.

She struggled to stand, making it to wobbly feet. "I've got to get to Otherworld. To Cam."

"First you've got to eat, get some strength up. Come on, I'll feed you." He turned and strode out of the room.

Her stomach growled, as if his words had spurred on her hunger. But he was right. Dying and reanimating had left her completely empty.

She trudged out of the bedroom to find Logan. She was in a hell of a lot better situation than Cam. Would they lock him up like they'd planned to do to her, afraid that he'd run again? Probably. They'd plotted against him before, after all. The idea gave her the extra bit of strength to pick up her pace near the kitchen.

There, she found Logan putting together a simple sandwich. He set it down on the table, a can of Tennant's next to it.

"Eat." His tone was annoyed, but at least he was helping her.

"Thanks." The sight of it made her stomach turn, but she had to do something to regain her strength. So she took a bite. "You recognized Cam. And he recognized you. Why?"

Logan leaned back in his chair until two feet hovered off the ground, crossed his arms over his chest. "We met a long time ago. When he was Camulos. And I was a god."

Holy shit. She hadn't seen that one coming. She forced her gaping mouth shut. "You're kidding. Seriously? I've never heard of a Logan Laufeyson as a god."

He shrugged. "Logan's not my real name. And no, I won't share it. This isn't exactly my real face, either. I like to keep my secrets."

"But Cam knows who you are."

"Because we share blood from a vow we made long ago. As a result of that, he can't harm me. By deed or word. You, however, aren't bound by that promise."

Fates, she'd been screwed all along. The brusque man across from her was already a freaking god, and a shifty one with his own mysterious agenda.

"Cam knew you couldn't take my place in Otherworld."

"No dual citizenship allowed." He frowned thoughtfully, a clever gleam in his eye that she hadn't noticed before. It made him a bit less scary. "Though I might have tried it."

"I've got to get to Otherworld." She pushed her chair away from the table and stood, considerably more stable for having eaten.

"Don't see how you can. You're a demigod now, so you can't aetherwalk."

"Can you take me?" She gripped the back of the chair.

"No. My aetherwalking has been bound."

"Bound?"

"Long story." His mouth flattened.

So Logan had problems of his own. Maybe that's why he'd said he understood why she wanted out of Otherworld. Why he'd helped her, even if he'd been a moody bastard about it. But he didn't look like the sharing type—not even a little—so she didn't ask.

"Before I forget," Ana said. "You have a bow and arrow that my friend wants. You stole it."

He shrugged. "Your friend can't have it. I don't even have it anymore."

She could tell he was lying, but also that he wouldn't tolerate more questions. She glanced out the window to see the gray light of a cloudy dawn stretching over the mountains. "How's the weather?"

"Good enough for your vehicle. Got a place to go?"

"Yeah. But having a place to go isn't the problem. Getting there is."

Comprehension flashed across his face. "Shit. Of course you can't drive. No cars in Otherworld."

"Bingo. I always wanted to learn to drive, but I'm never on earth long enough. I don't suppose you could...?"

He sighed. "Yeah, sure. To get you out of my hair."

"Thanks, really. Let me change my clothes"—she plucked at the fabric now stiff with dried blood—"then could we get out of here?"

"In a hurry to start your life on earth?"

The opposite. "I've got to see a Druid priestess about a trip to Otherworld."

CHAPTER TWENTY-SEVEN

Cam's body lay chained to the windswept tor while his mind hurtled nearly three thousand years into the past. To a time centuries before he'd ever met Ana.

Or so he'd thought.

As fist-sized hail pelted his battered body and left bruises that would heal so that others could form, the memory of a night he'd long forgotten rose in his mind, spurred on by the sight of Ana on the floor, her chest drenched in blood from his arrow.

Pain and delirium fueled the hallucination. Or memory. Which, he couldn't tell.

In his mind, he was no longer chained to a rock in the worst of the elements of Otherworld. He was standing in a clearing, observing the drunken debauchery of his fellow gods. It was an enormous party, and it appealed to his senses on every level. Joy and lust and other things that he'd never believed he'd felt as a god all surged through him, fueled by the wine that flowed freely.

All facilitated by the High Priestess Druantia, who he'd thought a worthless upstart following the last battle. After this night, he'd have to change his opinion of her. She was still just a servant, but one who attempted to make amends for her failures.

And oh, how she did. Wine, food, dancing. And she directed him to a nymph, a Dryad of the oak trees, who sat off to the side. Lovelier than any woman he'd ever seen, with shining gold hair and green eyes.

Ana. Every hair on her head, every expression on her face. It was Ana. His dream self didn't know to find it strange that a mortal who had yet to be born was here in this forest with him. Drunk on the wine and the revelry, he gazed upon her, his eyes tracing her athletic form draped in fine blue wool and reclining against the roots of the oak.

"Are you enjoying the evening?" he asked once he reached her.

She glanced up at him, stood slowly, and smiled. "Perhaps I will now."

"You haven't been enjoying the festivities?"

She shrugged. "Our presence was required by our mistress, Druantia."

Of course. Oaks were sacred to the Druids, whom the Dryads served.

She turned toward the deeper part of the forest and waved her hand. "Come with me. I tire of the noise."

He followed her as she led him back through the trees, away from the madness and revelry reaching a fever pitch in the clearing behind. Her hips swayed gracefully as she walked and her hair tumbled down her back. His eyes traced over her form, unable to look away.

She stopped at the base of a graceful old oak and turned to him. Her eyes were brighter now, and a smile curved her mouth.

"You prefer it here, away from the noise," he said.

"I do." She smiled wider, and the sight sent a jolt of pleasure through him. Good wine or victory in battle usually did that, but never the smile of a woman. Why should he care that she was happier now in the quiet of the forest?

But he did. He hadn't cared about anyone else's feelings in years. Maybe ever. But with her, he cared very much, though he didn't know why.

"Tell me about being a Dryad," he said, anxious to know more about her.

She tucked her hair behind her ear, and after giving him an appraising glance, spoke of the spirit of the trees and midnight dances through the forest.

Under the light of stars and with revelry sounding in the background, he set about wooing her, coaxing a smile and a laugh that filled his chest with more light and joy. The more she spoke, the more entranced he became. It was something in the air or floating on the wind. But it was her also. She was unlike any woman he'd ever met. She was someone special, and he liked her immensely.

His eyes traced over her face and curves as she spoke, his mind turning toward earthlier pleasures. What would her skin feel like beneath his hands? Would she taste as sweet as she looked? It became difficult to focus on her words as her forest scent wrapped around his mind.

In the distance, the sounds of the revelers increased in volume and tempo. Her words trailed off, and he realized that the heat in his eyes must be apparent.

His cock hardened when he realized that she looked at him with the same interest. She wet her lips and laid her fingertips upon his arm as the noise and energy of the other revelers rolled through the forest, carried on a dark wind.

The heat in his blood spiked, a combination of her touch and something else he'd never felt before. A push of tearing energy and need, something fierce that he recognized might be unnatural. It flowed on the wind, carried from the site of Druantia's gathering.

With need riding him hard, he pulled her to him. She didn't resist, wrapping her arms around his neck and fusing her soft mouth to his. His cock jumped and his mind fogged with something that was more than normal lust, but he was too far gone to care. Her hands were frantic on his clothes, ripping and tearing. Through the haze, he realized that she was as caught up as he.

Unconcerned that something foreign and dark had overtaken them, they tore at each other's clothes as the moon rose high above the sparse scatter of oaks. The noise of the party faded as they grappled in the moonlight, hands sliding over damp skin, hot and frantic for each other.

When he had her naked before him, he hoisted her up and pressed her back against the oak. Her legs wrapped around his waist.

He could barely see her as he thrust into the wet heat of her body, his vision darkened by the unnatural trance that had overcome him. He tried to fight it as he pounded into her. He liked her—he shouldn't be treating her so roughly, even if her wetness and her cries of passion told him that she liked it.

But he couldn't throw off the mantle of insanity that was overwhelming him, nor could he fight the pull of her. It stole conscious thought, vision, hearing, and eventually feeling. The glorious feel of her body accepting his began to fade. The joy that he'd taken in the act, in the victory of winning her affection, became hollow. Soon, his mind wasn't there at all.

He awoke from his befogged state in a thick forest of oak trees, confused, for there had been far fewer trees before. All had been home to the Druid's sacred mistletoe. The new trees were darker than the others, bigger and stronger, with no mistletoe hanging from their branches.

The sound of revelry had died, and the forest was silent. It was so quiet that he swore the other gods must have returned to Otherworld.

His gaze was drawn to the forest floor. At his feet lay the bloodied body of a beautiful blond Dryad. Yet he looked at her the same way he'd looked at the trees—with only the vaguest interest.

Had he killed her? Perhaps. There was a strangeness in his chest at the thought, but it too was uninteresting. As this night had become. He felt nothing and didn't realize that it was strange.

Detached, he watched as her blood soaked into the ground and her body grew to form a great oak tree. The roots plunged deep into the black earth, while branches reached skyward as if the tree were desperate to escape the hold of the earth. But even that bit of magic held little relevance to his life, so he picked up his bow and quiver and returned to Otherworld and his duties. He really should be getting back.

Cam's eyes snapped open, his consciousness returned to Blackmoor and the rock upon which he was chained. Madness tore at the edges of his mind. *Ana.*

CHAPTER TWENTY-EIGHT

Ana hopped out of Logan's Range Rover in front of Druantia's building and looked behind her at Logan. "Thanks for the ride."

"Sure." He nodded, then pulled away as soon as she shut the door.

Not too friendly, but he'd saved her ass.

Determined to get to Cam no matter what it took, she headed toward the wooden door of Druantia's shop. The knob was cold under her hand, and she was grateful to step into the warmth of the shop.

"Can I help you?" Druantia asked as she appeared from behind a tall shelf. "Oh, Ana. I didn't expect to see you here. How is Camulos?"

"Not good. The gods found us. I don't know how, but he's back in Otherworld."

Interest glowed in Druantia's eyes, and her mouth curved to an odd smile so fleeting that Ana was sure she imagined it. "That's awful. Come on to the back, tell me what I can do to help."

A sigh heaved out of Ana's lungs. She followed Druantia to the back room, weaving around the little tables and under the archway. The zip of magic that sang across her skin was stronger now, almost painful.

"Ouch. You really upped the power on that spell that protects this room." She rubbed her arms.

"Really? I'm sure I didn't." Druantia turned and smiled sweetly at her. "Tea?"

"Um, sure. Thanks."

"So, tell me what happened and how I can help." Druantia gestured to the chair that Cam had sat in for his tattoo.

Ana sat. She looked around the room, which was still fairly empty with the exception of the bookshelves. They'd been here just yesterday, so full of hope. And now everything she'd feared had happened.

Ana shook away the miserable thought and told Druantia about the gods while the other woman made tea at a little counter in the corner. The *ding* and click of the electric kettle made Ana's mouth water for something warm after being in the frigid wind.

"Here you go." Druantia handed over the steaming mug and Ana took it gratefully. She smiled at Druantia and sipped.

"Thanks." She sipped again, luxuriating in the warmth that spread through her as she dredged up the energy to finish her tale. Her status as a demigod was making her hungrier and more susceptible to cold than she'd ever been as a god. "Cam took my place in Otherworld. He's trapped there now."

"Oh, what a shame."

Ana blinked, certain that Druantia's voice had changed. And was she smiling?

"And what do you want from me?" Druantia asked. Yes, her voice did sound strange.

Ana blinked again and rubbed her ears. A buzzing bee was trapped in her head. "I need to get to Otherworld." She tried to keep talking, to tell Druantia that she had to find a way to save Cam, but her tongue had become so leaden.

"You—the tea—" Her hand relaxed on the glass, and it fell to the ground. The shatter of ceramic on stone floor echoed in her ears.

"Aye. The tea. You gods always think you're cleverer than we mortals. Why you're so arrogant, I have no idea. You've no reason to be." Druantia *tsk*ed and leaned back in her small chair, a smug cat's smile stretching across her face.

Ana's mind scrambled to understand, to make sense of the woman sitting across from her and all that had happened.

"You—you sent Cernowain to us." She wished the damn bee in her head would die. "Not... his spies."

"Of course. Idiot gods always need my help. And it suited my purpose to have Camulos found and punished for desertion." Hatred thickened her voice.

"But you... helped him Fall. With tattoo... and potion." Speaking was becoming harder.

"Of course, you imbecile. I'd do anything to see that arrogant bastard lowered from his godly status. Had I been able to kill him, I would've. But he's too damned strong, and I never knew where he went once he fell from godhood. I couldn't believe my luck when you walked into my shop. Of *course* I set the gods on you. I'd have done it right away if I could have, but I didn't want to alert Camulos. He's still strong enough to kill me." Bitterness and fear flashed across her face. "So I gave him the damn tattoo. And I added a tracking spell I'd recently devised. It was only a matter of time before Cernowain found you."

"But..." Ana's voice trailed off as fog clouded her mind.

"I've been waiting ages for this. And now I've got plans for you." Druantia reached out. Her hands were cold and strong, biting into Ana's flesh.

With what felt like a herculean effort, Ana heaved herself off the chair and onto the floor and the broken mug. Druantia crashed on top her, and Ana felt the bite of glass into her arm. They grappled, but no matter how Ana struggled, the dark and deep of her mind dragged her under until she could hear nothing but the buzzing in her head.

Something brushed over her arm, light and quick. The tickling woke Ana. She jerked upright from the hard floor, breath sawing in and out of her lungs, and her eyes popped open wide.

Darkness. All she could see was darkness. Air whistled through her throat as she tried to get it together. *Blind.*

She blinked frantically, shaking her head. No, she wasn't blind, she realized as her eyes adjusted to the gloom. A tiny window high on the wall let in just enough light through heavy streaks of grime.

A streak of pain pierced her skull. She rubbed her aching head, then winced when the cuts on her arm burned. She poked at the slices in her flesh that peeked out from the holes in her shirt. From the mug, she remembered. And her fight with Druantia.

Blood was dried on the fabric. What the hell? She was a demigod. If the blood was dried, enough time had passed that her wound should have at least started to heal.

Yet it was still gaping and ugly, slowly trickling blood. She prodded the lump on her head. Had she gotten that when she'd been thrown into this dark room? Demigods didn't heal *that* much slower than regular gods.

She looked up, more concerned with where she was trapped than with her wound. What the fuck? Druantia had drugged her. And thrown her in a cupboard or a butler's pantry, from the look of the shelves. The sound of rustling and chattering drew her attention to the corner.

Rats. One must have crawled across her arm. But it wasn't tiny rat feet that bothered her. No, this shit was far worse.

She glanced at the ground, desperately hoping to see her bow but knowing it was likely as futile as hoping for an unlocked door to the cupboard. *Nothing*. Her hands curled into fists on the stone floor, and she tried to slow the panic that threatened to suck her under. Even her bow wouldn't help her get out of here.

With an ache in her bones that felt wholly unnatural, Ana climbed to her feet and went to the door. Tried the knob.

Fuck. Of course it was locked. She gripped it hard in both hands and pulled, straining and cursing when it didn't budge.

Why couldn't she open it? She should be at least strong enough to break down a door.

But she wasn't. And without her strength or her bow or godly magic, all she had was her mind. *So figure out if you can get past this door.* Carefully, she ran her hands over the wood and metal fixtures, down to the base of the door to sneak her fingers under and measure its thickness.

Her throat and eyes burned when she realized it was a heavy wooden door with sturdy metal hinges and a lock. The old kind, built to really keep people out instead of just marking space with a piece of hollow plywood that could be broken through.

So Druantia really wanted to keep her locked up. But why? She'd helped Ana and Cam before. Given Cam his protection charm and the demigod potion. But there was no way around the fact that Druantia was clearly playing toward an endgame that Ana didn't understand. There was more at stake here than just her life or Cam's, at least for Druantia.

Options raced through Ana's mind as she explored the dark cupboard. It took her only minutes to feel around on every surface and determine that it was basically empty with the exception of some canned goods and books. Nothing to help her.

She sank down against the wall and dropped her head back. Had Druantia locked her up as bait to draw Cam back here? Or would she try to ransom her back to the gods?

Ana groaned and rubbed her throbbing temple. The cold, stale air in the cupboard wasn't helping. She closed her eyes and let her mind drift on waves of horrible thoughts and plans and futile attempts at escape. There was a chance she drifted off at one point, but after what felt like hours, she realized that Druantia probably wasn't coming to let her out.

And even if she did, it wouldn't be good. Without her bow, she'd have a hard time defending herself if Druantia appeared. Ana looked at her wounds again, her gut sinking when she noticed that they were still as open and angry as before. She wasn't healing. Not like she should be if she were a demigod. Had the potion not worked?

It hit her then, like a piano from the sky in an old cartoon. Only this wasn't funny. Whatever Druantia had given them had turned Ana *mortal.*

That's why she'd been feeling so cold and tired and slow and hungry and all the other things that mortals felt that gods and demigods did not. It was all so twisted, and Druantia's motivations so confusing, that Ana couldn't wrap her head around it.

Wow, she'd really fucked this up. Cam was in Otherworld, most likely being tortured, and she was here, a puny mortal locked in a cupboard. Things had really come full circle. They'd started out with he a god and she a mortal, and now they were back to it. Only in arguably a much worse situation.

But the fact remained: She was mortal. If Druantia had just given them colored water for the potion, Ana would have woken in Otherworld and realized they'd been scammed. Instead, she'd woken up mortal.

Which meant that there was a way for her to get to Otherworld.

Death.

She rubbed the scars on her wrists. There were risks to the plan, no doubt. She could end up in Otherworld like all the other mortals. An unfeeling automaton. If that happened, would she retain the desire to save Cam?

But there was no guarantee that she would end up like other mortals. She was mortal, but she had knowledge of the reality of the world, Mytheans and afterworlds, gods and monsters. Having that knowledge was halfway to being Mythean, anyway.

No, the worst of it was that if she failed, she might never return to earth. Not even for the rest of her miserly mortal years. But there was no question.

Ana heaved herself to her feet, slowed by the weakness of her mortal body. She searched the room again, patting down every surface for something sharp. After a few minutes, though, nothing. Still just a few old canned vegetables and a couple of cookbooks.

The light from the corner window caught her eye. Far too small for an escape effort, but perfect for her purposes. She grabbed the heaviest can and climbed onto the counter until she could reach the window.

The view through the grime revealed an empty alley, as she'd expected it would in this type of old building. No one to hear her scream, and what would it matter? She couldn't drag a mortal into this. She'd committed to her plan and she'd see it through.

She fumbled with her jacket until it was wrapped around her hand and the can. With all her strength, she punched her fist through the glass. Searing pain sang up her arm, but the glass shattered.

Gasping, she set the can on the counter and grabbed the biggest piece of glass she could find. It was still small, given that it was such a tiny window, but it would do.

With the glass pinched between her fingers, she climbed down from the counter and knelt on the floor in a position not dissimilar to how she'd sat two thousand years ago at the feet of the gods.

How appropriate. She'd done this once before, too young and stupid to extricate herself from the mess she'd gotten herself into. Only that time, she'd been heading to Otherworld to kill Cam. Now, it was just the opposite.

She sucked in a deep breath, held it in her lungs, then raked the glass down her wrist, pushing deep and hard and gasping at the pain that sliced through her. Coming full circle hurt. She fumbled to do the same to her other wrist, and though the cut wasn't as deep, the blood poured onto the floor.

The glass clattered to the stone and she sat, her head bowed, and watched her warm blood seep onto her thighs. So similar to the past, yet not.

As if it had been fated all along.

CHAPTER TWENTY-NINE

Guilt tugged on Logan's conscience, strong enough that he pulled his Range Rover to the side of the empty mountain road and leaned his head against the steering wheel. This wasn't his business. He had shit to do that was more important than whatever mess his uninvited houseguests had gotten themselves into.

He'd dropped Ana off at the bitch Druantia's place a couple of hours ago. The idea of Druantia noticing his Range Rover in the street had him driving off immediately, wishing Ana the best. She was a big girl. A goddess no longer, but in the world of myth, it was each Mythean for himself. A law he lived by.

He couldn't help but feel for her, though, heading into the lair of that harpy he'd been stupid enough to sleep with for a few weeks. His brain had followed his dick, though it wasn't until he'd seen some of the weird shit that she'd been into that he'd finally left.

With a groan, he swung his car into a U-turn on the empty highway and headed back toward Druantia's place. Ana probably knew what she was getting into, and fate knew his ass had been on fire to get away. But he couldn't fight the nagging guilt. Druantia probably wasn't as fucked up as he suspected she was. But what if?

Two hours later, he stalked through the door of her shop. Empty, but the eerie feel of the place made him shudder. He hadn't felt it when he'd first started sleeping with her, but over time it had begun to give him the creeps.

"Druantia!" he yelled when she didn't appear in the archway from the back room as she usually did.

Fuck it, he wasn't going to wait around for her. Maybe she had helped Ana, but he'd driven all this way on a hunch and a dinged conscience, and he was going to at least have a search around.

Her back room was empty, as was the little kitchen and sitting room. She lived above the shop, and he'd turned toward the stairs when a narrow door caught his eye. He'd skipped it when he'd walked through the room, figuring that it was a closet, but no stone unturned and all that shit.

The doorknob didn't twist under his hand. *Locked.* And suspicious as hell. So he yanked on the knob hard enough that the lock broke and the door swung open to reveal a larger space than he'd expected.

Ana's collapsed form lay on the floor.

Shit. He was kneeling at her prone form in seconds, her blood soaking through to his knees. He gently tugged at her to roll her onto her back.

Dead. *Fuck.*

But how? A demigod shouldn't be able to die from sliced wrists. Yet the shard of glass next to her body confirmed that she'd indeed killed herself.

Whatever the fuck had happened here, it had happened because he'd dropped Ana off with Druantia, ignored any niggling concerns he'd had, and hightailed it away. Druantia had some kind of stake in this, but it was beyond him to determine.

But it was his fucking fault that Ana lay dead, covered in blood. She'd been this desperate to go after Camulos? He hadn't spoken to Camulos in nearly a thousand years, not since he'd been a god. But he'd liked Camulos, who'd been a decent enough fellow.

Decent enough that he didn't deserve what happened to gods who ran from Otherworld. Logan could empathize with that desire and felt like shit that the guy might end up chained in the Celts' miserable, archaic punishment. It was a fucked-up system. And now Ana had run off to Otherworld after him in the only way she knew how.

Logan heaved a disgusted sigh and climbed to his feet. There was nothing he could do for Ana's body—not that it mattered, anyway—but he could try to help her in Otherworld.

He made it out of Druantia's shop without being noticed and drove all the way to the first abandoned patch of gravel along an empty Highland road. Private enough, he figured, so he climbed out of the car.

Mountains rose on either side of him, low and sloping in this part of the Highlands, and empty of mortals. Already regretting his decision but tugged by his conscience, he shed his mortal form for that of a black falcon.

Once the rippling pain of the change had faded, the lightness of being and the wind beneath his wings made his heart fly even as his mind dreaded what was likely to come.

He soared through the air, higher and faster, until his mind freed itself from the shackles of earth and he entered the aether, and through it arrived in Otherworld.

He couldn't aetherwalk as other Mytheans could, but he could travel in one of his alternate forms. Shapeshifting had always been his gift, and as the black falcon, he could travel through the aether.

After flying over Otherworld for hours, alternately over mountains and pastures, he neared the desolate land that had to be Blackmoor. It lacked the beautiful sweeps of colored heather and waving grass that dotted the other moors. He spied a flock of black birds circling over a tor and sped toward them, wind whistling past him.

Camulos. As he had feared. The man lay chained to the rock, eyes squeezed shut and struggling as if he were living out a vision within his mind. Poor bastard.

CHAPTER THIRTY

Ana gasped and opened her eyes, blinking rapidly to regain her sight. When her vision cleared, she looked around and realized that she was kneeling in the same grove of oaks that she'd arrived in two thousand years ago when she'd come here to kill Cam.

Fitting.

She looked at her wrists. Two scars now. A grim smile stretched across her face. It was a macabre way to travel, but she was lucky that it had worked.

Gracefully, she rose to her feet, no longer burdened by her mortal body. Though it didn't feel the same as godhood, it was certainly better than being mortal.

Her fist closed longingly around air, and she wished she had her bow. It was still in Druantia's creepy shop, gone forever because she'd never escape Otherworld to retrieve it.

She shook away the pang of grief. At least she wasn't an unfeeling automaton like she'd feared. And there were bigger things to worry about, such as getting through the forest and out onto Blackmoor without any of the gods realizing she was here. Luckily, despite the vast size of Otherworld, she was only a few hours from Blackmoor. She'd learned every patch of Otherworld in the centuries she'd been trapped here.

She set off through the oaks until eventually she stood at the edge of the tree line, warily eying the vast, open expanse of the moor. If the gods were still out there, it would be easy for them to find her.

But she was so close to Cam she didn't want to wait.

Her eyes scanned the rolling hills, barren brown with ever-dead heather. Great granite tors punched up through the ground, hulking over the horizon as the sun set behind them. It lacked the beauty of Otherworld's other moorland, but for good reason. This was the place of punishment.

In the distance, she caught sight of a flock of birds circling a tor and set out toward them. The sun had nearly sunk beneath the horizon, and the coming dark would shield her as she walked across the too-open space. She couldn't wait any longer for dark, not being as close as she was now.

She set off at a jog, slowly because of the deceptively boggy and uneven ground. About halfway to the tor, one of the birds cut away from the rest and joined her. A pitch-black falcon—feather, beak, and eyes. Strange looking, but prophetic.

By the time she reached the base of the large hill that supported the tor, it began to rain. She picked up her pace, sprinting now that she was out of the boggy valley. So close. Her heart pounded and cold fear raced along her skin.

The tor was a jumbled pile of massive granite rock, too complex to identify an outline of Cam in the low moonlight. But he was here—he had to be. She climbed, scrabbling for purchase on the smooth surfaces. The falcon veered left and she followed, climbing to reach the highest point of the tor.

There. She sobbed in relief when she spotted the barest outline of Cam only ten feet in the distance, straining violently against the chains that bound him to the rock. After a last mighty effort to heave herself onto the top of the tor, she fell to her knees at his side.

"Cam." She grasped his thrashing head. The chains had rubbed his skin raw, and blood seeped beneath him to soak the granite. Great circular bruises dotted his battered muscles, purple and blue and black.

"Ana." A tortured moan escaped his mouth.

He wasn't here. Not mentally, at least. She stroked his face, his neck. "Shh. Shh. I'm here. It's me. I'll get you out of here."

She turned to the chain and jerked at it, pulling with all her might.

It wouldn't budge. In her haste and fear, she'd forgotten that she was merely mortal. Just one soul among thousands, with no special powers. If she had any hope of getting him out, she'd have to leave and find help. Tools—or her brothers, if she could convince them. Anything.

Cam's moan tore at her ears. Could she leave him like this? He was going crazy. Her head whipped around, searching futilely for help, and she caught sight of the same black falcon. It sat near Cam's side, its eyes rapt on them.

Her brow furrowed as she watched it, her mouth dropping open when it pecked at the chains with its black beak. It was no normal falcon, for the chain began to shatter beneath its blows. Finally, the chain snapped. Grateful beyond measure, she pulled the chain away from Cam's chest as the falcon pecked at the others.

Within minutes, she was pulling the last of Cam's bindings away. She turned to the falcon, only to see it fly off into the distance.

"Thank you," she whispered, awed by her strange luck. She turned back to Cam.

"Come on, Cam, you have to wake up." She smoothed her hands over his face and chest, watching gratefully as his wounds began to knit with godly speed now that his body wasn't fighting the chains.

He moaned, a pained exhalation that tugged at her heart, and finally opened his eyes.

"Ana." Confusion wrinkled his brow as he reached up to touch her face. His eyes were vacant, the way one's were after a dream. "But you—you're dead."

Dead? She frowned at him. Mytheans didn't use that term. Death or dying, maybe, to talk about crossing over to the next life. But few people were ever truly dead, their souls blinked out of existence.

"I'm in Otherworld with you. My mortal body is gone, but I'm here." And here, she looked and felt as if she were flesh and blood. "Come on, we've got to get out of here."

Cam shook his head hard and leaned up on an elbow. He looked up at her again, his eyes clear. He yanked her to him, burying her against his chest. "Fuck, Ana. How did you get here?"

"Same way I did last time." She hugged him hard, then pulled away and held up her wrists, each now bearing two long scars. One for each time she'd come to Otherworld for him, for two vastly different reasons.

His big hands cupped the sides of her face, and he kissed her hard on the mouth and with so much gratitude that she could all but taste it. He stumbled to his feet, still weakened by his injuries.

"We've got to get out of here."

She pointed west. "The closest cover is that way. A grove of oaks."

He shook his head. "Out of Otherworld."

Her heart plummeted. Of course. "I can't leave Otherworld. The demigod potion didn't work. I'm mortal. I'm stuck here."

"You're not mortal, Ana. At least, not entirely."

What? Before she could speak, he wrapped his arms around her and she felt the familiar pull of the aether.

When they appeared in Esha's flat, Ana gasped. She'd never expected to make it back to earth. When a mortal went to an afterworld, they stayed there. No exception. "How? How am I here?"

Cam kissed her hard, then pulled away from her and limped toward the bedroom, presumably looking for Esha. "The gods cannot come here, right?"

"Of course," Ana said. "The gods hold no sway at the university."

"Excellent. Gofannon will know that his magic chains have been broken. Soon the gods will know I'm gone."

"But how am I here? I should be trapped in Otherworld. You can't give life back to mortals." She shivered. It had been the hardest part of slitting her wrists back in Druantia's pantry, the knowledge that even as a god, he couldn't give her back the earth. But it had been the easiest trade she'd ever made.

"You're part Mythean, Ana. Not enough to make you immortal, since you were able to kill yourself to get into Otherworld." He reached for her wrist and rubbed his thumb against the new scar, then met her eyes. "But enough that combined with your knowledge of the world of myth, I could treat you as any other Mythean and take you from Otherworld."

Her brow furrowed. "Then what am I? This doesn't make any sense."

He pulled her over to the couch and they sat. His grip on her hands remained, his thumb slowly stroking as if to confirm for himself that she really was there. The story that followed was surreal. Her mind raced as he told her about an enormous party, every god from Otherworld in attendance—and she had been there with him in the forest.

"A Dryad?" she asked. Could she have truly lived another life? The Celts believed in reincarnation, but she'd always thought that if it had been her, she'd have remembered her past life. "But I don't remember any of that. And I shouldn't have a body. I killed my earthly body. Even as a Dryad, my soul should have stayed trapped in Otherworld."

"That's strange, and I've no idea how that worked. But it *was* you, Ana. You're identical to the woman from my past."

Her eyes raced over his face. He believed this. "But how did everything change? You went from feeling to unfeeling. How is that even possible?"

"Very powerful magic, in which we gods played a part. That night, I woke long after the others, farther into the forest where the magic couldn't reach me as quickly. I witnessed the bones and blood of the Dryads form the oaks in that macabre glen. Your blood and your bones. But the spell made the memories fade until they felt unimportant. When I saw you covered in blood at Logan's house, it looked horrifyingly familiar. I couldn't get it out of my mind. When I was chained up on Blackmoor, I remembered."

"Holy shit," she breathed. She didn't remember any of that. She'd had another life? Where she'd known Cam? "You killed me?"

Grief darkened his gaze. "I'm sorry, Ana. I couldn't control it."

Her mind struggled to recall anything from her past, but she could remember nothing. Flutters of panic rose in her breast, that she had a whole history with Cam that she knew nothing about.

"Ana, I'm sorry."

She blinked and met his gaze, realizing that she'd disappeared into her mind, searching for memories. "It's fine. Really. It was a spell, of course you couldn't control it. And I can't believe it was me. I don't remember anything."

"It was you. I'm certain of it. She looked like you and she felt like you and smelled of the forest, like you do."

"I—I believe you. I just can't remember. But it's fine. I wouldn't be here in this incarnation if you hadn't killed me in the past. I like being me, even if my situation is currently a nightmare."

"We'll get out of it."

"How? If you step foot off the university campus, the gods will get you."

"They'll have to find me first."

"They will, eventually." Then they'd be separated—presuming the gods didn't kill her.

"Not if we can figure out a way to break the spell on Otherworld. It's got to be one of the reasons that the gods feel so bound to the place. None of the other religions are like that."

"True. You said before that Druantia hosted the party where the gods lost emotion?" When he nodded, she said, "I think she cast the spell. When I went to her for help to come after you, she locked me up. She hates the gods. She hates you. With the kind of hatred that lasts millennia and spawns intricate plots."

He cursed, vile and low. Then nodded. "Fucking idiot. I was so damned arrogant back then, I never realized. The last time I saw her before that terrible night was after a battle. She'd taken tributes that were meant for me. Now, I don't give a damn about them. But back then I was enraged. I was obsessed with myself and what I thought she'd taken from me. I threw her into the mud. Humiliated her in front of her followers."

"But you're not like that now."

"No. I think having my emotion taken from me changed part of the way I think. I couldn't care about anything enough—even myself—to dredge up arrogance. Once you gave me back some of my ability to feel, I think I wised up some."

"But she still hates you."

"And she's determined to have her pound of flesh. My pride didn't allow me to see what she was capable of. What she took from us. All emotion. Locking us in Otherworld."

"No longer. You have it back."

"Because of you." He reached for her, drew her face up to his. "Thank you, Ana."

He gave her the sweetest kiss of her life, all soft lips and grazing touch. Eventually, when she was breathless, he drew away and looked down at her.

He ran his thumb across her cheek and said, "I don't think I have the full capacity for emotion that I once did, but everything good that I feel is wrapped up in you. I couldn't kill you all those years ago when I found you in the forest because I recognized you. Not my eyes or my mind, but my heart."

Something in her chest cracked open. She almost felt like she should speak words of love. They simmered within her, ready to boil free, but the gaping hole in her memory and their past kept her silent.

What she felt already was enough to give this situation an edge of fear. Their odds of getting out of this free and together were so slim that she couldn't speak those words.

He grasped her wrists and raised them to his lips, pressed a kiss to one, and though she tried to jerk away, he pressed a kiss to the other as well.

"No," she whispered. "They're my failure."

Her failure to extricate herself from the mess she'd made so many years ago, her failure to live the life she was meant to. At least, that's how she'd always thought of them.

"And they're my savior," he said against her wrist. "You came to Otherworld for me. You wanted to escape, but you killed yourself and came back, thinking you'd be stuck there for good. How can I not love these scars for what they did for me?"

264

"Honestly, I didn't even think about it. I just had to get to you. And you're the one who saved me from godhood. Thanks for shooting me with my own arrow." She smiled wryly.

"It was my place all along. Even if it wasn't, I'd have done it for you. I could never let you suffer like that."

She kissed him, delighting when he reached out and pulled her toward him.

"Will Esha come back soon?" he asked against her lips.

"No. She said something about a vacation with her sister. I think she's gone."

"Good." He stood and swept her up into his arms.

"Wait, your injuries."

"I've healed. Enough."

She still had so many questions and so much worry about how they would keep the gods from hunting them, but they flew from her mind when Cam started for the bedroom.

Tomorrow. They would deal with them tomorrow.

He strode into the dimly lit room and set her on her feet near the bed. With a gentle hand, he lifted her chin so that she could meet his eyes.

"This means something, Ana. This is about what's between us. No more lying to ourselves about what's really happening. No matter what tomorrow brings, we'll have this."

Ana's heart leapt and she nodded. Everything they'd had until now had been hard and fast and full of fear, running from what could be and lying to each other about what there really was. The mess of their past and the fear of their future had put them on either side of a chasm.

She didn't want to run anymore, no matter how terrifying this was. Whatever came tomorrow, she'd have tonight.

He smiled and lifted her up, laid her upon the bed. He was so strong she felt weightless in his arms. She reached up to welcome him down to her, and he sank between her thighs with a groan.

His mouth found hers, lips seeking and tongue sinking deep. She moaned and opened for him, wanting to be as close as possible to this man who'd come to mean so much to her.

"I want you naked," he muttered, and stripped off her clothes until she lay in nothing but cotton underwear.

Every time before this, they'd removed just enough clothes to finish the job. Now she wanted to see all of him. The glorious hard muscles and lean strength. She tugged at his shirt, her hands trembling, and he obliged, yanking it over his head. In seconds, the rest followed.

She grabbed for his shoulders, but he slipped lower, kissing his way down her body, first to the scars on her wrists that he so loved, then to her thighs, which tightened when he neared their juncture. He nuzzled the fabric and she quivered.

"You are what I want," he murmured.

She shuddered and parted her thighs.

"That's it," he growled, and pulled aside her underwear to stroke his tongue along her pussy.

She jumped, keening low in her throat, and then reached for him. Her hands sank into his soft hair. "I want to see your face."

He relented, but not before he yanked her panties down and threw them across the room. She suddenly felt vulnerable, completely naked before him with her heart opening in a terrifying way.

He loomed above her, huge and hard with his warrior's face tight with concentration. Pale moonlight shone through the windows, highlighting the harsh planes of his face. He looked as if he never wanted to look away from her. The openness of this moment, of him staring down at her, was more intimate than anything they'd done before. Saying that this was *something*. Suddenly she was aware of how exposed she was.

She'd laid everything on the line for him. Her life. Her future. As he'd done for her.

She pulled him down for a kiss, sighing as his lips, the only soft part of him, pressed against hers. The rest of him was hot and hard, all smooth skin and firm muscle.

His big hand gripped her hip and she shifted, parting her legs so that his cock fit tightly to her pussy. She moaned, arching beneath him.

"I want you," she begged. She wanted to forget about what was coming and their terrible odds of success.

She felt his fist against the insides of her thighs as he gripped his shaft, and her muscles tightened in anticipation. She gasped as he pressed inside her, spreading her thighs to take more of him. He sank into her, hot and hard and oh so right. The feel of him blasted her defenses.

He shuddered on top of her, then met her gaze with his as he began to thrust. Chills broke out along her skin, from the pleasure and the realization that this was real and so were they. Together. Whatever happened tomorrow, they had tonight.

She cried out when his thrusts picked up momentum, dragging her along with him toward a finish line she was desperate to reach. The flutters of an orgasm started low in her belly. Desperate craving followed.

Cam fucked her like he might never have a chance to again. As his hips lost their grace, pleasure crashed over her, sucking all conscious thought from her mind.

CHAPTER THIRTY-ONE

Cam woke for the first time in centuries with a woman in his arms. His woman. He tugged her close and looked down at her. A chasm of fear opened within his chest.

She was mortal. There was no way to turn her immortal.

He shook his head to make the thought disappear. There was too much riding on today to be pulled under by such thoughts. Instead, he pressed a kiss to her forehead and rose to shower.

When he got out, he tugged on jeans and walked into the kitchen. Ana leaned against the counter, looking like the best thing he'd ever seen, swamped in his shirt and smiling. She handed him a cup of coffee.

"Thanks," he said.

"Tell me you've got a way out of this mess," she said.

"I do. But first, how did you get me out of those chains?" He'd been thinking about it in the shower. There was no way she could have broken through Gofannon's shackles.

"It was the strangest thing." Her brow furrowed. "I was running toward the tor, and suddenly a black falcon flew down and joined me. It had black eyes, a black beak. It didn't look like a real bird. When it pecked at your chains, they broke."

Cam frowned. "That sounds familiar. But I don't know why. There are no black falcons in Otherworld."

"I know. It's crazy. It flew off after it broke your chains, like its job was done."

"Damn. We could use help like that with what's coming. As it is, I think we should go to the University Council. And I'd like to call Esha back from her vacation."

"Good," she said. "I don't like the idea of the gods finding me, nor do I want you ending up on the run again. Or worse, chained to that tor."

"That part of my life is over. No more running." The idea felt as foreign to him now as emotion once had.

"I'll call Esha now. She can aetherwalk and be here within minutes."

"Could she pick up someone else?" They'd need all the help they could get, and Harp was good in a battle.

"Sure, I suppose. As long as you're willing to give her some of your power to refuel. A long trip really takes it out of her, and she'll need all the power she can get if this is going to be a fight."

"It's going to be a fight. She can refuel off me." He wouldn't like it, but it was the least he could do if the soulceress was helping him. He'd go get his phone and call Harp— "Shit. We need a phone. My charger was in my bag at Logan's. Does Esha have a landline?"

"Yes." Her brow furrowed. "By the way, do you know which god Logan was?"

"Is. Logan is the god Loki."

Ana's jaw dropped. "You're joking. He's one of the most famous in the world. He's been hiding and no one recognizes him?"

"He's a shapeshifter. I haven't heard from him in nearly a thousand years, not since he was Loki, but I'd guess he's been holding that form as Logan all this time, avoiding discovery for whatever reason. Whatever he's working toward, it's probably big. He was never subtle."

"But you could see through it back at his rental place."

"Yeah. Because of our blood vow, his illusions don't work on me. I can see him. But I also can't harm him, by word or by deed. And neither can you."

"I wouldn't."

"I know, else I wouldn't have been able to tell you his identity. It's a clever vow."

Ana showed him to an old phone on the wall near the refrigerator. He called Harp first and determined that his friend could come—along with the fact that he had located the origin of the *Rosa McManus* sample.

"Esha will meet us in the historian Lea's office in twenty minutes. With her sister Aurora," Ana said when she hung up the phone.

"Excellent." Two soulceresses would be better than one.

They knocked on the door to Lea's office twenty minutes later.

"Come in!" The voice echoed through the door and Cam and Ana stepped into a very Dumbledorian office. Cavernous and filled with bookshelves and statuary and furniture, it looked well lived in.

"Andrasta. Camulos." A translucent female gestured them inside.

Before entering the office, Ana had told him that Lea insisted that she absolutely was not a ghost. But he had no idea what she was.

She didn't come close enough to shake their hands. He wasn't even sure if she could touch others.

"Thanks for meeting here." Lea smiled warmly. She led them through her huge office to the group sitting around a table in the corner. Bookshelves towered around them, giving the illusion of a separate meeting room.

"Thank you for coming," Cam said as he and Ana sat at the head of the large rectangular table. He stiffened when he caught sight of the blond woman watching him from the other end.

Aerten. Celtic goddess of fate, and the one who'd been at Blackmoor when he'd been chained to the tor. She'd watched curiously then, a strange expression on her face, as she did now. Her head bobbed in acknowledgment, and his shoulders relaxed infinitesimally.

She'd hear him out, at least. Because she presided over the Mythean Guard, she left Otherworld more often than the other gods. The exposure might make her more inclined to believe him.

"We couldn't gather very many council members on such short notice," Lea said as she took a seat.

In its entirety, the university council was made up of nearly twenty university department heads. Together, they made the decisions that not only ran the university, but kept the peace between the major afterworlds created by European beliefs. A task that might have once been handled by war was now handled by knowledge and diplomacy. Other regions, such as Asia, had their own governing bodies.

He recognized some of the individuals at the table, though Esha and her sister had not yet appeared. A pink-haired witch named Cora introduced herself. Next to Aerten sat Warren, her right-hand man and the one in charge of day-to-day operations for the Mythean Guard because Aerten was forced to stay in Otherworld most of the time.

A dark-haired woman smiled and said, "Hi, I'm Vivienne. I'm a Sila Jinn. I'm new to the university, but I work with Diana. When she mentioned this, I thought I'd come along."

"Thanks, I appreciate it," Cam said, and looked at the woman she'd gestured to.

"I'm Diana," the red-haired woman said. "I'm the reincarnate of Boudica."

Cam's brows shot up. Fuck, he really needed to keep in touch with the university a bit better. The Celts' most famous warrior had been reincarnated and he hadn't realized?

She noticed his shock and said, "It's a recent development. But Ana was Boudica's patron goddess, and I appreciate everything that she did for me in that life and in this one. I want to help however I can."

Cam nodded his thanks, then glanced at Ana to see her smiling at Diana.

"It was nothing," Ana said. "When you were Boudica, you were my first big case. And you were, and are, a total badass. I'm glad you won your immortality."

Diana looked up at the man seated next to her and smiled. "Me too."

The man next to her was a Mythean Guardian that Cam recognized as Cadan Trinovante. He was a Celt born to a town that had worshiped Cam before his departure from Otherworld. They'd met once, long ago. Cadan nodded at him.

Fiona, the Acquirer, sat next to Cadan. She smiled at him and nodded her head.

"Thanks for coming," he said to her.

"Not a problem. I'm certainly not a representative of my department." She laughed. "They'd never let me be that. But I feel invested in your success. And I'm not bad in a fight."

He nodded gratefully.

"Okay," Lea said after a moment. "I think that Esha and—"

Two women appeared at the entrance of the room, along with Harp, who'd hitched a ride with Esha via aetherwalking. Harp nodded at him and Cam nodded back.

"And here they are," Lea said. "Good timing. That's everyone."

The women approached the table with equal swaggers. Harp followed.

"So the party started without us," Esha said. Her familiar glared at them with citrine eyes.

"Somebody invited the rabble." Aurora knocked her chin toward the pink-haired witch. Her sleek midnight cat hissed.

"Oh, shut up," Cora said.

"Make me," Aurora shot back.

"I did, once." Cora smirked.

"Please, you needed a whole coven to help you out. You're nothing without your—"

Esha elbowed her sister in the gut and her mouth snapped shut.

"Sorry we're late," Esha said, and they took a seat, Aurora still glowering at the pink-haired witch.

Great—his team was already fighting. Still, he was lucky to have them.

"Right. Thank you all for coming," he said. He introduced himself, Ana, and Harp. "We need your help, if you're willing to give it."

There were murmurs of assent from around the table.

"Hear me out first." He looked specifically at Aerten, the only other Celtic god in the room. "Ana and I think we've discovered why the gods of the Celtic afterworld feel no emotion."

Aerten's face showed no surprise, and he had to wonder at that. As goddess of fate, perhaps she knew more than he'd thought?

"Here's the situation," he said, and told them about the spell that Druantia had cast over all of them, including the part about Ana, as she was the entire reason that he'd ever remembered his past in the first place.

"I know nothing of this spell," Aerten said, frowning.

"You were bewitched with the rest of us. How could you?" he asked.

"But I am the goddess of fate. If there was a spell that needed to be broken in the future, especially one of such importance to our people, I'd have known about it."

"Perhaps. But Druantia's magic took my memories as well." Cam watched her closely, still on edge that she might flee the table for Otherworld and bring the rest of the gods down upon his head.

Instead, she spoke. "You think you have a way to break this spell?"

He nodded. "Druantia was mortal. *Was.* She's obviously not anymore. She's getting the power that fuels her immortality from somewhere, and I think it's from the forest that grew up from the blood and bones of the Dryads."

He felt Ana's hand clasp his under the table. He squeezed, grateful for the connection. "I believe that the power of our emotions, part of our very souls, is trapped in those trees. Along with the souls of the sacrifices. It's a macabre place, a dark forest that's protected by dark beings. But if we can cut down all the trees, I think that we can break the spell."

There were murmurs throughout the room.

"So, like, lumberjacks?" Aurora asked. She was even more irreverent than her sister, but he chuffed a laugh, grateful for the bit of levity.

"Essentially," he said. "But the forest will be protected by creatures and magics that will want to keep us from chopping it down. With all of us, and all our powers, I think that we could manage."

"And you say this will restore emotion to the gods of Otherworld." Aerten's voice sounded strange. Almost hopeful.

"That's what I think."

"We can't tell the other gods," Aerten said. "They wouldn't believe you. Coming to earth to oversee the Mythean Guard has made me question our ways. But for them, who see no reason to come here, they're mired in their superstition."

"I believe that's part of the spell," Cam said. "Druantia took our emotion as vengeance, but ensuring that we stayed in Otherworld gave her incredible power as the only intermediary between the gods and mortals. They're committed to the status quo because they've been enchanted to be. So, I agree with you. We don't tell them."

"Excellent," Esha said. "I say we get down to planning who does what. We'll see who else we can get from other departments. When will we do this?"

"I think we should leave for the forest tomorrow, at first light," Ana said. "Druantia already knows that something is up because she has most likely found my body in her pantry. She'll know what I did to my mortal body to send my soul to Otherworld and Cam. We want to get there before she can interfere."

"How do you have a physical, earthly body if you killed yours in Druantia's pantry?" Aerten asked.

"I don't know. There's something strange about that."

Lea frowned. "I can't explain it, either. But we need to move on with this. While you all plan, I'll look through my books, see if there's anything about the forest that can help."

The group set about sketching out a basic plan for the next day, though the details of what they would actually face were still a mystery. They finished by determining a meeting place for the next morning.

"Thank you for your help, everyone," Ana said. "We'll see you tomorrow. Oh, but before you go, does anyone know of a black falcon that can break magical chains with its beak? It helped us in Otherworld, but I don't think that kind of bird exists there. Or on earth, for that matter."

Everyone shook their heads.

Damn. "Right, then. Thanks for the help. Really."

Everyone nodded, said their goodbyes, and filtered out of the room. They met Harp in the hall.

"Thanks for coming." Cam clapped his friend on the shoulder. He introduced Ana, and the three of them walked down the hall as a group, passing beneath the watchful eyes of the portraits that lined the walls.

"Wouldn't miss it," Harp said. "What do you think our odds are tomorrow?"

Cam met Ana's gaze. It held the darkness he felt in his own heart. He finally had something to really live for, but would they survive? "I've no idea."

"That's what I figured. But I've narrowed down the location of the *Rosa McManus* to a thirty-square-mile area. So you've got a real reason to succeed tomorrow."

Cam felt a grin stretch across his face. He hadn't thought he'd smile until this was all over. "Excellent. Good work."

"Not a problem."

They pushed through the huge oak doors and stepped into the waning sunlight.

"I'm over at guest quarters," Harp said. "I'm going to head there now. There's a nymph who looked lonely earlier."

"Have a good time. And Harp?"

His friend turned back to him and met his eyes.

"Thanks again."

Harp nodded and spun, strolling off across the lawn with a lightness to his step that Cam could hardly remember having himself. He turned to Ana, pulled her toward him, and pressed a kiss to her lips.

When he pulled away, she looked up at him and asked, "Do you think we'll get out of this?"

"I don't know. But I know I've got a damn good reason to try. We've got a hell of a lot of things standing in our way, but if we make it out of this, I want a life with you."

CHAPTER THIRTY-TWO

Ana looked out over the valley and gripped her borrowed bow so tightly that her knuckles burned. It felt wrong. Terribly, horribly wrong compared to the bow that she'd made herself and used for two thousand years. She'd imbued it with magic to withstand the test of time so that she'd never have to be without it. But it was trapped at Druantia's house, and she was going into the biggest battle of her life with a borrowed bow.

She stood on the summit of a windswept mountain in the Highlands and gazed upon the dark forest below. Today would be either all victory or all defeat. There was no middle ground. She was likely mortal enough that she could die and end up in Otherworld. If they failed to break the spell, Cam would be found and chained to the tor again. Either way, they would be separated.

"The rest will be here soon," Cam said.

His hand enveloped hers, hard and strong, a bulwark against her fears. She looked up at him, so tall and fierce, with his bow strapped to his back and his brow furrowed as he looked at the forest. He looked so natural with a bow in his hand again. From the way he'd looked at the bow when he'd picked it up, he'd clearly missed it tremendously over the past millennia. A hard lump formed in her throat and she squeezed his hand.

She was amazed by what he'd come to mean to her in these short days. Their history was long and fraught, but they'd come so far since she'd cornered him in that jungle bar. And now they had only minutes before the rest of their party arrived and their lives were changed forever.

He jerked on her hand and pulled her until she was pressed against him. His eyes met hers and set her heart to galloping. This was more than just attraction. More than just affection.

"I'll make this right, Ana," he said. "I'll fix what Druantia has broken. Because I want to, because it's my responsibility for pissing her the hell off with my pride, but mostly because I want to be with you. And that can't happen until we break the spell so the other gods change their minds about the rules of Otherworld."

Her heart pounded harder, as if to make up for the oxygen that her lungs were failing to absorb. He wanted to be with her. And he wanted her to say the same. Fates, the things she felt for him. She swore it could be love, yet a part of her couldn't make that leap. Not yet. Not even in the face of all that stood before them.

She pulled his head down to hers and kissed him. With everything she had in her, she tried to banish her fears of failure and what it would mean for them. She broke away and said, "We can do this, Cam."

He nodded, determination in the set of his brow, then turned to face the people who had just arrived. Esha and Aurora held onto Warren and Diana respectively. The two soulceresses nodded, then disappeared again to retrieve more of their party. Though all gods could aetherwalk, it was a talent not all Mytheans possessed. Those who did could bring one or two people at a time along with them.

Before long, Esha and Aurora had brought Cadan and Vivienne. Esha returned for Fiona, the Acquirer, who grinned at her. Cora arrived with two other witches shortly after. Aerten was the last to arrive, directly from Otherworld. She tilted her head toward Cam, her expression a combination of wariness and hope. Still waters ran deep with that one.

When the full thirteen of their party all stood on the crest of the hill, Cam addressed them. "Thank you for coming. This is too great a task for Ana and me alone. If Lea is correct about the extent of protective magics in this place, it will be dangerous even with our greater numbers."

"She's correct," Esha murmured. "Never wrong, that one."

Cam nodded, a grim set to his mouth. "For that reason, if anyone should wish to depart at any time, you're free to go."

Aurora barked a laugh. "Not ditching you now, mate."

"Then we go," Cam said.

They set off down the hill, their plan from the previous night in place. The oaks loomed huge as they approached the wood, thick trunks supporting limbs that reached for the sky. Too large and too numerous to ever chop down with axes before the creatures of the wood killed them all. No, magic had created this place and magic would destroy it.

"To the center, witches," Cam commanded.

As a group, they moved to the center of the pack, surrounded on all sides by the warriors armed with bow and sword. Guns wouldn't fire in a place so thick with ancient magic, else they'd have used them. But tools of the present couldn't be used in the past, and this place was imbued with a magic so thick that it hadn't changed since the day it had been made.

They neared the wood and the shadows of the trees reached out toward them, carrying unnaturally cold air. Humans would never approach this place. Nor would Mytheans, not if they didn't have to. As it was, their band of warriors suppressed a collective shudder as they entered the shadows of the trees.

Esha and Aurora moved away from the group, striking ahead on their own. Their black familiars stuck close to their sides. If they'd stayed with the group, they'd have sapped their fellow warriors' strength and speed and magic. By forging ahead, they could cut a path through the monsters, weakening them for an easier kill, which both were handy at delivering.

"Dark in here," Ana muttered to Cam. It was as if night were only minutes away, and too cold and too silent.

They led the pack, with Aerten, Cadan, Diana, Warren, Vivienne, Harp, and Fiona surrounding the witches. Dead leaves and twigs crunched beneath their boots. A heavy tension shrouded them.

"There's nothing here," Vivienne whispered.

She was right, and it made the hair on Ana's arms stand on end. There should be monsters of the wood, creatures enchanted by Druantia into protecting the oaks. Instead, there was silence.

As if they were waiting to strike.

Perhaps Esha and Aurora would be able to repel them all until the group reached the center of the wood, where the witches would cast a spell to make the oaks break at their trunks.

Eerie whispers tickled Ana's ears as they crept deeper into the forest. Silence had turned to the rustle of oak leaves. It almost sounded like words. Were the souls of the Dryads speaking to her?

She strained to hear, but instead of whispers, a sudden shriek echoed through the forest. She slapped her free hand to her ear. Her fellow warriors stiffened, turned in tandem toward the shriek that came from the west. Another joined it, and another, growing ever closer. Ana clutched her bow and nocked an arrow.

"Caoineag," Cam said.

Highland banshees, foreseers of doom. To hear their cry meant death or tragedy for the listener.

Ana's gaze scanned the forest, looking for whatever monsters or attack the banshees prophesied. But instead, three horrifying women swept down from the trees to the west, wingless but possessing command of the air. They were gaunt, skeletal things with stringy hair and tattered dresses. The magic here was darker than even she'd expected, for the Caoineag were only meant to be heard, not seen. To prophesy doom, not deliver it.

Yet Druantia had given them form and rage and set them upon anyone who dared enter the forest. Ana aimed her arrow at the nearest Caoineag. Shot. Watched in horror as the banshee kept flying toward them, arrow protruding grotesquely from its chest. She reached for her quiver to nock another arrow, but a tree root snapped up from the ground and tripped her.

She crashed to the ground. In her peripheral vision, she saw Cam's arrows fly at the Caoineag. Ana heaved herself to her feet and reached for another arrow, but before she could shoot the banshee that was nearly upon them, Diana leapt from her place in their group and charged the Caoineag, swinging her sword at its neck. Its head tumbled to the ground.

Only then did the wailing horror disappear in a wisp of smoke. Cadan and Warren took their cue, charging after the other two and swinging their swords to decapitate. The banshees fought back, sentient enough to recognize their sister's fate and fight it. A great bloody gash appeared on Warren's chest from a swipe of its claws, but after a struggle, his sword hit home and she turned to a wisp of smoke. Cadan's Caoineag followed. Vivienne and Fiona worked as a team, doubling up on one banshee at a time.

Silence fell, but for the briefest second. The banshee's howl ripped again through the trees. But instead of a banshee swooping out of the west, a horde of short, grotesquely muscled men poured from behind the oaks on all sides. They had long arms and wild red hair. Ana fired in tandem with Cam, slaying two of them. But two more poured out from behind the oaks in their place.

"They're Pechs," Cadan yelled. "They'll crush you if they get their arms around you."

Fireballs flew through the air, thrown by Esha and her sister, while bursts of colored magic shot from the witches' hands, throwing the Caoineag off-track. Swinging swords took heads while Ana and Cam fired arrows through hearts.

But the Caoineag never stopped wailing and the Pechs never stopped coming, as if there was an endless supply of them.

"We need to keep moving. We're close to the center," Ana yelled. She could feel it, a tug like that which she'd experienced in Otherworld when she felt compelled to seek out her family. If they could just keep moving through the Pechs, fighting them off as they traveled. "I think—"

A root reached up and tripped her again, catching her ankle so that she fell hard onto her hands and knees.

She cursed and pushed herself to her feet. The trees tripped only her, the roots snapping out of the dirt to reach for her legs. She kept a wary eye on them as their group made slow progress to the center of the forest, toward whatever was pulling at her. Were there fewer Pechs? Or perhaps it was her mind, tired and terrified and hoping for an end.

And then she saw it. A great oak, split down the middle by lightning. One side dead, the other alive. *That* was what had been calling to her. That tree, specifically.

"Here!" she yelled, and the group ceased their slow forward movement, still fighting the Pechs. Though she wanted to go to the tree, to explore it, she and the other warriors would have to up their game now that the witches would be casting a spell to destroy the forest instead of defending against the Pechs.

The witches formed a small cluster in the middle of the group, joined hands, and faced outward toward the forest. As they chanted their spell, Ana and the rest began to shoot and stab and throw fire at the Pechs, barely holding them off. The Caoineag continued to wail, louder as the branches of the oaks began to tremble.

A symptom of the spell? Ana had no idea, and was too overcome by Pechs to dwell. She'd shot so many already, and they still came in such great numbers that there would be no end to them. Not until the spell was broken.

"It's not working!" cried one of the witches. "The spell won't hold!"

Shit. They had no backup if the spell didn't work. Cam had been right; the forest was far too vast and the defenses too strong for them to cut the trees down by hand. Magic was the only way, but it wasn't working.

Ana had no idea what to do, and the Pechs were driving her farther from the group. She'd been cut off when four had charged her. There was a hole in their defenses now, and she was surrounded on all sides by advancing Pechs. They stalked toward her, arms outstretched and ready to crush her.

One was only feet away, reaching out with its long arms, when a hard arm jerked her about the middle and lifted her into the air. High, higher. She realized that it wasn't an arm at all, but the limb of the great half-dead oak tree. She thrashed and kicked, desperate to break its grip.

When it tucked her against its trunk as if it were holding a doll, the eeriest sense of euphoria and calm overcame her. It filled her every vein and every cell, a warmth and knowledge of incomparable strength.

I am this tree or this tree is me. She gasped and seized as memories filled her mind. Memories of the night with Cam in this forest, memories of a life before the one she knew. As a Dryad. Part of her soul was trapped in this tree. It was protecting her from the Pechs who clamored below. And it was probably the reason she had a second chance at a physical body. She was still attached to the earth through this tree.

"Free us," it whispered in her mind. It filled her with a rage and desire to chop down every tree. For she wasn't just fighting on behalf of Cam and the gods, but for her brothers and sisters whose souls were trapped in these oaks. *The spell must work.*

She whipped her head around to find the witches, but their faces were just as desperate and strained as before. The spell still wasn't working. Cold terror spread across her skin.

What she caught sight of next made her stomach drop to the roots of the tree. Druantia was striding through the forest, visible only to Ana from her vantage point in the oak. An unholy light surrounded her as her features twisted with rage.

"Cam!" Ana screamed, pointing toward Druantia.

But he couldn't hear her. No one could hear her over the din of the Caoineag that still swooped around the trees, reaching for her friends with outstretched claws.

Cam continued to hold off the Pechs, desperately trying to buy time for the witches. His back was to Druantia. She would sneak up on him. Ana clawed at the tree limb and screamed his name. No matter how wonderful it felt to be so close to the other half of her soul, she had to get to Cam.

But the tree wouldn't budge, as if it knew something great and terrible were about to occur, and her cries were lost in the din. She strained to see Druantia. The priestess neared the group, only a dozen feet from Cam, and raised her hands as if to perform a spell. Just as she opened her mouth, Logan swept out from a tree behind her and snatched her up by the waist.

Ana struggled harder to escape the oak, kicking and punching and screaming, but never taking her eyes off Logan and Druantia.

Logan carried Druantia's thrashing form toward Cam and yelled, "Hey, Camulos. I don't know what the hell is going on here, but I think you want this one."

Cam turned and cursed. Druantia shrieked and waved her arms. Tree limbs followed her motion, whipping out to knock Cam off his feet. Another swooped and yanked Logan off his. Druantia surged free and waved her arms, sending the oak limbs into a whipping frenzy that targeted Ana's friends.

"Is that the witch who enchanted this forest?" Cora yelled as she ducked beneath a branch.

"Yes!" shouted Cam as he rose to his feet and sighted an arrow at Druantia. He shot, but she didn't fall, just laughed maniacally with the arrow protruding from her chest.

"You can't kill me," she screamed, a wild, feral look in her eyes. "These trees feed me from the power and emotion trapped inside them. *Your* power!"

Cora stopped chanting to yell, "Make her bleed! Into the ground! Her blood is needed to seal our spell."

Of course. Blood sacrifice had been needed to create these trees. It was required to end them as well. Druantia screeched and waved her arms once again, directing a hail of flailing tree limbs that struck Cadan and Esha off their feet, as well as several Pechs. It was chaos below, yet Ana was trapped up here.

"Please," she whispered to the tree. "Please release me. I'll free you. I'll free you all."

She felt the tree's resistance and begged again. It shuddered and dropped her, and she had a feeling that it was the strength of her desire to be freed that had done the trick, not her plea. With hard ground finally beneath her feet, she yanked out three arrows and cut down the three Pechs closing in on her. She ran toward Cam, who fought off whipping tree limbs as he tried to get another clean shot on Druantia.

"Cam!" Ana screamed at him. "Use your sword. I'll cover you."

He had to be the one to take Druantia's blood, and an arrow would never be enough. Cam plucked the short sword from the scabbard at his waist. Ana ran up behind him, shooting at the tree limbs to make them snap back temporarily. Cam advanced on Druantia, who still waved her arms frantically to direct the trees. But with Ana as cover, the tree limbs couldn't land a decent hit.

When Cam neared Druantia, a tree limb swiped him across the back, opening a great wound that poured blood. Druantia laughed and sent another limb at him. He dodged, but not before it sliced his arm.

Finally, he reached her. Cam kicked Druantia to the ground and stabbed her through the chest so that the sword pinned her to the ground, her blood soaking into the dirt. She shrieked and writhed, but wouldn't die.

But the tree limbs stopped fighting, and Ana felt their relief like a physical thing. The witches chanted louder, faster, as Druantia's blood soaked into the earth. The Pechs stopped fighting, but the tree trunks didn't snap as they were supposed to.

Free us. Ana heard it again and turned toward her tree. The magic just needed a boost.

She ran toward her tree, pulling her borrowed short sword from the scabbard at her hip. She took a great swing at the trunk as if the sword were an ax. It sank an inch into the wood, and Druantia howled louder. But a reverberation flowed through the forest, stretching outward toward all the trees.

The Caoineag finally stopped screeching, and with the silence, the witches' chants carried through the forest. Suddenly, the sound of cracking wood punctuated the chants. The trees began to topple.

Ana darted toward the witches and Cam to get out of the way of falling trees, hoping that they wouldn't topple toward the witches creating the magic. It worked. The warriors stood in a cluster as the great oaks crashed to the ground around them.

Ana looked down at Druantia. She lay still now, with hatred gleaming in her eyes. When she caught sight of Ana looking at her, she gritted her teeth and swung her arm in an arc. So quick that she barely saw it coming, the branch of an oak swung toward her, whipping around until it pierced her through the chest.

Incredible pain tore through her as the limb yanked free of her flesh, leaving a great gaping hole. Through the pain, Ana swore she could feel the oak's regret. But all she could see was the glee on Druantia's face.

Ana fell to her knees, then toppled backward, lying so that in some cruel twist of fate, she could watch Druantia's face as her blood seeped into the earth in an ugly parallel of what had happened here so many years ago.

The distant sound of Cam's roar of pain echoed through her as he fell to his knees beside her.

Mortal. She truly was mortal enough to die. Trees crashed around her, the ground trembling with the impact.

She felt Cam's shaking hand on her cheek, tilting her face toward him. "Ana, Ana, Ana."

She tried to talk, but could only cough.

"Damn it, Ana, I love you." Pain laced every syllable.

He loved her?

"You're so close to having a life on earth. Fight this," he said, grief for her loss clear on his face.

Fight it? There was no way to fight a giant hole in her chest. She would die.

Though her vision was going black, she caught sight of her tree looming behind Cam. So close to the rest of her soul and to Cam, yet so far away.

Her tree stood strong, as if waiting for its compatriots. Finally, as Ana's vision became nothing but a blur, the trunk began to crack and lean. The oak crashed to the ground, and as it did, a *whoosh* of something glorious filled Ana's being. It filled in the hole created by Druantia's last strike until the pain was but a memory. It continued to flow through her, filling holes she hadn't known existed.

Her soul. Half of it had been trapped in that tree, and she'd never had any idea she'd been missing it. But everything was so much brighter now, so much fuller. And she was healing. As a Mythean would. No longer mortal.

She gasped, the first decent breath she'd taken since her wound, and opened her eyes to see Druantia's withered form. She was halfway to mummification. Within seconds, she was nothing but dust, as if she'd aged 2,600 years in a minute. Behind her, Ana could see the wisps of souls flying from the downed trees, up into the air and away toward freedom and peace.

"Cam." The words were rough in her throat.

"Ana, you're healing." His voice was awed.

She turned her head to look at Cam. His cheeks were wet.

She reached a shaking arm up to touch his face. She could see him now. Could really, truly see him. In the light of understanding and their past. All the hesitation that she'd felt over her feelings hadn't been about him. They'd been about her. About her being unable to feel so much because she lacked half her soul. But, oh, how that had changed.

With the last oak fallen, the witches ceased chanting and silence fell upon the forest.

"Cam, I—"

His voice rode over hers, thick with concern. "We need to get you back to the university."

"We all need to get back," Cora said. "The worst is over, but the forest must settle. It's dangerous here."

Cam nodded and swept her up. Ana realized that the time for speaking her heart had passed.

CHAPTER THIRTY-THREE

Cam laid Ana upon the bed in the infirmary at the university, worry wrapped around his heart like barbed wire.

"I'm fine." She coughed, a bit of blood marring her lips.

"You're not." He pushed gently on her shoulders when she tried to sit.

Behind him, Esha demanded that a nurse help her sister, while Cora helped a wounded Vivienne to the bed in front of her. Bright light shone through the windows, illuminating the long room studded with narrow beds placed at regular intervals.

Healers rushed to the beds, inspecting Vivienne's crushed torso, a testament to the strength of the Pechs.

He felt a pair of hands brush at the wound in his back and reached around, pushing them away. "Help Ana first."

"Really, I'm fine," Ana said. "I think the other Dryad souls helped me heal. I'm a bit tender is all. See to Cam's back. And Aurora's arm."

"We'll be able to save it," the healer said from two beds down. He was a huge man, burly with great ham-like hands.

Yet he was delicate and gentle when he touched Aurora. "It's not entirely severed."

"She'll be all right, won't she?" Worry was thick in Esha's tone as she hovered at her sister's bedside. The Chairman yowled his support.

"Shu- up," Aurora slurred. "F-fine."

"You're not fucking fine and you know it," Esha shot back.

"She'll be fine," the healer said.

The rest of their party sat on or leaned against hospital beds that were lined up along the wall of the white-on-white room. A third healer tended to the deep gash on Cadan's chest while Diana looked on worriedly. Fiona held an icepack to her bruised face. Aerten stood off to the side, shell shocked, and Cam wondered vaguely if she felt as overwhelmed as he did. Loki hadn't returned with them, but Cam wasn't surprised. He must have followed Druantia to the clearing, though why he'd helped them was still a mystery.

Cam wanted like hell to get Ana alone, but he needed her checked by a healer first. A second later, a small, gray-haired woman bustled over from where she'd been tending Cadan to check on Ana. She looked like she should be baking cookies for her grandchildren, but in Cam's estimation, age meant experience, and the more of it, the better.

"I really am fine," Ana said as the woman inspected her abdomen. The skin was unblemished and smooth.

"Aye, you are. Right as rain." The healer looked up at Cam. "You can let her up now, son. And you can let me tend to that arm and back."

Cam scowled, then realized that his blood was dripping to the floor and he was feeling vaguely lightheaded.

"Just a few butterfly bandages. I'll heal up soon." Sooner, now that he was a god again.

"All you need is a bit of a spell, and you'll be all right," the healer said from behind him.

A vague warmth spread across his back where she touched him. He realized he wasn't in the jungle anymore, treating himself haphazardly with whatever he had on hand. The university had a top-notch healing staff.

"Good as new." The grandmotherly healer came around to his front. "Most of you can go. Aurora and Vivienne will need to stay. It'll be a while before they're healed."

"But they'll be fine, right?" Ana asked as she sat up.

She was the most beautiful, most precious thing that Cam had ever seen, and his heart expanded just to look at her.

"Aye, they'll all be fine. It'll just take some time to heal those bones and reattach that arm."

"Thank you, everyone," Cam said, gratitude thick in his throat.

"Well, then. I suppose I can ask if it worked?" Warren asked.

"Yes." Cam's voice was a little strained. Ana reached for his hand, and he squeezed hers.

Aerten rubbed her temple, then shook her head. "Yes. I... yes. It worked. I need to go. To see someone. I—I'll see you all later. And—thank you."

With a last blind glance around the room, Aerten disappeared. Otherworld would be in a frenzy right now, but Cam didn't care. The rest of the group was filtering out of the room, limping or walking tall. But all would be healed soon, thank fate.

"Let's get out of here." He helped Ana stand.

"Definitely." She nodded and grinned.

He wrapped an arm around her and aetherwalked them to the Amazon. Damn, it was good to be able to do that again.

The sun was setting over the canopy when they arrived on the deck of the *Clara G.*, and long shadows were being cast across the dark river. The boat was still tied off to the dock space he'd rented before they'd left. There were vessels on all sides of them, but none were inhabited at the moment. The familiar howling and rustling of the jungle animals was a welcome taste of home, and something in Cam's chest loosened. Being home, with Ana, who he'd never expected to see again, much less fall in love with, felt perfect.

Ana looked around at the boat and the jungle. "We're back on your boat?"

"It's not the finest accommodations, but it's home." He grinned.

"Good point. I like your home. And it's not like I have one of my own now that I'm no longer a god. I'm starting from square one."

He pulled her to him and hugged her close, reveling in the feel of her whole and healthy. "You have one now."

"Do I?"

"Didn't you hear me in the forest? I love you, Ana. I probably have for a long time, but I couldn't feel it. But I feel everything now, and most of that is love for you."

She wriggled so that she could meet his eyes. "Really?"

"Of course." He pressed a hard kiss to her lips. "I've been hiding from my fate. Hanging out alone in the jungle, ignoring life. You have such a passion for it that you made me realize I'd lost mine. Of course I love you."

"Good. Because likewise. One of those trees in the forest was me. Or at least half of me. Part of my soul was trapped within. When it finally fell and I was whole again, I realized I loved you."

His big hands cupped her face while he kissed her. He raised his head and asked, "You're full Mythean now? Immortal?"

"I think so. I was only part Mythean because half my soul was trapped. Now that I have it back, I'm a Dryad. I can hear the jungle trees like they're whispering. But it's been so long since I've been a Dryad that I'm not sure what it all means. I haven't spoken to another since my first incarnation. I don't even know how many are left after what Druantia did to us."

"We'll figure it out."

As she grinned, the last beam of sunlight of the day shined upon her face. Cam saw the potential of the future and all that lay before them, and for the first time in millennia, everything was perfect.

"We will," she said. "I'm just glad I'm alive. On earth. And you're alive. And the gods probably won't want to kill you now that the spell is broken and all the old rules are clearly shit."

"We'll have to see."

"It will be fine. I *know* it will. Aerten felt emotion back there in the infirmary. Give the gods a little while to adjust and then go back to visit. They'll see sense. Now we just need to figure out what the hell I'm going to do with the rest of my life."

"How do you feel about hunting cures here in the Amazon with me? We're close to finding *Rosa McManus*."

She grinned. "I do like plants. More than I'd ever realized. I could be good with that. And we'd live on the *Clara G*?"

"Yeah. You and me and the river."

She looked around appraisingly. "All right. But the cabin will need a bigger bed."

He pulled her to him and kissed her, the light of a thousand suns filling his chest with joy for the future. "Not a problem. Anything for the woman I love."

EPILOGUE

Amazon Jungle, Three weeks later

"Hey, Cam! I think I found it!" Ana called from her position in the jungle.

Cam turned from the foliage he was inspecting and trotted toward Ana. Her pale arm and shoulder were visible behind a tree about twenty feet distant. When he reached her, he slowed to a stop and crouched next to her. She was inspecting a creeping rose bush that crawled over a fallen tree limb.

Pale orange and lushly petaled, the rose looked exactly like the sample.

"You found it." A grin spread across his face.

"Not hard. I could almost hear it. It's crazy the skills I have as a Dryad."

He reached over and cupped the back of her head, pulling her toward him for a kiss. "Good work."

"Really, not hard. I did the same thing as before, but this time, it worked. I focused on the type of plant and asked it where it was. A really strong feeling led me to it since we were already close."

It made sense. This was the thirteenth spot they'd checked along the river this week. After Harp had given him the basic location, he'd set off with Ana to locate the rose. Every other time, they'd tied off to shore and searched the banks and the deeper jungle. This time, they'd actually tied off to the right spot.

"I'll go get the supplies."

"Good. I'll go look for more. I think this is the first rose species ever found in the jungle. I don't know how common it is."

He nodded, then jogged back to the boat to gather the sample bags, shovel, garbage bags, and buckets needed to safely transport the roses out of the jungle.

When he returned, he called out for Ana, who he presumed was deeper in the jungle searching for more roses. When she didn't respond, his heart kicked into a frantic rhythm.

"Ana!" He dropped the shovel and jogged through the forest, searching for her. Where the hell was she? The jungle was dangerous.

"Hey! I'm over here!"

He turned toward her voice and finally caught sight of her, stepping out from behind trees in the distance. He was at her side a second later, clutching her to him.

"Fuck, you had me worried," he said into her hair.

She squeezed him, then pulled back. "Don't be. Everything's fine now."

"I know. I guess it was just so close there for a while that I became accustomed to the idea of losing you. And it sucked."

"It's over. The gods are no longer pissed, Druantia is stuck in Otherworld, and I'm a Mythean. And I have my bow, thanks to you."

One of his first acts after they'd survived the forest had been to retrieve her bow from Druantia's creepy shop. With it, she could protect herself from anything. Remembering that when worry overwhelmed him… Well, that was harder. He pulled her to him and kissed her, leaning his forehead against hers. "I love you so damned much."

"As I love you. More than I ever knew." She kissed him hard, then drew back. "Now let's get those samples."

They walked back to the first *Rosa McManus* they'd found.

"I discovered a couple dozen bushes scattered around the immediate vicinity," Ana said. "I can feel more farther away, so I'd say we're safe to take two from the root and it won't hurt the population. Then we'll get the clippings of about a dozen."

"Good. We'll have them back to Scotland before New Year's, and testing can start on the first of the year." Cam set about digging up the bush while Ana prepped the bucket and bags. "Don't forget we're going to Otherworld after we celebrate the holiday with Esha and Warren."

They'd only been back to Scotland once since the fight in the grove three weeks ago, to check up on everyone and to thank them. Aurora and Vivienne had healed fully, thank fates. Seeing them under less dire circumstances would be good.

"I can't wait to see my brothers. It's just so different now that emotion has returned to Otherworld and they aren't automatons any more. It's like I have them back again." Ana patted the last of the soil in place around the roots in the bucket and grinned up at him.

Her joy was palpable and contagious. He still didn't love returning to Otherworld to see to the occasional godly meeting or duty, but he didn't mind it. And since Ana got to come along and see her family, it was more than worth the trip.

"If we get back in time, we could try to make it to Otherworld for the winter solstice celebration."

"Sure," Cam said.

"Hey! I should see if my brothers want to add a Christmas tree to winter solstice. And presents. It would really liven up the night. You never know, they might like it," she said.

"It'll be grand. First Christmas I've celebrated. And it will only be marred by one visit with the gods' council." He'd seen them once, a week ago, after the chaos had settled in Otherworld. With the spell broken, the gods had emotion and they no longer believed the lie that their presence was required in Otherworld to keep it functioning. Not that they were running off to earth to party—Cam was the only one who wanted to live here—but the laws holding him in Otherworld were no longer in place.

"They still love those meetings, don't they?" Ana asked. "Gotta say, I'm glad it's your job now and not mine."

She laughed and he grinned, thanking the fates for everything that had happened in the last month. He had a future now, and so did she. Together, they could face whatever came at them.

THANK YOU!

Thank you so much for reading *Rogue Soul*. I loved writing this story and hope you enjoyed reading it!

I love to hear from readers, so if you'd like to get in touch or to know when my next book is available, you can...
- Join my new release newsletter at http://linseyhall.com/subscribe/
- Connect with me on twitter at @HiLinseyHall
- Or find me on Facebook at https://www.facebook.com/LinseyHallAuthor

Reviews help other readers discover books. I appreciate all reviews, both positive and negative, and I really appreciate the time you take if you choose to leave one.

If you liked *Rogue Soul*, the next book in the series is *Stolen Fate* and it will be available on December 8th, 2014. Book 1, *Braving Fate*, and book 2, *Soulceress*, are available now.

AUTHOR'S NOTE

In *Rogue Soul*, I had a great time returning to the history that inspired my first book, *Braving Fate*. Historically, Camulos and Andrasta were both Celtic gods worshipped by the Celts of Britain. The Celtic kingdom of the Iceni favored Andrasta, goddess of victory, while the people of the Trinovante kingdom favored Camuos, god of war.

They are just two out of hundreds of Celtic gods worshipped by thousands of people from dozens of kingdoms and tribes. The Celts weren't one people in one place at one time. Rather, they were a culture that originated in central Europe and spread out to encompass most of Europe and the British Isles during the first millennium B.C. They spoke many languages and worshiped many gods, but were linked by their material culture and advanced use of metalwork.

Andrasta never replaced Camulos, however. I made that bit up, which I imagine was fairly obvious.

Something I think is really neat is the fact that the heroine of *Braving Fate*, Diana (the reincarnate of Boudica) worshipped Andrasta when she was Boudica. Cadan, the hero of *Braving Fate*, was born in the city that was named for Camulos—Camulodunum. This was purely coincidental.

Camulodunum was briefly mentioned in *Rogue Soul* as the city whose construction gave Camulos more power because it was built in his name. This is the event that convinced the other gods that Camulos was so powerful that he must be removed.

As for the Celtic history of the bow? To date, there is little, if any, concrete evidence that the Celts of Britain used the bow and arrow in the first millennium BC. For the purposes of this story, they used the bow for hunting but not for war. In the story, Camulos says that the bow was given to him by the Greek god, Apollo. The Greeks did use the bow for war at this time.

And last, Camulos' modified steamboat was inspired by another Klondike gold rush steamboat, the *A.J. Goddard*. He named his boat the *Clara G.* after a real woman named Clara Goddard. She helped her husband, Albert Goddard, build two 50-foot long sternwheel paddleboats during the winter of 1897/98. With the help of men and mules, they carried them over the mountains of southern Canada in pieces and constructed them on the bank of Lake Bennett at the headwaters of the Yukon river. Clara Goddard was the first female steamboat pilot on the Yukon river. If you want a good story, look up the *A.J. Goddard*. I promise that you won't be disappointed.

Books by Linsey Hall

Braving Fate
Soulceress
Rogue Soul
Stolen Fate

ABOUT LINSEY

Before becoming a romance novelist, Linsey Hall was a nautical archaeologist who studied shipwrecks from Hawaii and the Yukon to the UK and the Mediterranean. She credits the historical romances of the 70's, 80's, and 90's with her love of history and her career as an archaeologist. After a decade of tromping around the globe in search of old bits of stuff that people left lying about, she settled down and started penning her own romance novels. Her debut series, the Mythean Arcana, draws upon her love of history and the paranormal elements that she can't help but include. Several books may or may not feature her cats.

Printed in Great Britain
by Amazon